BAD BLOOD

Book 4 of
THE WARDEN

FELICIA JEDLICKA

For the ones who give second chances.

SISTER WITCHES
THE DEVIL'S SHADOW
THE DEVIL'S SOUL

DESTINY REJECTED
DESTINY RECLAIMED
DESTINY RAZED
DESTINY RESTORED

DÉJÀ VU

SAVE THE HUMANS

THE NECROMANCER'S CHILD

THE NEBRASKA APOCALYPSE NOVELS
CORN COWS AND THE APOCALYPSE
COW TIPPING AFTER THE APOCALYPSE
CORN HUSKING AFTER THE APOCALYPSE

THE WARDEN SERIES
SUCCESSORS
RIVALS
LOVERS AND LIARS
BAD BLOOD
TENANTS AND TYRANTS
THE RING BEARER
GODS AND MONSTERS
BEASTS AND BURDENS
MAGIC AND MAYHEM
FORK IN THE ROAD
DETAILS AND DEADLINES
*CURSES AND SACRIFICES**
*WITCHES AND WOLVES**
*SAINTS AND SERPENTS**
*ENEMIES AND ALLIES**

MARRIED TO DEATH*

Bad Blood

Felicia Jedlicka

# 1

C ORI TUGGED ON THE bridle lines to slacken the rope. A few yards away, Ethan cranked an oversized winch, tightening his wire base line. "How did we get stuck with this job again?" Cori yelled over the wind at him.

Aside from the gale, the arctic summer had finally arrived again, and the temperature was peaking at an astonishing 65 degrees Fahrenheit. With only a light jacket and the energy of a kid just released to summer break, Cori intended to spend the day outside exploring the local wildlife.

Danato and Belus had other plans for her.

"Gee! I wonder what it could have been that incited this punishment," Ethan taunted. "Perhaps it had something to do with you calling Belus a Cactus Toad!"

"He *is* a Cactus Toad!" she insisted.

"What the hell is a Cactus Toad?" Ethan's voice pitched with frustration.

"It's a plant. A plant that is best observed from a distance!"

"Cori," Ethan grumbled, directing his anger into his work. His biceps tensed as he gave the winch another turn. "How did you expect him to react to that? How did you expect Danato to react to you slandering his second in command? They have to maintain some form of discipline in this godforsaken place."

"You could have at least defended me." She continued to play tug-of-war with her rope. It usually took several men to do the job, but as part of their punishment, it was just the two of them. The guards had gone so far as to vacate the roof for the task, but that might have been as much to avoid gigantic dragon droppings as to preclude their assistance.

"Defend you? You called him a Cactus Toad right in front of Danato. There was no defense."

"No, before that! No one believes me about Efrat." Cori put all her anger into her strength and the rope finally gave another foot. When she looked back at Ethan, he was looking at her severely.

"No one?" He said it quietly, so she barely heard it, but she could read his lips.

"Besides you." She slumped her shoulders to match the frown on her face.

"Cori, they checked with the military. He never left. So, either they're lying to cover up their ineptitude or the trauma that you went through has skewed your memory. I think we both know which one is more plausible in Danato's eyes."

"But you didn't even—"

"I took you to see Cleos. You know how much I hated doing that. He verified that the memory is yours and not a leftover." He continued to look at her even as she pretended to be occupied with her work. "Cori." She waited a moment before looking back at him. "I believe you, but at the moment, there is no use fighting about it. Efrat is currently locked up and secure. I doubt interrogating him will result in an admission of his escape."

Cori huffed and twisted the rope around her elbow to get a better grip on it. The huge wooden spool it was coming from was as ancient as the rest of the prison and hardly provided the spin that was required to get the slack she needed to fasten the other end. The other three ropes were already in place, but four were required per prison guidelines for "walking" the dragon.

"Cori!" Ethan hollered at her.

She looked back at Ethan. He was still waiting for an acknowledgement of his efforts. He was right, of course. He had gone above and beyond to get an explanation for her memory of Efrat.

"I'm sorry. I know you did what you could. It's just..." She paused, debating whether she wanted to admit her concerns. Normally, she probably wouldn't have, but she was making a concerted effort to tell Ethan everything she was feeling. The open and honest communication had resulted in more arguments, but in a way Cori liked that they were back to themselves. It was fighting for Twinkies all over again, only when push came to shove, their physical altercations concluded in the bedroom.

"It's just what?" He stopped his work to give her his attention. He could probably sense her reluctance to speak. As much as she hated putting all her emotions out on a platter for him to see, she was thankful that he never judged her for them or brushed them off as overreactions.

"It's just—" She shrugged, trying to make the statement seem more casual than it felt. "—he killed me." Ethan's expression was sympathetic, but she could see the wrinkles of confusion forming in his brow. "I basically flatlined in the infirmary that day, more than once, if I recall correctly." She wasn't sure if he had ever gotten the full run-down of her injuries from Daniel, but the anger that flashed in his eyes suggested he hadn't. "I just need to be sure that he is locked up good and well." She cleared her throat, trying to keep her tears away. She had already expressed her feelings. She didn't want to display them on her face, too.

She could tell Ethan wanted to move to her, to comfort her, but his winch needed attention. He cranked through another cycle to draw their scaly pooch closer to the building. "I'll double-check with the guards. Maybe they've seen him and just assumed they were mistaken." He looked her over with new worry etched on his face. That was what she'd wanted to avoid. She didn't want him to be worried about her. She already gave people enough reason to worry about her. She didn't want to add to the list. She was tired of being the damsel in distress.

She smiled warmly to let him know she was okay. He returned it, but it faded. "Don't wrap that rope around your arm like that. She's going to take every last bit of slack when she gets back down here."

Cori looked up at the female dragon soaring above them. She had been flying around the high skies for nearly an hour and she didn't want to come home. Whether or not she knew it, she was tired and they were dragging her in for a nice, long nap. Eventually, she would settle down and they would use the bridle lines to draw her toward the hangar door on the side of the building. Cori had one more line to secure in her sheave and they could tow her to the edge of the building, where, God willing, she would choose to go to her warm pseudo-cave to sleep off the exercise.

The dragon dove in for a low swoop. The gust her massive wingspan provided was no less powerful than the windy day they were already enduring.

"Cori, get that secured." Ethan barked the order at her as if she was one of his guards.

"Okay." She laughed at the urgency in his voice and started to unwind the mess of rope she had spooled on her arm.

"Get it off your arm!" Ethan blustered, sounding remarkably like Danato.

"I am," she shrieked back at him. She didn't understand why he was so mad.

The dragon swooped in again, heading east against her guidelines. "Cori!" Ethan raged and started barreling toward her. She stared at him, baffled by his actions.

When her arm was hauled from her side with enough force to pop it out of the joint, she began to understand.

Her feet left the roof before she could even contemplate a scream. She caught one last glimpse of Ethan's face, pinched in effort as his clenched fists flanked his futile charge.

For a split second that felt longer than it was, Cori hovered in the air, staring at the sky. A beautiful blue sky, unobstructed by the dismal white ceilings of the prison. She missed being outside. She missed the warmth of the sun. They needed to have a BBQ or a picnic. Something to mark the summer as it deserved.

Cori finally deciphered her predicament as her body started to descend again.

The tension temporarily holding her up was just the last of her coiled rope snagging on her dislocated arm. She had been pulled up into the air by the lassoed bridle line and now it was unraveling. With her arm out of socket, she didn't have the strength to hold it. She was falling.

The additional height from the seven-story building guaranteed her death. She wanted to scream, but the time for panic was gone. There was only enough time to pray that Ethan would be okay without her.

She closed her eyes, resigned herself to enjoy the drop like a roller coaster. At any rate, she didn't want to see the ground coming toward her.

Her arm snagged again, stopping her descent with another painful yank on her already stressed shoulder joint. She waited for the rope to give way again, but she realized it wasn't the rope that was pinching her wrist. She opened her eyes and looked up.

Ethan loomed above her, panting. His biceps were thick with the strain of holding the rope in one hand and her wrist in the other. His legs clamped around the rope, maintaining his stability.

He said nothing as he pulled her up with his impossible strength. When she was high enough, she latched onto his neck with her good arm. He repositioned and assisted her rise with a firm grip on her butt. Similar to many evenings in bed, she wrapped her legs around his waist so she was essentially sitting on his lap. He grabbed the rope with both hands behind her back and slowly climbed down.

She looked around to see where he was taking them. The rope was hanging just over the edge of the building. The dragon was happily circling above, oblivious to the insignificant increase in weight on her ropes.

As they reached the building edge and the bend in the rope, Ethan leaned back, creating the momentum for them to swing. She obliged by leaning with him. He still hadn't said anything to her, but she imagined the stupefied stare on her face was telling him she wasn't all there at the moment.

Once the rope was in full swing, he pressed his hand to her back. She reached around his torso and gripped tightly with her functional arm. She shifted her legs as well to get the maximum adhesion to his body.

His legs dropped out beneath her, and she closed her eyes. She felt the drop, and with a grunt and scuffle of gravel, Ethan landed on his feet. She didn't release him right away. Even as his hands started rubbing her back, she clutched tighter.

"Your arm is dislocated," he said, as if he had just taken a cursory look over her wounds.

She released him and slid down his legs. Back on her own feet, she took a step back and looked the roof over.

"Are you okay?" He asked it as if he had already asked her once before. Maybe he had.

She moved to the edge of the building to look at how menacing the drop would have been. Seven floors was nothing to scoff at, but she did anyway. She looked at the rope they had just come from.

She played back the incident in her head, without her deluded, shock-induced timeline. She realized he had followed her right off the roof. He leaped off behind her to grab her and the rope. She looked back at him, flabbergasted. "You jumped off the roof."

He didn't answer. He was still panting.

She came up to him and pointed vaguely to the edge of the roof. "You just jumped off the roof after me. You could have died."

His face marred with confusion. He wasn't being cocky about his feat. He honestly had no idea why she was surprised. The risk of jumping off the building meant nothing to him. His task from the moment he saw the danger was to save her at any cost.

She came at him, hooking her foot behind his and shoving him with her good arm. "Cori?" He windmilled for a half second before bending his knees to drop onto his butt, instead of flat on his back. "What are you—?"

He didn't finish that statement. She dropped down on him and kissed him. She pulled away and used her good hand to unbuckle his gun belt. After a brief moment of shock, he returned the favor by assisting her with hers. The black pistols fell away, and she bit her lip, struggling to undo his pants with one hand.

He pulled her face down again and kissed her fervently. His hand slipped down between her legs and offered her some abatement to her frustrations. She moaned, wanting so much more than that.

She wished her arm were functional so she could properly rip his clothes off. She was not nearly as patient as he was in that department. Months of her waffling sexual appetite and reluctant compliance to aggressive advances were biting her in the ass now. She didn't want to make love right now; she wanted to—

"Ahem."

2

CORI'S LIPS FROZE. ETHAN'S did too. He had obviously heard the same unwelcoming interruption. His hand slipped from its goal and she groaned for new reasons. As they broke away from their lip lock, Ethan grazed his teeth on her lower lip. A consolation prize for the time being, but hopefully a promise as well.

She looked up at the intruder as she pushed away from Ethan's chest. "Belus," she announced, partly as an accusation. "Please tell me this disruption is not an attempt to get back at me."

"Ethan has a visitor," he said flatly. "Danato wants him downstairs right away."

"It couldn't wait until we were done walking the dragon?" she asked.

Belus eyed her position on top of Ethan. "We don't want to keep her waiting. She needs to leave on the same the truck she came in on."

"She?" Cori felt her defenses rise as she removed herself from Ethan. "Sophie?" she asked, glancing down at her husband. He seemed just as confused by the female visitor. He looked at Belus for the answer as well.

"I haven't met her before today. Just come downstairs so we can get her out of here."

"I need to take Cori to the infirmary first." Ethan rose and dusted off his butt. He picked up his weapon and handed Cori hers. The pistols were a recent addition to their wardrobe. After the transmorph incident, Danato gave them permission to arm themselves. Danato and Belus still didn't arm themselves, but Cori wasn't about to stand on tradition when she was usually the one in danger.

"What happened?" Belus looked her over, his eyes settling on the obvious slump in her shoulder.

"I tripped," Cori said with bitter sarcasm.

"She dislocated her arm," Ethan said firmly, reprimanding her with his militant gaze. She looked away. She hated being reminded that she had to be good, especially by the same man who loved it when she was bad.

"What caused that?" Belus probed.

"She got caught up in the ropes," Ethan said.

"We have detailed instructions on the dos and don'ts of this procedure, Cori. Perhaps you should read them again," Belus drawled, stone-faced.

"I almost died, you cantankerous ass!" Cori flailed her good arm. "Not that you would bother to sidestep my rotting corpse!" She turned away as soon as she said it. She didn't want to show him how much it hurt that he had no consideration for her safety other than the paperwork it might cause.

She clenched her jaw and took in a few breaths to calm the anger that was threatening to transform into the emotion it was blocking. Ethan grabbed her hand, but she shook her head and moved away. He was never a good vaccine for her blubbering, slobbering, pathetic reactions.

"I'll take Cori to the infirmary," Belus stated. "You get down to the office."

Ethan looked back at her to see if she would be okay with that. She wasn't, but she nodded anyway. After he left, she gathered her strength to face Belus. She turned around, but he was gone.

"What the hell?" she mumbled. Why was such a point made to take her if he was just going to leave?

She headed to the stairs leading off the roof. When she reached the door, it opened, and Belus offered her passage through. When they reached the elevator, it was just opening. She realized he must have run down to hit the button, so they didn't have to wait forever for it to arrive.

She stepped inside and he followed, pushing the button for the animal level, which also held the infirmary. She was far too familiar with the wretched place. She never seemed to be free of it. If she made it a month without going there, it was likely going to be saved up for a long stay later.

She leaned against the wall and tried not to think about how extremely uncomfortable it was for her to be alone in an elevator with Belus. He had never been the easiest man to start up a conversation with, but she remembered a time when they had bonded briefly over tequila. Regrettably, her betrayal during the elemental escape had put a stop to anything resembling friendship between them. She respected him and wanted to earn back his trust, but his antisocial personality made it impossible for her to know if she was making any progress.

Ever since she had been designated Ethan's second, he treated her like the scum on his shoes. He barked orders at her, with no hint of appreciation, when she complied. Minor mistakes were pointed out immediately and major achievements were outright ignored. She was in Belus's own personal boot camp. However, his efforts to make her more disciplined and dutiful were only driving her to buck against his authority.

Her insolence caused him to seek out Danato's support for appropriate punishments. That, in turn, put a rift in *their* relationship. Since Ethan was caught in the middle of all three of them, he was doing his best to mediate, but in the end, that just added to the number of men trying to dictate how she behaved.

The doors graced them with a *ponk*, and Belus stepped out of the elevator. She moved out, but held out her arm to block the doors from closing. "There's really no need to accompany me. You can go to the office with Ethan and Danato if you want."

Belus perked an eyebrow. "Thank you for the permission, but Ethan would probably like a report when I arrive."

Cori rolled her eyes and released the doors. "Fine."

They walked to the infirmary entrance. Belus opened the door for her and they moved through the short galley waiting area to the nurse's station. The reception hub was just a pitstop on the way to the lab rooms, exam rooms, and windowed patient rooms.

The ever-poised medical staff erupted into a frenzy of arguments. She wasn't sure what the specifics were, but evidently they had been placing bets on when she would be back again. Once they had settled on who owed whom a shift cover, she was placed in a tiny windowless exam room.

Belus joined her and leaned against the wall rather than utilize the small chair designated for guests. She situated herself on the crinkling paper of the exam table. She knew no one would be in a hurry to come check her. She was familiar with the routine anyway: muscle relaxants, pain meds, yank, scream, sling, *"have a nice day"*—and in her case—*"come again soon."*

She unzipped her jacket and attempted to slip it off her shoulders, but she couldn't get it off either arm without the help of the other. Belus pushed off the wall and waved her off the table. She slid off it and kneeled before him. He pulled the jacket off and placed it on the chair.

He palpated her shoulder, checking the position. He might have been considering twisting the arm back into the socket himself. He was familiar with the procedure, and despite what he admitted to, he had the strength to do it. Instead, he stepped away from her and leaned back against the wall.

Cori took up her spot on the exam table and stared at the floor. When she finally glanced up, she saw Belus watching her. "What?" she sneered.

"Did you want to say anything more to me before the surgeon gets in here?" he asked. "You might as well get it off your chest now, while we can still blame your attitude on the pain."

Cori shook her head. She wouldn't fall into his trap. "I don't want to fight with you, Belus."

"Your history says otherwise."

"Don't bait me. I never wanted you as an enemy. You took that position up all on your own."

Belus didn't respond to her accusation, but his chin jutted forward in disapproval. "What is a Cactus Toad, anyway?" There wasn't any sarcasm in the question. She waited to see if it was an opening for another attack, but he tipped his brow, waiting for her answer.

"It's a succulent." His brow furrowed—apparently he was unfamiliar with the terminology. "It's like a cactus, but it doesn't have any needles."

"I understood the cactus reference, but one without needles doesn't seem to be much of an insult."

Cori looked him over, wondering if his punishment for her insult had more to do with his offense than his ire. "It has a pretty bloom. Unfortunately, the flower smells like rotting flesh. Flies will actually lay eggs in the petals because they think it's dead meat. It's a lovely plant..." Cori broke from his stoic gaze. "...but damn if you don't regret getting close to it."

Before Belus could respond, the doctor's arrival liberated them from the conversation. He blew in with the speed and indifference of a politician. Equipped with trivial chitchat and a passive aggressive undertone, he examined her shoulder. She did her best to stifle her yelp as he manipulated her shoulder into its socket, but the pain was greater than her pride.

The doctor pulled a bottle of muscle relaxants and pain pills from his jacket and tossed them to Belus. He explained all the instructions to him instead of her. She didn't waste her time explaining to him that her ears weren't dislocated. With her sling in place, and sexism taking the place of her good-patient lollipop, she slipped off the table and headed back out of the infirmary.

Belus arrived late to the elevator holding a paper-cone cup of water and two pills for her to take. Given the residual throbbing pain from the relocation, she didn't pretend to not want or need them. She took the pills and downed them with the water.

She hadn't realized how thirsty she was until the cup went dry before her thirst was slaked. She crushed the cup and looked around for a disposal shoot. Belus took the cup from her and jogged it over to one.

The elevator *ponked* while he was gone. She thought about jumping in and pushing the button before he could get back so she didn't have to endure the long silent ride, but propriety left her standing in the doors to keep them open. He jogged back and followed her in.

The descent of one floor seemed to take twice as long as five floors had. She was starting to suspect that the elevators had a life of their own. She would have to consider taking the stairs when she wasn't mortally wounded.

She thought at some point Belus might make a comment regarding the definition of her insult, but he was content to lean on the wall ahead of her, keeping all eye contact unavailable. When the doors opened, he led the way to Danato's office. He didn't look back to see if she was keeping up, nor did he slow his pace. She didn't need any such assistance, but it was just another difference between the way he treated her versus Danato or Ethan.

When she made it to the office, he was holding the door for her. She slipped her pistol off her hip and placed it next to Ethan's in the bin Danato had installed next to the door. He didn't want guns in the office at all. Actually, the phrase he used was, "You *can't* bring guns into this office." Either way, the implication of an ass-ripping upon dispute was conveyed.

Cori stepped into the office and smelled the fragrant perfume of their female guest. Despite the floral nature of the perfume, the small room magnified the mannish undertone of musk. Her legs went weak and the hair on the back of her neck stood on end as she remembered the last time she had smelled that combination.

Ethan and Danato barely glanced at her as she entered the room. The woman, sitting with her back to Cori, wore a dark gray business suit that clung to her like leather. The business-inappropriate short skirt had slits up the sides that added focus to the chiseled legs extending from beneath the hems.

The previously short black hair was now long enough to pull into a loose bedhead up-do. She turned her head, revealing the bold plum-colored lipstick. It looked well with her coppery brown eyeshadow and black mascara. Her lips slanted in a partial smile that looked like a precursor to a snarl.

"Cori," her arch-nemesis drawled with a smug undertone.

"Leona." Cori took in a deep breath to steady her voice. Whatever importance the current conversation had, it was forgotten as all eyes volleyed between the two women. Everyone was trying to figure out how they knew each other.

"I thought I smelled something familiar on the hunter." Leona stood up slowly and turned to face her. It wasn't a threatening movement by any means, but Ethan stood, and Danato's chair squawked as he pushed himself back from the desk.

Cori noticed the rounded belly that was hiding under Leona's pluming gray silk top. The new girth was unassuming, but since Cori had remembered her as being scarecrow-thin, it immediately drew her attention.

"You look well." Cori struggled to find something to say, so she didn't blurt out the question that was looming on her mind.

Are you going to kill me?

Cori's skin erupted in goosebumps as her adversary approached her. She couldn't put her jacket back on because of the sling and she was just realizing she had forgotten it in the infirmary anyway.

"So good to see you again." Leona grabbed her shoulders, paying no heed to the grimace of pain it elicited. She pulled her forward and kissed each of her cheeks, most likely leaving a purple smooch on either side. She tightened her grip and planted one directly on her lips as well. Though it wasn't an open-mouthed kiss, Cori could still taste the petroleum chemicals in her lipstick, and the flavor of her toothpaste.

Leona withdrew, revealing three confused faces in her background. Little did they know; Cori had no explanation to offer for this display. She could hardly repel the woman's affections. A not-so-chaste kiss from another female was a far superior discomfort to having her throat ripped out.

"I always wondered what happened to you," Leona said with her thick French accent. "I take it Vince has passed on?" She glanced back at Ethan. A hint of understanding hit the room as everyone realized the connection.

"Yes, sadly he has."

"I had hoped to spare you that pain, you know." Leona released her grip on Cori's shoulders and she relaxed.

"I know. It was all for the best, though."

"Oui." Leona looked at Ethan again. "I see that it was." Ethan didn't react to Leona's ogling, but Cori didn't like her observation or her approval.

"Ethan is my husband," she blurted out without any prompting that would have made it a reasonable contribution to the conversation.

Leona looked back at her with a smile of subdued irritation. Cori knew very well that husband or not, it made no difference. If Leona wanted something, she took it. No matter who got in the way.

However, it did matter when Cori was in the way. She was the reason that Leona had never mated with Vince. Cori was probably the only woman from here to Portugal who had ever dared oppose her. Certainly the only one who had won.

Unfortunately, that was what made the meeting so tense. Cori didn't know if Leona was still mad about what had happened. Was she seeking revenge? Or would she let mutual respect maintain their razor-thin civility?

"Leona," Danato spoke up. "We should really get on with this if you want to get back on the truck."

Leona kept her eyes on Cori. "I'll take the evening truck."

"I would really prefer if you left as soon as possible."

"I don't give a damn what you want, Warden," she said, eyes still locked on Cori. "I'd like to reminisce with my friend before I go."

Cori looked at Danato. She had hoped he would be red-faced and on the verge of throwing her out of his office, but he wasn't. Frustrated, maybe, and discontented, but he seemed to know that there was absolutely no point in arguing with a female werewolf. That was probably why they wanted her out of the prison as soon as possible.

"Can we at least get on with business, then?" Danato tapped his pencil. The small noise seemed to break Leona's concentration.

"Of course." She returned to her chair. "Let's discuss my terms, and you may decide a price."

"Price for what?" Cori didn't mean to interrupt, but she was curious why Leona was here, of all places. Female werewolves never entered into part-time contracts like males did. She wasn't sure if that was because the prison couldn't hold them, or if they just had a better hold on their monstrous appetites.

Leona looked back at her. "A price for your *husband*."

3

ORI COULD FEEL A prickling heat of panic climbing up her spine. Unlike the creepy, hair-tingling nervousness that Leona was causing, this was pure fear. Ethan could see her wide eyes and he shook his head.

"We are negotiating for Ethan's services as a hunter," Danato clarified. "And I would like to get it done with *before* the cat fight, please."

"Dog fight in my case." Leona laughed at her own joke, but no one joined in.

"Belus." Danato looked at his second, silently demanding that he fix what he had broken.

"Come on." Belus grabbed her hand, a rarity in and of itself, but the forceful tug he used to drag her from the room was a good deal rarer.

She managed to grab her pistol and catch a glimpse of Ethan mouthing, "*I love you,*" before he shut the door behind them. She knew that should have been a comfort, but it wasn't. She was being dragged down the hall by her one good arm, leaving her husband in a room with her hot, lustful, stronger-than-superman arch-enemy.

"Belus, stop, you're—" She was about to say, *hurting me*, but since he wouldn't have any sympathy for her pain, she changed her mind. "—pissing me off."

He let her go as they reached the stairs so she could grab the railing. "This way," he said when she mistakenly turned to go to the elevators.

"Where are we going?" she asked, following him to the entrance.

"I'm taking you home."

"Seriously! Every time a beautiful woman visits Ethan, I have to go home. This sucks!"

Belus grabbed his jacket from his locker and slipped it on. "Damn it, I forgot your jacket in the infirmary." He dug in another locker and pulled out one of Danato's many spares. "Here." She crouched down, and he draped the oversized windbreaker over her shoulders.

"You do realize she could break both of their necks, quite literally, with the flick of a wrist." Cori imitated the flicking in case Belus still didn't understand the gravity of her concerns.

He gave her a "no duh" head waggle. "Why do you think he wants you out of there? A female werewolf provoked by female bickering is not a good work environment."

"I wasn't bickering," Cori protested.

"Let's go." Belus opened the door and steered her through. She tromped out the door, ignoring the fact that she probably looked like a disappointed six-year-old.

Cori entered the house and hung up Danato's coat. She made it half-way to the kitchen before she remembered Belus's restriction. "Crap, come in."

"Thank you." Belus came in and shut the door, but he stayed close to it.

"Remind me why the house doesn't let you in?" Cori asked as she pulled leftovers from breakfast out of the fridge. Cold French toast was better than waiting for microwaved popcorn.

"I don't live here. Plain and simple," he said tersely.

"Yeah, but you used to." Cori stuffed a quarter of her toast into her mouth. "Doesn't she remember you?" she mumbled over her full mouth.

He chuckled at her stuffed face. "It was a long time ago, and her memory is short. I'm sure she's forgotten all about me since then." His voice trailed off as if he were a little disappointed by that.

Cori noticed he hadn't removed his jacket. She stopped chewing and watched him examine the room. "Aren't you staying for a drink?" she asked.

He turned to her and faltered through his answer. "I wasn't sure you... It's been a long day. I thought maybe you'd want to be alone."

She swallowed the remainder of her bread. "I'm pretty sure when Ethan is in the hands of an attractive, evil woman, you and I get to rob a few drinks from the liquor cabinet."

He gave a curt nod and took off his jacket. He headed into the living room and opened the wall panel to access Danato's liquor stash. He poured two glasses of ouzo and handed one to her as she sat down on the couch. "You probably shouldn't have this with your pain meds," Belus said, but made no attempt to take the glass back from her.

"What is this?"

"It's Greek liquor. Licorice. You'll like it." He sat down in Danato's usual chair and sipped it. She did the same. It was as much like rubbing alcohol as all the other liquors she had tried, but the licorice aftertaste was rather pleasing.

"Mmm, I like it." She coughed on the fumes.

"I can see that." Belus laughed. "I'll make a liquor connoisseur out of you yet." He watched her take another sip, which she smacked between her lips. "So, do you want to talk about what you said to me up there?"

Cori felt the warmth of her face add to the warmth in her throat. She didn't want to talk about anything, but she could hardly avoid it. She took a bigger drink of her ouzo and coughed on the fumes again. "I'm sorry. I shouldn't have called you a Cactus Toad," she admitted.

"That's not what I meant." He leaned over his knees and rolled his glass between his hands. "Something about me not bothering to sidestep your corpse."

Cori downed the rest of her drink and fought back the cough. "What about it?" She could feel him looking at her, but she didn't want to get into a staring competition she knew she would lose.

"Is that what you think of me?" he asked coolly.

Cori shrugged. "I just got pulled off the building to my impending death. I was a little wrung out. A little sympathy would have been nice."

Belus went back to the cupboard and pulled out the ouzo again. Without asking if she wanted more, he filled her glass a quarter full. He waited beside her, holding his glass in one hand and the bottle in the other. "Is that what you want?" he asked. She looked up at him. His rugged features reminded her of the brawny man on the paper towels. A lumberjack in midget clothing. "Do you want me to coddle you? Tell you everything is going to be okay? Kiss your boo-boos?"

She knew he wasn't trying to be an ass, but he was taking his reverse psychology too far to the extreme to sound like anything less. She tried to keep her tongue civil, but in the process of controlling her anger, she lost the battle against the tears that had crept into her eyes. "I want you to give a damn whether I live or die." She wiped away the tears discreetly and leaned back on the couch. She took down her new liquor portion in one shot. It didn't make her feel better, but the strong taste gave her something to concentrate on other than the uncomfortable conversation.

Belus sat down on the coffee table in front of her. He put the bottle of ouzo beside him along with his glass, which he had barely touched. "Hey." He tugged on her pant leg. "I certainly give a damn whether you live or die," he said sternly.

She wiped away another tear and nodded. She didn't believe him, but what else could she say?

"I've been in this job for a lot of years, Cori. I've lost some good friends, including Danato's wife. They made mistakes. Mistakes that cost them their lives. I know I'm a hard-ass. I know you don't like me most of the time, but I don't want you to meet the same fate as them. The only way I can protect you is by training you. My empathy is not going to make you stronger, faster, or smarter. If you want praise and reassurance, then go see Danato or Ethan. That's not the way I do things. I can't change who I am."

"And yet you insist on changing me?" Cori put her glass back to her lips, but there was nothing left to drink.

"Every serendipitous discovery you have made in this prison has been accomplished by spitting in the face of the rules. It's all well that ends well... until it doesn't. I don't want to see you hurt." He pointed to her arm. "It does pain me, but not because your arm is in a sling. It pains me because I am responsible for you. Your mistakes are my failures."

"I'm going to have accidents, Belus."

"They aren't accidents when you aren't following protocol. Then they're stupidity at the hands of arrogance."

"You can't change, and neither can I." She leaned forward to face him properly. "I keep trying to make you proud of me. I strive for it every morning, but you are so relentless and closed-mouthed that by the afternoon I want to strangle you. You can't be my mentor if I hate you! I don't want to hate you, Belus!" She took his drink from the coffee table and downed it, but it didn't make the tears go away. She buried her head in her knees. She wondered how long it would take for him to get uncomfortable and just leave.

He took the glasses from her hands and set them back on the coffee table. She waited for him to get up and put away the ouzo or make some attempt to change the subject, but he didn't. His coarse, tiny fingers patted the back of her head. Her tears subsided, but she didn't lift her head. The gesture was too precious and unusual to disrupt. After a minute, he paused and moved his hand to her shoulder. The gentle pressure that eased her up wasn't insistent, but it was enough of a reason to show her face again.

When she looked up, he removed his hand. His face was calm in the face of her blubbering. She'd expected to see a note of ire in his eyes, but for once, he seemed sympathetic. "My intent is not for you to hate me. On the contrary, I rather like you, actually. Well, not when you're like this." He smiled to let her know he was joking. She laughed, wiping away the remnants of her stalled tears. When the moment of levity passed, he spoke again.

"I like you, kid. Damn if I didn't try not to. You're arrogant, belligerent, and clumsy, but you're headstrong and resilient, and you've made me proud... often."

Cori drank in the compliments like the water she was still thirsting for. She knew this was probably a moment that wouldn't be repeated in the future, and she wanted to memorize it, so that when he scowled at her or made a biting remark, she wouldn't have to be so hurt by it.

"Well." He grabbed the bottle from the coffee table and put it back in the hidden paneled cupboard. "I hope that's what you wanted to know. It won't make much of a difference to my curmudgeon façade, but as long as it saves you a few tears in the future, then I suppose it's worth it."

He gave her a sympathetic smile as he leaned over to grab the glasses off the coffee table. She grabbed his hand and squeezed it. She hadn't intended to, but she couldn't think of anything to say that would express her appreciation outside of smothering him with baby kisses, which she knew was well beyond his tolerance.

He paused and squeezed her hand back. She had already gotten more from him in this one afternoon than she could have ever hoped. He leaned over and kissed her forehead, and she released his hand. "You should take a nap, kid. Between your meds and that booze, you'll feel better if you do."

She mumbled in agreement and grabbed the blanket from the end of the couch to snuggle in. She listened to him whistle as he washed up the glasses. When he was finished, he slipped on his jacket. She sensed that he was waiting by the door. She wasn't sure if he was debating on if he should say goodbye or perhaps just fiddling with his coat.

When the door finally clicked shut, she smiled. There was a throbbing pain in her shoulder that the pain meds hadn't even touched. The muscle relaxants combined with the alcohol were adding to her tipsy dizziness. Her stomach was roiling, rejecting the triple mix, but she was happy.

4

E THAN LOOKED AT DANATO's discomfort across the desk. He had seen the big man mad; he had seen him worried, and he had seen him sad, but Ethan couldn't remember a time when he had seen him uncomfortable. He looked like he needed to use the restroom and couldn't quite find the right position to hold it. If Ethan hadn't thought it to be impossible, he would have assumed that Danato was afraid of the woman.

Ethan might have blamed his discomfort on Cori's association with Leona, but Danato had been antsy long before that interaction. Oddly enough, Ethan discovered he had a history with the fem-wolf as well. All the times he had chased after his illusive fem-wolf, it was apparently Leona he was tracking. According to his friends, the chances he could have caught her were beyond astronomical. Yet, it was those chases that had brought her to the prison.

The meeting revealed that Leona needed assistance to get her son back from her mate, a task which she deemed worthy of Ethan's expertise. "Forgive me, Leona, if this is a loaded question," Ethan spoke up after the debate about money had lent itself to passive aggressive insults about the institution Danato held so dear. "Why is it, with all your strength and prowess, you can't retrieve your son on your own?"

It must have been an offensive question, because the four eyes that landed on him were angry. Ethan shrugged, pleading his innocence for the ignorance. "I'm not questioning your abilities. It's because of my understanding of them that I can't quite get a grasp on why you're asking for my help."

Leona's expression hardened, translating the anger into resignation. "Because I am with child." Ethan thought there should have been drums leading up to the statement since she confessed it rather than announcing it.

"I'm sorry, still not understanding. You can't retrieve your son by yourself because you're pregnant." Ethan looked at Danato for the answers. He had read the book on werewolves through and through—for obvious reasons—but the topic of females was vague, bordering on myth.

Danato looked between Leona and Ethan as if asking permission to proceed. "Female werewolves can't change while they are pregnant. They are often weaker in their human form than the males during this time as well." Danato settled his gaze on Leona. "It's also very unusual for a female to get pregnant while she is still nursing, but I suppose that is why he took the child."

Leona nodded. The scowl on her face told him she wasn't happy about the path her life had taken. "My beloved mate is forming a pack. He was so impressed with my attributes that he has decided to use me as his sire. He kidnapped my child and sent one of his minions under my nose during my mating season. Now I am pregnant again, and he will likely attempt to steal this one while I am still nursing and weak."

"He sounds like a piece of work. Have you consulted with any other hunters?" Ethan asked.

"They tend to run away from me." Leona leaned over to Ethan. "You're the only one who chases me."

Ethan smiled, though he was pretty sure she wasn't trying to be funny. "So, you want me to hunt down your ex and fetch the baby?"

"No." Leona rolled her eyes. "I know where he is. If it were simply a matter of fetching, I would do that myself. I need you to keep his goons off my back while I get my baby back."

Ethan looked over at Danato. He understood why Danato was being uncooperative in this discussion. "You want me to be bait?"

5

C ORI WOKE ON THE couch a couple of hours later. The dizziness was gone, but it had been replaced by a headache. She probably shouldn't have played doctor and bartender on the same day. Lucky for her, the throbbing pain was back in her shoulder, so she could start the process all over again.

She hoped against hope that Belus had remembered to leave her pain meds behind, but she didn't see them anywhere. Since she had to fetch her coat anyway, she decided to head back for them as well.

She grabbed Danato's spare jacket and headed straight to the prison. The air was already starting to cool, but the sun was still up. She was tempted to explore the grounds before it got too dark, but her shoulder demanded otherwise.

Cori arrived at the prison and put Danato's jacket back into his locker. She headed to the elevators and pushed the button. She considered taking the stairs instead, but she didn't want to aggravate her headache. When it finally arrived, the doors opened and Belus stepped out, carrying her jacket.

"I was just coming to get that," she said, taking it from him.

"I was just heading back to get you."

"I was coming to find you. Please tell me you have my pain pills."

"Yeah, come with me. Danato wants to talk with you." He moved past her and headed toward the office stairs.

She groaned and followed. "I just woke up. I can't possibly be in trouble already."

"You're not in trouble and yes, it's possible." He looked back at her with a smirk, so she knew he was joking. It was true, but it was still funny. "He wants to talk to you about Ethan."

"What about Ethan?" Cori slowed as they entered the narrow hallway.

"Exactly," Belus said. She started to ask another question, but he interrupted. "Danato will answer your questions." She sighed and followed him to the office.

When she arrived, she found Danato strumming his fingers on the desk. He looked exhausted. She sat down in front of his desk and tried to discern his mood: tired, angry, worried?

Belus brought over a set of pills and a cup of water from the water cooler that wasn't cool. She downed the pills and leaned back in the chair, already feeling better.

"Cori, I'm going to have to let Ethan leave the prison to help Leona."

She stopped feeling better. "What?"

"Leona is in need of some assistance and—"

"Bullshit. She's a freaking werewolf! The only assistance she needs is picking the meat from her teeth after a kill."

"She has requested Ethan's help, because—"

"No shit, she wants Ethan! She wants to get back at me for ruining her chances with Vince. She wants revenge."

"Leona is unable to—"

"She can—"

Danato slammed his fist on his desk. "Don't interrupt me!" he bellowed, showing the short fuse the day had left him. "Leona's baby has been taken by the father. Werewolves have particular rules on mating and child-rearing. This is a violation of those rules. I'm not going to go into detail, but we are obligated to protect werewolf children."

"Why?" Cori asked, succeeding in sounding as bitter as a six-year-old—her designated theme for the day.

"It's part of the deal; old, longstanding prison rules. We originally housed werewolves during their moon cycle to protect them. In exchange, they would hunt down troublesome supernaturals for us. The origin of our employee hunters is from those original contracts. The first hunters didn't hunt werewolves. They *were* werewolves."

"Since when do werewolves need protection during their moon cycle?"

"There was a time when they were rendered nearly extinct by human poachers."

"Did we ever house female werewolves?"

"No. Females don't change while they're pregnant. They also aren't as strong during pregnancy and while nursing. Since the mating cycle to weaning is a minimum of one year female werewolves are virtually harmless until they go into estrus again."

"Harmless?"

"Don't get me wrong, they still have superior human strength and senses, but they are at least manageable."

"Leona is not manageable. We have a history. I can't trust her with Ethan."

"She wouldn't dare hurt one of my hunters. The Council—"

"I'm not worried about her hurting him!" Cori interrupted.

Danato slowly gleaned her meaning and glanced back at Belus. "Do you trust Ethan?"

"Of course, but—"

"Then that's all that matters."

Cori furrowed her brow. "He's already agreed to this, hasn't he?"

"Yes." Cori threw her head back. "But I didn't exactly give him a choice. The old rules may be antiquated, but keeping a good rapport with the werewolf population is important. Aside from income to the prison, they aren't exactly a group you want to be in opposition with."

"I suppose what he's about to undertake is highly dangerous."

Danato waffled as if he were rolling a few different phrases for "yes" around on his tongue. "Yes." Apparently, there wasn't any sugar to coat it with.

"Goddamn it," Cori whispered. "I lost six weeks of my marriage to a transmorph. Now we're going to be apart again."

"Days, Cori. You'll have him back by next week."

Cori's body shot up in the chair. "He hasn't left yet, has he?"

"No, he recruited one of the guards to finish tucking our dragon in," Danato said.

"When is he leaving?"

"Tomorrow," Danato said.

Cori wasn't much happier at the sound of that, but at least she got one more night with him to properly say goodbye. Unlike the last time he'd left.

6

E THAN FINISHED CLOSING THE building's exterior doors with Duke's help. The dragon was already curled in a heap behind him, sound asleep. She would likely be out for the next few days. Belus had told him the creatures were like big cats, but Ethan thought they were more like bears. They spent much of the cold months in a half hibernation mode. The only exercise she got was when they dragged her out for training, which was only a few times a month. "Walking" the big creature was only a once-a-month thing, and only when the temperature was reasonable or she simply wouldn't leave her cave.

"Is that locked?" Ethan called over to Duke.

"Yeah, boss." Duke gave him a thumbs-up as he headed out of the hangar and into the gym. "Wouldn't want anyone to steal our dragon."

"No, we wouldn't." Ethan stepped over the creature's massive tail. "We aren't insured for that." He caught up with Duke and patted him on the back. "Thanks man."

"No problem. That's as close I get to a rodeo these days."

Ethan chuckled. As they cleared the shadows of the dragon den, he noticed Cori standing at the front of the gym. He could tell by the peevish look on her face that she had spoken to Danato. "Duke, hit that lever on your way out."

"Sure thing." Duke jogged on without him.

Ethan slowed to a stop well before he had reached Cori.

Duke pulled the lever by the gym entrance. A shudder of activation echoed through the room before the interior hangar door lowered.

"Ma'am." Duke gave Cori a wide, friendly smile. The only thing missing was the tip of a cowboy hat, which was unfortunately not part of the guard uniforms.

Cori gave him a civil nod, which was appropriate since she barely knew Duke. Ethan hadn't explained the integral part he had played in saving her life a few weeks prior. He hadn't meant to diminish Duke's credit, but there was so much to tell, and recent days were not allowing for detailed conversations about anything.

Duke left and Cori strolled over to him. She took a bit more time than necessary to close the gap. As it was, she left several feet of void. All awkward conversations required physical space, no matter how many times the participants had seen each other naked.

"So," she said, letting the conjunction speak for itself.

"So," he added to the loquacious exchange.

"Leaving me for a werewolf. Kind of ironic."

Ethan knew she had meant it to be funny, but something still stung about that topic, and possibly always would. He turned away, changing his position to hide his displeasure. "I'm sure you know all the arguments already."

"Yup, and I don't care. I don't care that she needs your help. I don't care that we are contracted to help werewolves. I don't care about anything but you."

Ethan was surprised she had said that. There was no doubt in his heart that Cori loved him. She had professed it many times. He just hadn't expected her to be so honest. Normally, she would skirt her emotions and try to win the argument on merit or volume. The fact that she wasn't yelling already was another surprise. "It isn't my preference, but it is for a baby. I think we can both agree that a child has the right to be with his mother."

He could almost see her shoulders slump. He had played the baby card. She could argue from now until dawn, but in the end, Ethan wasn't leaving to go fetch some groceries. Nor was he taking revenge in Leona's name. He was retrieving a kidnapped child.

"Ethan, she is dangerous." Cori stepped forward. "I know Danato understands that, but I don't think you do. Vince was terrified of her. He... I don't want to get into details, but when Vince and Danato are afraid, I think you should rethink being anywhere near her."

"She's lame right now. She's pregnant again. She isn't likely to pick a fight."

Cori looked away. "It's not a fight I'm worried about. I'm worried she may want to take revenge on you because of me."

"What is it between you two, anyway?"

"I sort of spoiled her chances of mating with Vince." Cori hadn't shared the details of her life with Vince, and for obvious reasons he never asked, but he was curious about this. "Vince told me he could either agree to be with her, or suffer the consequences. Either way, he was going to have to mate with her."

"She refused to choose another?"

"She couldn't, something about scent targeting. Once she's set on a mate, she can't change."

"What stopped her?"

"I poisoned her with colloidal silver." Cori said it casually, as if it were a low point in her life. Like a man admitting he had to kick a fellow man in the balls to win a fight.

Ethan smiled and withheld the laughter he wanted to bluster. "That's amazing." He wondered how many times he had used that word to describe her. Every time he said it, he meant it.

"Maybe, but I can't imagine she won't take my punishment out on you."

"Well, if you want to confront her, she's still over at the docks. Truck doesn't leave for another ten." He could see her repulsion at the idea of seeing Leona again, but that faded and was replaced by determination. "Come on. I'll wait by the door, just in case." He winked and extended his hand. She linked her fingers in his and they headed over to the docks for a showdown—or at least some verbal bitch-slapping.

7

E VEN BEFORE CORI WAS through the door, Leona was up from her crate and meeting her half way. Her business suit left nothing to the imagination. Even the high-necked, billowing blouse undercut her breasts. The woman evoked the image of respect and sex in one antithesis style.

Ethan stayed by the door to give her privacy. Cori knew he didn't want to have anything to do with a discussion involving her past with Vince. Even the mention of his name made Ethan wince. Luckily, he understood how important the relationship had been for her. Without it, she would not have overcome her insecurities. However, if he hadn't died, she might still be with Vince, and that was no doubt where some of Ethan's bitterness stemmed from.

There were three dockworkers loading the truck with empty boxes. With so many runs in and out of the prison these days, they had taken to loading empty boxes on the trucks to hide their passengers. With that much traffic coming out of no-man's-land, if a cop pulled over a truck with only one woman stashed openly in the back, they might see fit to investigate where the truck had come from.

Leona stepped up close to Cori. This awkward conversation was apparently not going to be given the space that Ethan and Cori had afforded each other. Leona did so love to breach personal space. "I knew you'd come see me. Couldn't resist, could you? I suppose you're here to ask me to protect Ethan."

"Actually, I came to ask you to stay away from him."

Leona scoffed. "Really? And what makes you think you have the right to ask me for anything?"

Cori licked her lips. "I think I've earned your respect as a *frenemy*. I asked never to see you again. I know this was unintentional, but I need you not to interfere with my life here. Ethan is too important to me. There has to be another person who can help you with this."

"The promise I made does not take precedence over my son. Ethan is the best at what he does, and I need the best. Besides all that, *you* owe *me*."

"How's that?"

"The father of my son, the one who has kidnapped him. He is the mate I took after Vince." Cori shifted, feeling the backlash of karma smacking her in the ass. "If I had mated with Vince, I would have been pregnant already when I met this man. Since he turned out to be a violent oppressive pack hunter, I think it only fitting that you now release *your* man to help me be rid of him."

"I'm sorry for your trouble, Leona. I know it seems like a petty thing now, but he meant everything to me. I took no pleasure in defeating you."

"Defeat?" Leona's eyes widened with a flare of rage. She stepped in closer, softening her voice. "You got lucky, little girl. Never forget that." She touched Cori's arms, rubbing them gently. Leona directed a glare behind her. Ethan must have shifted to intervene.

"I know what you're really afraid of," Leona whispered, her hot, minty breath tickling Cori's face. "I know you're afraid I'm going to seduce him. You think I'll take revenge on you by sleeping with your new love?"

Cori nodded. She couldn't find the voice to respond anymore. She wasn't afraid, but the only thing she could contribute was dense, feeble gestures.

"I want you to know that I could and I might, but what you need to understand—what most of you *still* don't understand—is this: If I want it, I take it. I will make no more promises to you. I will not bind myself to you in any way, friend or foe. If it pleases me to have your husband, I will." Leona squeezed her arms. "If it pleases me to have *you*, I will. There is not one thing you could do to stop it. Understand?"

Cori understood her words, but she was a little confused about when her feet had stopped touching the ground. They dangled inches from the floor, held up by Leona's inexorable strength. To add to her show of power, she kissed Cori. It was an eerie mix of sincerity, sexuality, and more than a fair share of intimidation.

Though her feet had returned to the ground, and Leona had long since dismissed herself to the truck, Cori could still feel her lips pressed against hers. She forcefully pulled herself from whatever trance she was in and returned to Ethan.

He was standing against the back wall with his foot propped and his hand clasping his mouth. The glimmer in his eyes was a tell for the smirk he was hiding.

Cori shook her head at him. "Shut up."

8

DANATO AVOIDED THE SPLATTER of cream of mushroom soup as Cori plopped the contents of her can into her noodles. He handed her the tuna, which she ungratefully ripped from his hands and dumped in. He gave her a questioning look, but she turned her burner on and stirred the casserole until she was satisfied with the consistency.

Ethan had gone upstairs to pack for his trip. The two of them were alone, as they would be for the next week. It wasn't unfamiliar territory, but even one meal was excruciating when Cori was in a foul mood. It didn't help that he was the cause of it, or at least, to blame for it in her eyes.

"Cori—" Danato started.

"I don't want to talk about it. You're right; he's right; I'm selfish. It doesn't mean I'm not going to be pissed. I love him. I don't want him near her. I hate her. You're just going to have to live with me like this until he's back. Okay?" She finished her rant and gave him a determined chin up.

"I was just going to say that we should put Parmesan cheese in there."

Cori looked down at the tuna noodle casserole in her pot. She looked back at him. "Yeah, let's do that."

He grabbed the shaker out of the fridge and let her liberally apply the cheese. "I know how you feel, you know?"

"I know you're just as concerned about Ethan as I am," she said, taming her tone enough to sound sympathetic. "I know you wouldn't send him if it wasn't very strictly part of his job." She stirred the pasta and tasted it. Satisfied, she turned off the burner and dug out a potholder.

"No—yes, but I mean, I know how it feels to have a spouse in danger." Cori's interest perked, and she neglected her pasta. "If you remember, I had a wife."

"Of course I remember," Cori scolded, putting her hand on her hip. "How could I forget such a thing?"

"Well, she was often in dangerous situations. I imagine you feel the same frustration I did. You want to just close your eyes and make all the bad stuff go away, but you can't because that's who they are. Taking away the danger takes away the reason you loved them to begin with. Ethan wasn't half the man he was until he was fighting dragons and hunting vampires. You can hardly ask him to go back to being meek and unassuming now that you have a reason to protect him.

"And take it from someone who knows: it won't make it any easier on Ethan for you to be overly upset about him leaving. The last thing he needs is to be concerned about how you're doing instead of concentrating on his job."

Danato took the potholder and the casserole to the table for her. As he placed it on the table, he thought it was missing a food group since the mushrooms were few and far between in the soup. "Why don't we whip up a quick lettuce salad?"

He headed back to the fridge for greens, tomatoes, and cucumbers, courtesy of Cori's genius in the greenhouse. Cori grabbed a big bowl, and they both started ripping lettuce into it. She glanced at him several times, but said nothing. When her hand came to rest on his in the bowl, he looked over at her. "What's wrong?"

She looked sad, but in a different way than before. It was directed at him. "Do you think you'll ever feel comfortable talking to me about what happened to her?"

For a half second, he had no idea what she was talking about. When he realized his wife was the topic of discussion, he had to block out the thousand and one thoughts that accompanied her memories. "Cori," he whispered, feeling her eyes on him as he spoke. "You know I love you. You being here means the world to me, and I would give you anything in the world—within reason." She nodded, taking the sentiments like heavy bags of groceries. "But that part of my life is over and I will not discuss it."

Her eyes flickered over his, trying to discern his temperament. She might have suspected he was mad, and she could easily assume he was sad, but there would be no way for her to place the third emotion that always accompanied his memories of his wife's death.

Guilt.

He had no intention of reliving any of his history. Not for the sake of empathy or understanding. Certainly not to entertain curiosity.

The moment was interrupted by Ethan tramping down the stairs. They broke hands and continued to slice the cucumbers and tomatoes to add to the lettuce. "That smells good." Ethan dropped his duffel bag by the door. It was rather small, Danato thought, even for a week, but since Ethan rarely escaped his black t-shirt and cargo pants, there really wasn't much of a wardrobe to pack. "Any wine, or are we saving that for my triumphant return?"

"Wine it is," Danato agreed. He did prefer to save the wine for special occasions, but goodbyes were as much an ordeal as hellos, so why not? He wiped off his hands and pulled a choice bottle from the wine rack on the counter beside the fridge. Ethan practically ran to fetch the glasses. He grabbed three, even though Cori usually just sipped hers to be polite. Ethan never noticed that she poured most of it down the sink at the end of the meal.

He popped the cork just as Cori finished the salad. They sat down at the table and started devouring the food with hardly a word of conversation apart from groans of appreciation to compliment the cook. Though Danato would never burden her with supper duty every night, he preferred her cooking to Ethan's and even his own. It was a benefit he was loath to be rid of, but he had put off the hard conversation long enough.

"I have something I want to talk to you both about. We should probably discuss it before Ethan leaves."

"What's up?" Ethan said with a mouth full of noodles.

"I assume the house has finally decided on your apartment?"

"Yes," Ethan said, swallowing. "It's the perfect combination of modern and comfortable."

Cori nodded in agreement.

"At some point, we will need to consider other accommodations."

After an exchange of glances, Cori and Ethan dropped their forks. They both swallowed hard and stared at him. "Are you kicking us out?" Cori asked.

"No. Me. Other accommodations for me."

They once again shared a glance before returning to him. "But this is your house," Ethan pointed out like Danato had gone senile.

"I know that, but you are going to be warden. This is your house."

"No," Cori said. "This is *our* house."

Danato shook his head. "You two are married now. You don't want me cramping your style."

"Do you want to leave?" Cori questioned, with notable pain in her voice.

"No, I love it here." Danato put his hand over hers, so she didn't think he was trying to escape them.

"Danato." Ethan looked at Cori. "I think we both agree that we don't want things to change." She nodded fervently at him.

"But this house could be your house. The way you want it. Your style," Danato insisted.

"We like this house because it's home. We like it for the contents currently in it." Ethan pulled up his napkin and tossed it on his plate. He motioned to the table. "Do you see the three unoccupied chairs at this table? I don't want more empty chairs at my table. I want more butts in the seats. I don't want fewer people in my home. I want more."

Danato smiled. He had expected them to demur as any polite person would, but he didn't expect them to outright refuse to let him leave. He'd thought he was offering them a way out of their awkward cohabitation. He'd had no idea they actually preferred being with him.

"I guess it's settled," he said, raising his glass to drink.

"Damn right it is." Ethan toasted the air and joined him for a swig.

9

ETHAN WOKE TO THE soft pressure of lips trailing his belly. He wasn't sure what time it was, or how long it had been since he had finally laid down to sleep. Between saving her life that morning and him leaving on the next, Cori had already made advances on him twice that night.

Cori rarely instigated sexual advances, but since her amnesia incident, she had been more open to his advances. He knew part of her would always be a little temperamental about it, and he had long since accepted that. He couldn't smell her emotions like Vince had, so he had to rely on good old-fashioned instincts.

Ushered once into the throes of passion, he didn't question. Twice he was still not surprised by. However, as she made her way beyond the horizon of his elastic waistband, he was wondering what else might have prompted her devoted attention.

He cupped his hand on her cheek before she could begin her ministrations and change his mind. She looked up at him, baffled that he might refuse her generous offerings. "Hey, why don't you come up here and talk to me?" he whispered, still half asleep.

She balked, but eventually slid back up to face him. Her old t-shirt and sweatpants were far from the sexy lingerie that men fantasized about, but he preferred the honest soft cotton to silk and lace. Cori may have been an emotionally complex person, but her vanity was simple.

"What's wrong?" she asked. The question was loaded with undertones of: *I thought you liked that. Aren't you attracted to me? Don't you love me anymore?*

Ethan tucked a flaxen wave behind her ear so it wasn't blocking her view. "I was about to ask you the same thing."

"What do you mean? Are you too tired?"

"Probably, but that's not the point. Why so much attention?"

"You're leaving tomorrow. She glanced at the clock on his side table. Today."

"For a few days, not a month."

"If you don't want me, just say so," she grumbled and flipped back over to her side of the bed.

He let out a growling sigh and reached under her to drag her back. He rolled himself on top of her and pinned her down beneath him. He could already see the panic in her eyes and feel the wrenching in her muscles as she fought against the submissive position. He knew he was playing with fire by handling her this way, but he didn't have time to thread through her walls and labyrinths.

Despite years of familiarity and months of intimacy, she bucked against him, trying to free herself. He could feel her heart racing through his chest. She panted from futile exertion.

After a moment, she stopped struggling, but he could see she was resisting the urge to yell or cry. He relaxed the tension in his grip and she looked up at him, begging for a complete release, but not willing to admit defeat to him.

"I don't have enough time to weed through your crap, Cori." He wasn't mad, but his frankness still gave her pause. "Tell me what's got you coming back for thirds."

"I thought..." He could almost see her give up on the sentence, like she knew he wouldn't believe it. "I don't want you to sleep with Leona."

He chuckled. "I wasn't planning on it, but I'll put you down for a vote of nay."

"I'm serious!" Her neck muscles strained as she lifted to head butt him. Just short of her goal, she settled back into the mattress. "She'll seduce you. I know it won't be your fault, but I don't like it."

"Cori, werewolves have no particular power for seduction, although you might be the exception to that rule. What is with you and the girl-on-girl hypno-kisses?"

"I don't know," Cori grumbled, bucking to get away again.

"It seems to me the only person she wants to sleep with is you." He smiled.

"No, she doesn't. She just does that to intimidate me and throw me off."

"Are you sure? If you want, I could get her number for you."

"Shut up!"

He laughed, feeling her give one last-ditch effort to get him off. "Why do you fight so hard when you know all you have to do is ask me to get off?"

Her face blanked and her body froze. She looked over his face suspiciously. "If I ask you to get off me, you will?"

"Of course. You know I'm your slave once we enter this room." He winked.

Her body relaxed, and she started breathing normally, even though he hadn't actually changed anything about his position. "She's beautiful, you know. Sexy long legs."

"You have a hangup about legs, don't you?" He released her left arm and reached down to grab her thigh. "I like your legs."

"They're chicken legs."

"I don't know what that means, but if it means they're strong enough to ride a man into ecstasy, then hurray for chicken legs." When she didn't smile at his quip, he realized this was more than simple jealousy. "Don't you trust me, Cori?"

She nodded. "Yes, but I don't trust her. She's going to sleep with you just to get back at me."

Ethan could see that she was already steeling herself for the inevitable downfall of his marital vows. Nothing he said was going to ease her mind. He released her and sat up, pulling her along with him.

In a position not so dissimilar to where they had been that morning, hanging from a dragon leash, he linked his fingers in her gold-ringed fingers and kissed each of her hands. "What can I do to convince you that it won't happen?"

"Stay." She shrugged.

"Done," he said instantly. She stared at him, baffled, unprepared for the quick response. "I'll have to brave Danato's disapproval, but if you want me to stay, I will."

"You can't."

"I can do what I want. Short of Danato stuffing me in a box and shipping me to Leona—which might be the resulting punishment—I won't leave if that's what you want."

Cori sighed. She shook her head. "No, you have to go. It's who you are. I can't just pin you down and make you be boring and safe just because I'm affected by your risks."

"Wow, that's very mature thinking."

"It's not mine. Danato told me that. I just didn't really realize what it meant until now. I can't ask you to avoid danger because I love you. Your willingness to face danger is part of why I love you to begin with."

"And Leona?"

Her face melted, on the verge of tears, but she snapped herself out of the thought she was in. "I know you'll do your best. I hope it's enough." She touched his cheek as if he were the one that needed comforting on the subject. He had no doubts about his loyalties, but Cori did.

He shook his head. There was nothing more to be said. She had accepted his infidelity as retribution for her attack on Leona. He gave up on convincing her otherwise and reached up the back of her t-shirt to grip her strap-free shoulders. "Where were we before I interrupted you?"

She smiled and dove onto his mouth with a kiss that was as much anguish as it was lust. He reveled in her confidence, regardless of the motivation for it. He knew nothing would make him stray from her, and if it took a few days away from her with a werewolf to prove it, then so be it.

He leaned her back onto the bed, pressing his weight against her. He could feel her try to lift to get on top, but he wanted her under him. He released her long enough to remove her t-shirt and pants.

He stayed back a moment to look over her naked body. He knew her insecurities left her uncomfortable with his eyes on her, but she was beautiful. The legs she referred to as chicken legs were firm and muscular. Her belly and breasts were pale—lovingly referred to as milky. He had never thought much of the description until he had his very own creamy flesh to touch and kiss. The view made his mouth water.

Cori rolled her eyes and pulled a blanket over the top of her body. He promptly ripped it away. She looked perturbed by his gawking, but she just turned her head so she didn't have to see him.

He leaned down to her ear and whispered, "Touch me." His voice was trembling from the restraint he was exercising not to pounce on her. She reached her hand below his waistband of took hold of him. He gritted his teeth against the pleasure and gently turned her chin to look at him. "Do you feel that?" She nodded and started to caress him. "That's what you do to me," he said, trying to keep his focus on her instead of himself. "Just looking at you turns me on. I am a slave to you, and only you."

He could see her eyes flicker between his. She released him just long enough to remove his pants and push them down with her feet. She pressed on his lower back, begging for him. "Then give me what I want, slave." She smiled.

He descended on her, giving her the embrace they were both aching for. He watched her as she climbed to ecstasy again and again until he could no longer resist his own. Collapsing against those milky white breasts, he murmured, I love yous and promises of fidelity until he fell asleep.

10

THE NEXT MORNING, ETHAN roused to the feel of a cold bed. Cori had long since slipped out of the room. He looked at the clock. It was nearly 9:00 a.m. He only had a few hours before the afternoon truck came in.

Ethan got dressed and headed downstairs. He could smell bacon and eggs before he hit the first landing, and suspected Cori was making him a goodbye breakfast. He was surprised, given what he had put her through last night, that she was even awake, let alone functional.

Cori wasn't the best morning person and late nights of lovemaking usually made for a grumpy-butt in the morning. It was a small sacrifice that was well worth the irritated looks and sarcastic tongue.

As he came out of the hall to greet his blushing, bitchy bride, he found Danato hard at work making breakfast. Danato looked up as he entered. Ethan must have been wearing a terribly disappointed expression because Danato deepened his brow in confusion. "What is that look for?"

Ethan shook away whatever look he was giving him and proceeded directly to the coffee, which was always the first thing Danato prepared. "I was expecting Cori to be in front of the stove."

"Sorry to disappoint you."

"Oh, I'm not disappointed," Ethan said as he grabbed a mug from the cupboard. "Anyone making me breakfast is welcome, but I just didn't expect my morning kiss to involve whisker bristles that weren't my own."

Danato laughed. "You should be so lucky."

Ethan poured his coffee and sat down at the end of the counter on one of the bar stools. "Where is she? I thought she would be here to see me off. I only have a couple of hours."

Danato nodded. "Yes, that was a hot topic this morning."

"What now?"

Danato shrugged. "You know who you married."

"Yes, I know who I married." Danato flipped several pancakes, a side of bacon, and two over medium eggs on a plate and handed it to Ethan. He preferred his eggs over easy, but anything that wasn't burned to a crisp by Danato, he was grateful for. "What did she say?"

"Something about last night being the perfect goodbye and not wanting to spoil it with tears, arguing, or yelling."

"What?" Ethan moaned, even though he knew exactly what she was talking about. He slammed his fist on the counter. "I thought we dealt with this last night."

While Danato loaded up a plate for himself, that was nearly double the size, Ethan smothered his pancakes in peanut butter and honey—a rather strange concoction that the big man had introduced him to. And addicted him to.

"What did you deal with last night? Or is that private?" Danato added. Ethan assumed since Danato had broached the subject of moving out that he was trying to make a concerted effort not to get between them. It was a noble effort, but again, unnecessary. Ethan wanted privacy for the happy parts of his relationship, but for the not-so-happy parts, he wanted second and third opinions.

Although Ethan was younger than Cori, he often felt more mature than her. She was so reckless with her emotions. She was easy to anger, quick to tears, and rarely did she show the level of reserve he did when dealing with a difficult or uncomfortable situation.

However, when it came to being in a marriage, he really had no idea what the right and wrong ways to handle things were. He often sought out Danato's advice. At least he had been married before. He should at least have the insight of what not to do.

"No, it's fine," Ethan assured him. "Cori apparently thinks Leona has a vendetta against her."

"How is that? I never got the story on that one."

"Leona chose Vince as her mate, while Cori was with him. He had the choice of volunteering for it or fighting it. Either way..." Ethan raised his brow and took a bite of his pancakes. Danato knew how that sentence ended.

"I imagine Cori wasn't okay with it either way."

"No." Ethan covered his mouth and swallowed so he didn't offend Danato's delicate sense of decorum. "She knew she was in an unwinnable fight, but she tried anyway. She met with Leona to *offer* Vince. She spiked her coffee with colloidal silver."

Ethan took another bite. The smile that curved on Danato's face was nothing short of a proud father. He knew how stupid and dangerous it was for Cori to pull such a stunt, but he also knew that she was just that stupid, and he couldn't be prouder. "I'm surprised Leona didn't kill her on the spot."

Ethan nodded and sipped his coffee to get his food down. "I guess they kind of have a mutual respect. Cori asked her to promise never to see her again. Leona, thinking she had won, agreed. For whatever reason, even after the poisoning, Leona kept her promise."

"Mmm." Danato nodded. "I can see that. Vince was always very reluctant to promise anything. Werewolves have a lot of very traditional values that are passed down from generation to generation. I won't say that all werewolves hold a vow so dear, but the better half of them take a promise very seriously." Danato started doctoring his own pancakes. "So, I assume Cori doesn't want you to go because she thinks Leona is going to hurt you as revenge."

"No, I think Cori knows I can hold my own against a pregnant fem-wolf." Ethan paused, wondering if revealing this part of the conversation went against Cori's privacy more than his own. "She thinks Leona is going to seduce me."

Danato gave a silent, "*ahh,*" as the statement revealed far more than a sticky plot point. "She's jealous. I assume you told her it was preposterous?"

The undertone of the question was not so much verification of what he told Cori, but rather confirmation that he was indeed devoted to his wife. Ethan gave him a look that said, "*duh,*" and probably bordered on "*how dare you?*" "Yes, but I can't do anything to make her believe me."

Danato paused and thought about the situation for a moment. It amazed Ethan that the man was leaving his food unattended for this long. He must have been determined to help him through his conundrum. "I think you've done everything you can. Words are lost on her right now."

"How can she think that of me, though? Danato, I know you see how much we argue, but..." He paused once again, debating how much of his marriage he wanted to reveal. Danato was like his father, his father-in-law, his mentor, and his friend all rolled into one. He already knew his whole life. What was one more detail? "I am always—" He lowered his voice as if there might be someone else in the house to overhear him. "—gentle and patient. I've never once given her room to think I am cruel or barbaric. How can she think that I would be ruled by my desires?"

Danato didn't wince at hearing the inference to their love life. He took in the information, just as he would the details of a report. Ethan was thankful for that. "I don't think Cori suspects that you are a lecherous man. I don't think she thinks that Leona will seduce you. I think she thinks she will rape you."

Ethan furrowed his brow and laughed. "Is that even possible?"

Danato tipped his brow and shrugged. "The male body is not without its faults. Even in the face of something as undesirable as wrecking your marriage, it is possible that your body would betray you against your will."

Ethan leaned back from his plate. He had just lost his appetite. "Do you think she could accomplish that in her pregnant state?"

"I think she would have a marginal upper hand, but that might be enough if you are in the least bit incapacitated by wounds or... mixed feelings."

Ethan all-out glared at Danato's second, underhanded accusation. "Stop accusing me, Danato. I love Cori too much to be that cavalier with her trust."

"I know, but sending you away isn't making just Cori nervous." Danato looked down at his cooled pancakes. He must have lost his appetite, too.

"What? Please tell me this isn't about danger. Our plan is sound. I'll be lucky to get a scratch out of this trip. I'll have the offending pack leader on your doorstep in two, maybe three, days."

"Yes, I know. I've never doubted your skills at hunting. You were always well suited for the violent profession. Perhaps better suited than for warden."

Ethan took in a deep breath. "So, my wife thinks I'm going to cheat on her, and you think I'm going to abandon you?"

"No, I know you will return." Danato leaned in on the counter. "I just don't think you understand how much guilt I have for bringing both of you here against your will. It was a choice made out of desperation, and I abhorred doing it."

"You're afraid I'll get back into the big bad world and resent being cooped up in here with you?"

"Essentially." Danato nodded.

"Well, I guess I could tell you the same as I did Cori: I love you and I will never betray you, but that isn't quite what you need, is it?" Danato arched an eyebrow at the sarcasm-laced comment. "Nothing is going to change, Danato. You've given me more in this confining lifestyle than I ever had in my life of foster homes and juvenile incarcerations. However, now that you bring up the outside world." Ethan grimaced. "There has been some discussion between myself and Cori about changing things up a little."

Danato crossed his arms and narrowed his eyes in preparation for the subject. "What changes?"

Ethan pulled his plate back to him, feeling his appetite re-emerge. "Just as I mentioned last night, Cori and I like having you around, but our evenings are feeling repetitive. We eat, we do dishes, you fall asleep in your chair reading, Cori and I play games. Frankly, we're bored."

"I told you I'd order new games."

"Yeah, no, the games are fine, but we want new people to play them with." Danato's face was vacant. He either didn't understand or he was still thinking of a response. "I wasn't sure how you would feel if I invited some of the guards for a poker night. Also, Cori has been talking non-stop about an outdoor BBQ." Ethan knew Danato was likely to decline both suggestions, but it didn't stop him from wearing his best pleading face. He probably looked like a teenager begging to borrow the car.

Danato's face fell. He looked admonished by Ethan's words. "I'm so sorry."

Ethan nodded. "I understand. I just thought I would ask. I'm sure Cori and I can come up with something to keep things exciting."

"No." Danato looked up at him with sad eyes. "Of course you can have people over. Of course, Cori can throw a BBQ. What a recluse I must seem to both of you." The disappointment Danato was directing at himself shocked Ethan. "I never meant to make you think you should be like me. Ever since..." He bit his lip and shook his head. "I've been wallowing in self-pity for a long time, Ethan. I'm sorry that it never occurred to me that you might want more to life than dinner and board games."

Ethan took in a deep breath and let it out. "Oh, thank God, I was about to chuck those damn things in the fireplace." Ethan laughed, and Danato joined him. If Ethan had had any resentment about being cloistered in this prison, it was gone now.

11

E THAN KNEW CORI DIDN'T want to see him before she left, but he couldn't leave without saying goodbye. It was only a few days, but since she was still upset, even after last night's effort to quell her fears, he wanted to make sure he did everything in his power to secure their future.

He already knew she would be hanging out in her greenhouse, preparing her plants for transfer to the wizard world. It had taken her nearly a month to get Danato to agree to that little experiment, and she was more than proud to have influenced his decision with a seduction of fresh tomato BLTs, crisp cucumbers drenched in ranch, and sweet corn dripping in butter. The man was a stickler for safety, but he had no chance when Cori came at him through his stomach.

Ethan charged into the greenhouse and caught her repotting a plant. Her face was already dismissive, but he ignored it. He turned her around and threw her over his shoulder. She yelled and hit his back harder than he had expected. He was certain she was going to be mad for a while. He just hoped not so long that he couldn't get a proper goodbye kiss to accomplish his purpose.

He took her outside and listened to her scream and yell at him to put her down. He tolerated her beatings, but when she bit him, he gave her butt a firm smack.

"Hey!" she yelped.

"Don't bite!" he said firmly. He could almost sense her pouting lips. She stopped hitting him, but he could tell she was still infuriated.

When he made it to his target, he kneeled down. She tried to get her footing, but he pulled her knees up so he could lay her down on the blanket he had spread for them. She grabbed on to his neck, afraid he was going to drop her, but she released when she felt the fabric beneath her.

She looked over the blanket and smiled at the basket of fruit he had put together, mostly strawberries and grapes. She looked back at him. He lay down next to her, leaning on his elbow so his face was above her. He could tell she wanted to be mad, but the gesture was just too damn sweet.

He grabbed a strawberry and fed it to her, after which he kissed her. "I'm sorry," she whispered as he withdrew from the kiss. He wasn't sure what she was apologizing for: the bite, the hitting, or just the overall mistrust. "I know I should trust you, but she is just so conniving."

"I understand why you're concerned. She is a very strong creature. She could force the issue, but I don't think she will."

"Why do you say that?"

"She wants her baby back. I think she will be so occupied with him, she won't even know I'm gone. Which I will be the second that kid is safe. Okay?"

"Okay." She nodded. "I never took you for a picnic kind of guy," she said, nodding to the display.

"I'm not. I hate sitting on hard ground. I hate eating food outside. I hate using paper plates and plastic silverware." He kissed her. "But I know you like it and that smile is enough to drag me to a battle, let alone a picnic."

"How did you ever come to love me that much? I feel like I am always struggling to find the core reason behind that devotion. You have to hate me sometimes, don't you?"

"Hate?" He fed her a grape. "You are stubborn and sometimes I want to put a clamp on that mouth of yours." He smiled when her face crumpled at his honesty. "But you're real. You don't have ulterior motives. The only thing you want from me is my love and devotion." He put his hand under her shirt to touch the soft skin of her belly. "After my parents died, I was always looking for somewhere to belong. It never occurred to me to look in Siberia." She smiled at him, and he went on.

"When I met you, I thought you were this beautiful, broken, wild creature. You were frustrating, but once in a while, when I would do something right, you would let your guard down. I fell in love with you, Cori, because I knew once I figured out how to disarm you, I would have someone to share my life with who understood how precious and fleeting love can be." He pushed her hair back. "I'm leaving today at noon. I expect you to be the last face I see before those doors close on me."

She nodded. "Okay."

"Good, now that that's settled, I have some good news."

"What's that?"

"I asked Danato about your BBQ idea." She paused with the same eager, hopeful enthusiasm he had shown Danato. "He gave the go-ahead."

She gasped and hugged him, planting kisses all over his face and neck. He laughed, wondering if he should be insulted that his soliloquy of love hadn't provoked as much excitement as Danato's permission to have a party.

The final kiss that prompted her to straddle him, however, seemed to be a response to his previous declarations. Though he had chosen a secluded area for the picnic, he did a double-check to make sure no one was stationed in view above them on the roof. Once he was sure they weren't to be interrupted or peeped on, he let her have her way with him. With such attentions, Ethan was certain that he would have nothing left for Leona even if she tried to force herself on him.

When their outdoor romp was complete, she walked him back inside for a proper clothed send-off. He wrapped his arm around her and kissed her forehead as they walked down the hall to the docks. "You are going to spoil me,

Cori. What am I to do with all this energy when you aren't giving me so much goodbye sex?"

She smiled. "There's always hello sex, make-up sex, and bored sex."

He smiled. "Do me a favor."

"Hmm?"

"Focus on your work for the next few days. I know your brain. I know you'll fret about me and what's-her-butt if you don't. There's nothing I can say to make you not, but try, for me."

Cori inhaled deeply. "For you, I guess I will bury my hands in dirt."

The dock manager was already checking the clock when they strolled in. He had already packed his duffel bag. He was just waiting for Ethan—impatiently. They were right on time, but the five minutes before they arrived, he'd no doubt been frantic that his shipment of empty boxes would be late.

Ethan gave Cori a long sensuous kiss that made the dock manager "ahem." Ethan mouthed, *I love you*, as he backed away. Cori mouthed it back to him. He pointed at her feet and then to his eyes. He still wanted her to be his last sight as the truck closed.

He was practically shoved into the truck by the dock manager, which he chose to ignore since he didn't want to interrupt his longing goodbye with Cori. It was short-lived, though. He saw Cori wave and the door shut.

He felt the truck move and he remembered how painful it was the first time he'd left her at those docks. He knew as well as anyone it was only for a few days, but when you were with someone nearly every moment of every day, it was surprisingly painful to be away from them for even a short time. It seemed like he was going to have to be the one submerged in work to keep from fretting over her.

12

CORI BARELY MADE IT in to report for duty. Her first night without Ethan by her side had left her tossing and turning. Consequently, she'd slept through the alarm. If it weren't for the house's subtle lighting changes and temperature drop, she may have still been comatose in her bed. She wasn't sure she was thankful for the goading, considering how tired she was, but she appreciated that the house took notice of her, even if she hadn't been doing the best job keeping her apartment picked up.

Decked out in black cargo pants—with more pockets than pants should be allowed to have—a white t-shirt, and a fitted matching black jacket, she strolled into the prison. She hadn't intended to join the black brigade, but her gun holster left her yanking up her *relaxed fit* jeans. Plus, the black was rather slimming.

Whenever she changed her outfit, Ethan had a fit. In fact, any small changes in her hairstyle or personality put him on guard. He had been paranoid ever since the transmorph incident. He was mortified that he had not been able to identify the culprit Cori and he was determined never to mistake her again.

She jogged up the short set of stairs and through the hall leading to Danato's office. It would only cut a few seconds off her late arrival, but every second counted. She opened the office door, but before she could enter, and even before Danato and Belus had looked up to see her, they both hollered, "Gun!"

She grimaced and backpedaled to remove her pistol and place it in the hanging bin by the door. She had been wearing the thing nonstop for a few weeks, so she often forgot it was there.

She entered the office and closed the door. Belus, for a change, was sitting in a chair in front of the desk drinking coffee, while Danato was filling out paperwork.

"Sorry I'm late," she said, plopping herself onto the arm of the free chair with her feet on the seat.

Danato looked up at the clock. "Five minutes? That's hardly worth apologizing for."

Cori looked up at the clock on the wall. It read 8:05. The black on white numbers were all in the correct order, but they certainly weren't reading right. She was at least forty-five minutes late, if not nearly an hour, by her calculations. She was certain the clock was wrong, but she wasn't going to argue the point just to win disfavor.

"Are we going to go into the time bubble?" She rubbed her hands in anticipation. After some convincing and a little of Belus's diplomatic skills, Cori had gotten permission to plant a garden in the wizard realm so they could grow food faster. With no animal competition, and the time difference, she could plant a seed or seedling and be back to pick fresh vegetables in less than three days.

"No. Sit on that chair right," Danato scolded.

"No?" She glanced at Belus for some support as she slipped into the chair. He gave her a barely noticeable headshake and sipped his hot coffee gingerly. It was his way of saying, "*Wait.*" It was also his way of saying, "*Don't open your mouth, and say something you'll regret.*" Either way, she held her tongue for Danato to continue.

"*We* are not going. You are," Danato said.

"Me, by myself?" Cori had been into the wizard world a few times since her original stint with Ethan, but only for a few minutes at a time to track entrance locations. She knew she could handle the world, but it didn't mean the prospect of being there for several hours didn't scare her just a little. Or a lot.

"With your gun, of course. I mean, that was the point of getting them, wasn't it? So I don't have to babysit you all the time."

"Babysit? I resent that."

"You know the risks of that, don't you?" Danato peeked over the rim of his glasses. "If a wizard gets the drop on you, that gun isn't going to do you any good."

Cori glanced at Belus again, searching for the reason for such animosity. Danato had always been a stern man when it came to safety, but he usually wasn't so forceful with her. Belus lifted his cup to his mouth. As he did, he brought his other hand under his chin and tapped it. *Chin up.*

If she expected Danato to approve of this pursuit of hers, he needed her to have the discipline and responsibility to complete it. She took in a breath and brought her chin up physically in preparation for doing it internally. "I'll be very vigilant. Do you have any preference as to the location of the garden?"

"I assumed you had a spot in mind," Danato said.

Cori bit her cheek so she didn't smile. "Yes, sir, I have an ideal location picked out. Moist, fertile, and in full sun."

"Well, have at it, you're the botanist. I wouldn't presume to know your job."

She couldn't help but grin. "Thank you, sir." She knew Danato was trying to maintain his stern face for the sake of professional separation, but she could see the pleasure he derived from making her happy.

"Get on with it, then." He waved her off. She jumped up, prepared to undertake her day. "You'll need to if you're going to get the paperwork done for it by the end of the day." She stopped short of the door and groaned.

"No, paperwork." She turned back. "Paperwork for vegetables?"

"Paperwork for everything," he practically chanted.

Cori threw her head back and resisted the urge to stomp her feet like a child. "Yes, sir." She saw a new pleasure on Danato's face: the pleasure all superiors held for their underlings as they undertook the duties they had once endured and hated just the same.

Before the door shut behind her on her way out, two voices simultaneously shouted, "Gun!" She growled and grabbed the weapon that she would have forgotten otherwise .

13

O NCE SITUATED WITH HER supplies, it only took Cori an hour to plant her seeds in excess of forty plants. She wasn't sure how well the plants would do, but even if half of them came up, they were still saving months of time waiting for them to grow in the greenhouse. Not to mention she had far more space in real ground.

After a quick overview of the surrounding trees for wizards, she looked out onto the clear, crisp, freshwater lake. She remembered her first time here with Ethan. She remembered how harsh it had seemed to be stuck here, and yet the moment she was taken away from it, she would have killed for more time.

With another hour, at least before she was removed, she decided to make the best of it. She stripped down to her bare essentials and dove into the water for a swim. There was nothing as refreshing as a swim in natural, unchlorinated water.

When the time was up, she wrung out her hair and slipped back into her clothes lest she be drawn back into the real world half naked. It didn't take long for the swirling images of a canvas in the rain to signal her ascent from the bubble.

The guard who pulled her out was already prepared with her designated tuning fork, which released the cotton from her ears. She thanked him, and he returned to the pseudo-watchtower that overlooked the bubble. The plethora of buttons, lights, and switches inside the small enclosure provided readouts of anything and everything bubble-related. It was the one area of the prison, save the infirmary, that was staffed 24/7.

She pulled her wet hair back into a loose bun, preparing for the most boring day ever.

She heard a grunt and a thump. She turned toward the guard station and saw the guard hunched over his workstation.

The double doors to the room clapped shut. Even before her eyes reached the door, she could feel static electricity drawing the hairs on the back of her neck up.

Efrat, in all his casual glory, stood by the entrance with his hand on the light switch. She didn't know what the rules for conductivity were, or if they even applied to a supernatural being, but somehow Efrat had knocked out the guard from twenty feet away.

He looked the same as he had nearly a year ago when she'd faced off with him. His jeans and t-shirt layered with a blue flannel reminded her of how out of place he seemed in the prison. He should have been sitting on a couch watching football and drinking beer, not trespassing through the prison, plotting his escape. His blond hair was still just a little long, making it flare away from his face. His face was handsome, but more so because of his brilliant blues; the same brilliant blues that were now staring at her.

His eyes widened, mirroring her surprise. He must not have expected to find her there. The time bubble was not often visited by anyone. The self-sustaining prison was a bit off the beaten path for sightseeing.

Efrat's surprise dissipated, and his eyes bloomed with predacious intent. She knew she had only one chance of surviving this. Her gun was inches from her hand, but her opponent's weapons *were* his hands. She needed to escape into the time bubble. It was a risk, but her odds were better in there than staring down an elemental at close proximity.

Just as his hands rose, she simultaneously reached for her gun and flung herself back against the bubble. The reverse swan dive reached the bubble just as the bolt of electricity hit her. She felt the recoil of her gun, and the sharp pain of Efrat's electrification. She felt heat resonating through her metal rings, burning her fingers. Her back arched painfully and anatomically wrong. She thought it might break, but as fast as the pain hit her, it left. *The world around her swirled into a watercolor painting.*

14

ORI WOKE IN HER bedroom. The room was chilled. The lights were on. Her alarm was quietly humming somewhere below the bed, where she had knocked it to when it had assaulted her sleep. She checked her body and hands for charring, blood, or missing digits.

Nothing.

The skin beneath her rings was blanched, as it should be. Her lower back was a little achy from her days spent lifting dirt in the greenhouse, but not so painful that she might suspect a recent performance from *The Exorcist*.

It had been a dream.

Unfortunately, the dream must have been premonitory because she was indeed late for duty. Like in her dream, she didn't bother with a shower. She dressed and grabbed a token breakfast of a granola bar and headed into the prison.

This was a fine start to her week. Her husband was no doubt shacking up with her fem-wolf arch-enemy; Efrat, her murderer, was now trying to kill her in her dreams; and Danato was likely going to gripe her out for being late. Granted, being late was the least of her worries, but when the background stress was so high, everything seemed like a kick in the head.

Cori bounded into Danato's office just as—"Gun!"

She retreated from the doorway and placed her firearm in the bin with a minor muffled scream. She couldn't believe she had forgotten again. She stepped into the office and shut the door. She hadn't slammed the door, but the glass shuddered a little, anyway.

Just as in her dream, Danato was doing paperwork while Belus sipped on his coffee in the chair in front of the desk. "Sorry I'm..." She looked up at the clock; it read 8:05. She was now certain it was forty-five minutes off. "...a little late." Danato glanced up at the clock and grunted his concession before returning to his paperwork. "This is so weird." She sat on the arm of the chair, with her feet on the seat.

"Sit right." Danato pointed to her feet. It wasn't foretelling to predict that Danato would have an issue with her feet being on the furniture, but it was uncanny that the events were happening very similarly to her dream. She repositioned and started to put her feet up on the desk. "Don't even think about it," Danato said without looking up.

"Sorry, just had to throw a wrench in my déjà vu. It was starting to overwhelm. So, are we going into the time bubble today?"

"No," Danato said. He even paused as if he expected her to object, but since she was already predicting his response, she saved her breath. "You will go by yourself. You're armed now. I think you can handle it."

Cori grinned at seeing the hard look he was giving her to defend his choice before she had even objected to it. "I understand completely. I think you're right. I even have the perfect spot picked out. Shouldn't take me more than a couple of hours, and then I can start filling out the paperwork."

The two men exchanged looks of surprise and suspicion. "Who are you, and what have you done with Cori?" Danato asked. He was only partially joking, considering her past.

"I'm me. I was just prepared for this. I had a dream about it last night."

"Dream?" both men asked as they shot looks at each other before turning their concerned looks on her.

"What?" She looked between them for who would best explain the excitement.

"Cori." Danato stood up, tossing his glasses on his pile of papers. "We don't get to keep our dreams. We have protections from that. If you remember dreaming, something is wrong."

Cori shrugged. She had forgotten how the use of the wrong word could get her into so much trouble. "I don't know. Maybe I just... I don't know." She knew at the house, her nightmares couldn't touch her. She knew in the wizard world she had no protection and she had awful nightmares, but it never occurred to her she shouldn't be having *any* dreams.

Danato came around the desk and grabbed her hand. "Tell me what happened." She didn't like the attention she was getting for one little dream. She looked at Belus. He nodded toward Danato. *Tell him.*

"It was nothing. I woke up. I came here. You told me to go to the bubble by myself. I did. I planted the plants. I swam." Danato's eyes narrowed at that part, but he didn't interrupt. "I got out of the bubble and Efrat was there. He shocked me, and boom. I woke up."

Danato's comforting hand slipped away. He meandered back to his chair, but didn't sit down. He stood there pondering the situation. "This might explain your sighting of Efrat before."

"Maybe the transmorphs left her open," Belus said, still sipping on his coffee calmly. Danato could have been climbing the walls, and Belus would still be sitting in that chair.

"Yes," Danato agreed.

"Open to what?" she asked.

"Dream feeders," Belus said. "They inject you with bad thoughts, fears, and traumatic memories. Nightmares, like the ones you had while you were in the wizard world. Anything that will get your amygdala into overdrive. They feed off the energy it produces."

"If that's the case, what would happen to me—besides having nightmares?"

"Eventually, the creatures would be able to inject you with psychic stimulation while you're awake. Long-term exposure to that will result in paranoid and delusional behavior. That, of course, spawns all sorts of trouble depending on how paranoid, and how delusional."

Cori let her mouth hang open, but the defaming word could not be put back in now that it was out. "It's just a *dream*," she whined. She could see Danato pondering, turning the entire situation over and over again. Soon, he would be so concerned for her safety that he would lock her in the house to keep her safe.

"A test," she blurted out and turned to Belus, who was still sane. For once, she could see the benefit of having one man around that was not overprotective of her. "There's always a test. A CAT scan of my brain. Say my ABCs backward. There must be some way to determine that I'm not going schizoid on you."

"Actually..." Belus turned to Danato. "A PET scan should show if the amygdala is active."

Cori nodded vigorously. "Yes, let's do that!" She wasn't even sure what a PET scan did, but she was desperate to allay Danato's fears, as well as her own. Bottom line, she was sick of having anything taking her over. Dream feeders, transmorphs, fear demons, they all sucked something from you: life, happiness, sanity. If she could do anything to hedge off an attack, short of a lobotomy, she was going to do it.

15

THE PET SCAN WAS painless and so far no one had suggested brain surgery as the next course of action, but they were still waiting for the doctor to reveal the results of the scan. They were in the small foyer ahead of the nurse's station that was laughably called a waiting room. There were only four chairs, none of which looked sturdy enough for Danato's large frame. Instead of sitting, he just paced back and forth between the entrance and the hub. His ominous presence was making the two young women behind the counter nervous. They tried to look busy by shuffling their papers repetitiously, but Danato wasn't even paying attention to them.

Belus sat across from Cori in a chair, looking positively bored. If it hadn't been for their most recent conversation on the topic, she would have assumed he simply didn't care about the danger her brain might be in. As it was, it was still the first conclusion she went to.

When Danato was on the far leg of his pace, Cori switched chairs to sit beside Belus. She pulled her feet onto the chair and hugged her knees to her chest. He looked over at her inquisitively. "Do you think I'm under the influence of a dream feeder?" she asked, resting her head on her knees.

Belus noted the whisper in her voice and glanced at Danato. When he was sure he was out of ear's reach, he spoke. "It is possible. Being inside the prison for six weeks of your abduction would have made you susceptible, but transmorphs are not prone to being affected by dream feeders, so I doubt that you would have been exposed to them."

"So, how would I have been exposed to them?"

"You wouldn't."

Cori pulled her head up to watch Danato make a U-turn at the door. When he was gone, she turned her attention back to Belus. "You don't think this is a dream feeder, do you?"

"No."

"Why is he even considering it, then?"

"Danato has his own reasons for being concerned. I don't share his conclusions."

"Do you care to expand on that?" she asked.

Belus looked her over as if he were debating that very question. "If you were protected from your dreams as you should have been," Belus said, lowering his voice even further, "then there is no way this is a dream feeder."

"Is there some reason to think that I would not have been protected from my dreams?"

Belus opened his mouth to respond, but a nurse interrupted, announcing that the doctor was ready for them. Danato nearly bowled her over, heading to the computer lab. Belus slipped out of his chair, but Cori grabbed his arm before he could go. "What is he so concerned about?"

Belus glanced back at the nurse, who didn't know if she should wait for them or catch up with Danato. He gave her a nod, and she shuffled off to find the warden. He turned back to Cori.

"The house protects you from all supernatural influences while you sleep. You know that dream feeders produce a psychic energy that is designed to invade your mind in an unconscious state. What you don't know is that humans produce a minor psychic energy while they are in REM sleep."

"Humans are psychic in their sleep?"

"Not exactly, although some, yes. The point is the house absorbs unconscious psychic energy."

"The house absorbs psychic dream energy, but why can't I remember my dreams?"

He paused like he didn't want to say more. "It eats your dreams." She must have been holding a horrified expression because he went so far as to touch her hand that was still grasping his arm. "It is essentially the equivalent of what Cleos does when he removes your memories, unobtrusive and harmless, but the difference is the house can't access your mind, only the psychic energy being dispelled during sleep."

"Why?"

"Sustenance. Energy is energy. Look, I don't have time to explain, but rest assured, I feel very confident that the house has always and will always protect you."

"But Danato isn't confident?"

"He's not thinking clearly. He tends to do that when you're the concerned party."

"What does it mean if the house was protecting me?"

"That it wasn't a dream." Cori's eyes flickered over his and her mouth opened to spill a hundred more questions at him. "I don't know," he said, putting his hand over her mouth. "Danato and I will figure it out. Trust us."

Cori wondered if he knew how hard that was for her. "Okay," she muttered through his fingers before he removed them.

They headed to the infamous, off-limits computer lab. She followed Belus into the darkened room. Multiple computer monitors showed images of her brain activity. The blobs of color depicting her emotions and stimuli looked like kindergarten coloring projects and "Doctor Dickhead" was as proud of them as any mother of said kindergartener would be.

Danato ate up his spoon-fed technical jargon. Meanwhile, Cori's comprehension had stalled back in the office when the word *amygdala* came up. She resented that the guy was so smart that he had been elevated above the normal standards of socialization. He probably didn't even know how much of a condescending ass he was. Unfortunately, she wouldn't get the opportunity to educate him on the topic since she was a revolving-door patient and needed him on her good side. She would just have to grin and bear it. Or in her case, sneer and bear it.

Rather than stand there and look vacuous while he explained everything, she wandered out of the lab. No one noticed. The conversation taking place was about her, but it didn't actually have to include her.

As naturally as life handed her opportunities to feel bad about herself, it was no surprise that her exit from the lab caused a collision with one of the nurses. A tray of vials flipped out of the woman's hands and broke on the floor. The dark red blood it contained puddled at their feet.

"Oh, crap!" Cori groaned, giving the nurse the expression one gives when they are not just sorry, but mortified to be such an idiot. "I'm so sorry!" She leaned down without thinking and prepared to pick up the mess.

"Oh, honey, no!" The nurse grabbed her hands before she could touch anything. "Bare hands and sharp bloody objects don't go well together. Let me go grab a spill kit. Don't touch anything. I don't want you to get hurt." The nurse bounded off to fetch the kit while Cori stood crouched by the mess, prepared to be the orange cone to avert passersby from stepping into the mess.

When she looked back down, she saw the blood against the white floor, but the shattered shards of the glass vials were gone. A body was lying next to it.

"Belus!" she exclaimed upon seeing the face of the body.

16

CORI GASPED, FALLING BACK on her butt. She crabwalked away from Belus's unconscious form. Blood seeped on the floor from his back. She could see a small hole dotted with red in his side.

A trail of bloody hand tracks followed her away from the body. She looked at her palms and saw the blood staining the creases in her hands and coagulating under her fingernails. One of her fingers looked disjointed, but she couldn't feel any pain from it since her arm hurt so much. She was trembling, but it wasn't from being cold.

The walls of the infirmary hall were gone. She couldn't immediately place what part of the prison she was in, but the large and small empty cells suggested she was on the part-time level. A row of armed guards pointed pistols and elemental weapons at her. They looked baffled, as if the orders they had been given weren't making any sense to them.

Movement on her left caught her eye. Efrat rose from his sprawled position on the floor and approached Belus's body. He paid her no heed as he passed her by. Awaking her muddled mind; she reached for her gun, but the holster was empty. She backpedaled further along the ground, ignoring the pain in her arm so she could escape his attack.

"Don't move!" Danato yelled on her right.

She whipped around and saw him pointing a gun at *her*. Another row of guards were lined behind her, waiting for an order, any order. "Danato!" she gasped in relief. "What's going on? What's happened to Belus?"

Danato's eyes were hard with anger, but she saw him cringe, as if he might cry. "Do it." He ground out the words to Efrat, but kept the gun securely trained on Cori.

Cori looked back at Efrat as he kneeled beside Belus. His hands hovered over the body, charged with electricity. "No! Danato, what are you doing? Shoot the bastard!" she screamed, but Danato didn't move his gun off her.

Cori gave up reasoning with him. He was obviously as stunned by the event as she was, and couldn't think straight. She pushed herself back to her feet and ran at Efrat to tackle him.

Her attack was not throttled by his bolts, but when she was close enough to push him away, he flipped her to her back, using her own momentum. He pushed her to the floor and gripped her wrists firmly and painfully over her chest. He pressed all his weight on to her hands, pushing them into her breasts. She struggled to bring her legs up so she could kick him, but he kept his body at her side, out of range.

"Corinthia!" he yelled at her.

She had been prepared for slurs and banter, but she had not expected to hear her birth name from his lips. As it usually did, the name froze her because she expected her mother to jump out and tell her to clean her room.

She met his eyes. A sea of beautiful blue—that had no business being on the face of a criminal—was conveying urgency and concern. "Let me save him!" He spoke the punctuated words as if she was deaf or dumb. It was probably for the best since, at that moment, she understood nothing.

Cori searched his face for the meaning of this statement. His eyes flickered over hers, searching for the permission to release his grip. His face pleaded the request that she didn't want to believe from his voice. "I need to defibrillate him, or his heart will stop completely and he will die," he explained further when she didn't visibly concede. "I will save him."

She knew she was lost down the rabbit hole, but why did the white rabbit look like the big bad wolf? She had so many questions: How did she get here? Why was everyone here? How had Belus been shot?

None of them mattered, though. Belus was over the threshold of death, and the man that had put her into a flatline nearly a year ago was offering to save him. "Why?" She voiced the only question that refused to be put off.

He released her wrists and backed away slowly, like she might be a risk to him. He distanced himself from her body before he answered. "Because you asked me to." Efrat turned and repositioned his hands over Belus. He pressed them to his chest like paddles, and Belus's body arched from the electricity.

"*Cori?*" *Danato called her name.*

When she looked up toward Danato's voice, his eyes were filled with concern and his hands were free of the gun that had recently been pointed at her. The cages of the part-time level were gone.

17

The stark white walls and crisp clean glass windows of the infirmary hallway surrounded her again. Danato was peeking out of the computer lab. "Why are you crying?" he asked.

Cori touched her face and felt the wet tears. "Belus has been shot."

His brow dove deep, trying to discern the purpose of this deception. "No, he hasn't. Belus, come out here."

Belus stepped out behind Danato into the hall. "What's—" He started, but observed the mess on the floor. "Seriously, kid, we can't take you anywhere."

"Oh, thank God!" Cori dove to Belus, dropping to her knees to give him an awkward midline hug. "I thought you were done for," she mumbled against his torso. "I thought..." She didn't finish, just in case the words had the power to make it happen again.

"What are you talking about?" he asked. She could sense he was on the verge of squirming from her embrace, but she gripped him tighter, refusing to let herself be deprived of her relief. She heard him sigh and his hand settled in on her head, petting her hair down. "Okay, kid, what happened?"

She sat back. Danato lent her a hand, and she pulled herself back to her feet. "I was waiting for the nurse to return, and I saw Belus on the floor, shot." She glanced furtively to Belus, as if the words might hurt him. "I was somewhere else in the prison. You were there too, Danato. And..." She paused, wondering if telling the whole truth and nothing but the truth was wise, since her first admission had prompted a PET scan.

"And?" Danato urged, as he crossed his arms over his chest.

"And Efrat was there."

"Again with Efrat." Danato glanced at Belus. "Your PET scan looked normal. Minor raise in the anxiety zone, but frankly, given the morning, that would be unavoidable."

"These can't be dreams if I'm wide awake while I have them," she pointed out. "Am I hallucinating?" She didn't like the sound of that any better than being assaulted by a dream feeder, but she wanted an answer before things got worse.

"That is the next most likely explanation," Danato said.

"Great, I'm back to being a schizo."

The nurse returned to the scene of the accident to clean up. Danato nodded for them to leave. They headed back downstairs via the elevator. Danato led the way down the hall, with Belus trailing her. Cori wondered if they were doing it intentionally to keep her in their sights.

She glanced back at Belus, trying to figure out what could have transpired to cause Efrat to save his life. "Cori." Belus rolled his eyes. "I'm fine. Stop checking me for bullet holes."

She grimaced. "Sorry, it was just so real."

"I'm fine," he said more reassuringly.

"As long as it stays that way, we don't have a problem." She smiled before continuing into the office.

"Gun!" she heard from in front and behind.

She deposited her gun and went inside.

Before she reached her chair, she heard a voice from behind say, "Watch your step." She turned to see its source and found Belus gone. The taupe walls of the office were replaced by fluorescent-lit crap.

"Efrat!" she yelped, staring into his baby blues again.

18

CORI DOVE BEHIND THE endless piles of junk in the "prop room." She didn't bother stammering about her sudden change in location or his appearance. Whatever was happening to her, regardless of its impossibility, was real enough to warrant self-defense.

She reached for her gun and happily found it in its holster this time. She ripped it free and pointed it at Efrat as he nonchalantly weaved through the junk after her.

"Stop right there!" she shrieked, resenting the fact that she sounded like a cop—and a rookie one at that. "I'll shoot."

"No, you won't." He picked up a few trinkets that were of interest to him, but tossed them away as soon as their entertainment value failed.

"Yes, I will!" she clarified. She wasn't sure she wanted the blood of a human being on her hands, but if it was between him and her, she was certain it would be him.

Efrat looked her over, re-evaluating her resolve. His eyes dimmed slightly from the assessment, but his smug sneer didn't. "Don't you want me to help Belus?"

Cori wanted to pull the trigger just for the cockiness he exuded in that statement. "Screw you! How do you know about that?"

He leaned forward a bit to reveal his secret. "You told me."

"No, I didn't!" She knitted her brow, glancing at the room. "I haven't even spoken with you since..." Cori wondered if he was having visions just like her. "How could I tell you what I don't even know? I have no frickin' clue what's going on!"

"Not yet, but you will." He stepped around the harp she was hiding behind, putting her in line with him.

"What does that mean?"

"You're having a bit of a fucked-up day, kitten."

"No shit. What do you know about it, pup?" She took a step back as he advanced another step.

"Do you want the short version?" he asked.

"The less time your jaws are flapping, the better."

"You're jumping through time." Cori raised her gun from his heart to his face in response to the obvious lie. "I didn't believe you either when you told me, but you seemed to know what you're talking about."

"It happens once in a while," she mumbled.

"Sometimes, you start over and overlap your timeline. Other times, you just blip out to a different part of the day. I can't really say I get it either, but I'll do my best to keep you apprised."

"Why are you helping me?"

"I haven't quite figured that out yet. It might have something to do with the gun you've had planted in my back all morning."

Efrat took another step forward, and she backed up another half step, bumping into another pile of crap that had no business being on the premises of a prison that held supernatural beings. Something fell at her feet and she kicked it away.

"What—" Before she could continue, a waft of smoke drifted up from the floor. With it came the image of a man. He was not a corporeal being, but rather a ghostly one. She and Efrat stared at the bronze, bald, tattooed man that was interrupting their all-important bad-guy, good-guy banter. "—the hell." She finished her sentence on a new thought.

"What is your command, Mistress?" the man's bass voice asked

"What?" she asked, glancing at Efrat for an explanation.

"Genie?" He shrugged.

"What are your three wishes?" the genie asked, bowing slightly to her.

Cori growled. "Are you freaking kidding me? Do you see the gun?" She pointed with her other hand. "I'm kind of busy right now."

The genie looked between her and Efrat, discerning the scene he had come upon. "You don't want three wishes?"

"No!" both she and Efrat barked.

"But they always want three wishes," the genie explained, almost forlorn.

"I don't have time for wishes. Go away."

"But no one has ever said no!" The genie's ghostly face started to glow red.

Cori repositioned her gun to point at the lamp near her foot. "I wonder if that lamp is bulletproof."

The genie looked down at the lamp and twitched his upper lip and the ring that adorned it. "This isn't over."

"Yeah, yeah, get back to me on a day I'm not traveling through time, enveloped by transmorphs, or being electrocuted by this asshole." She stabbed her gun in Efrat's direction, who dared to smirk at her sarcasm.

"Very well." The genie bowed again and was absorbed back into his lamp.

"That's going to bite me in the ass later, isn't it?" she asked, not really intending to get an answer.

"I would imagine so." Efrat took another step toward her, but instead of backing down, she took a quick step forward and jabbed the gun in his belly. He grunted and bent over, putting their faces in line.

"Did you shoot Belus?"

"No, I don't use a gun, remember?" He waved his fingers at her. "I don't know how he got shot. I imagine if you knew, you would have tried to stop it rather than recruit me to save him after the fact."

"I can't trust you," she seethed. "You killed me."

"Killed you? You're standing right here."

"I died more than once on the table from the damage you did to me." She pushed the gun again. "I want to pull this trigger, so bad!"

"Go ahead, if it means that much to you." His eyes glimmered with confidence. His hands were close enough to her to attack, but so far, he hadn't. Yet another *why* that was transfixing her mind. "I believe it was the wall that did the damage, not me."

"You may not have succeeded in killing me, but you are a murderer and no one would miss you."

His eyes narrowed at the statement. "Am I? A murderer?" He lowered his face, practically touching her forehead. "Is that what you read in my file?"

Cori's mind blanked, and she frantically tried to remember what she *had* read in his file. After a moment of gaping like a fish, she realized she hadn't read his file. She had never even seen a file on any of the elementals. She assumed that was because they were a military contract, but she was surprised that they were not allowed at least a cursory reading of the dangers presented by the inmates.

"I don't have to read your file. Danato told me how many guards you and the other elementals have killed."

"War isn't pretty, but if you're the enemy, you had better be prepared for sacrifice."

"*You're* the enemy!" she hissed.

"You're so sure about that." He leaned back, giving her breathing room, but his height looming over her was just as uncomfortable. "I almost envy your ignorance. It must feel good to be blissfully blind to the oppressed."

"Don't get sanctimonious with me. You aren't a goddamn war refugee. Every prisoner in this facility has killed or endangered a human's life. A good number of them have *me* on their resume, including *you*."

"That may be true, but I didn't start tallying my kills until after I was imprisoned." Cori's eyes flickered over his, trying to see through the lies. His gaze didn't falter. She knew she couldn't trust him. She had mistaken his actions for reverence for her life once before and nearly died for it. However, the statement left room for curiosity regarding his imprisonment. Perhaps there was a file to read, and she had just missed it.

"You're pretty early in your timeline, aren't you?" Efrat asked as he shifted a step away from her. She extended her hand, keeping the gun firmly at his belly, but he didn't seem concerned about it. He smiled as he looked her over. Her brow furrowed as she tried to figure out what his smile was about. "There's something I owe you, or depending on the timeline, I may have earned it. Either way." Efrat shrugged and slapped her across the face.

Cori fell back, feeling red-hot pain even before she landed on the ground. Before she could question her own actions, she pulled the trigger to her gun in his general direction. The gun clicked obediently, but there was no boom or kick back.

She looked at the weapon as if it had betrayed her. Efrat waved her clip at her. "Like I said. You won't shoot me because you've already given me your clip." Cori screamed and vaulted off the floor to manually rip his throat out.

By the time she reached the thick, muscled neck, she realized her target had changed. The pens on the desk beneath her dug into her belly. Her victim was virtually unaffected by her grip, but he was nonetheless unhappy with the surprise attack.

"Danato?"

19

"Cori!" Belus yelled from behind her as he grabbed her legs.

Danato gripped her wrists, pulling her fingers off his neck. She was back in the office, sprawled across the desk. The only thing more uncomfortable than the stapler in her hip was the look of shock on Danato's face.

"Oh God, Danato, what's happening to me?"

His face softened as he realized she was back to normal again—at least as normal as she got. She frowned and *thunked* her head onto the desk.

Danato stood from his chair and scooped her up with ease. He could have sat back down and rocked her like a child, and she would have gratefully curled into his arms and let him. Instead, he set her upright on the floor beside the desk.

She moved to the wall and closed her eyes as she leaned against it. Her head was starting to ache. She wasn't sure there were any known symptoms of time travel, but a headache seemed reasonable.

When she turned back to Danato and Belus, they were both watching her from opposite sides of the desk. Danato was noticeably concerned, and for once, so was Belus. Neither asked the obvious question. They just waited for her to begin.

"I had another vision of Efrat," she admitted.

"Another?" Danato asked.

"Yes, but it may not be just a vision. He's helping me, I guess. I don't understand it, but it has something to do with the other vision I had of Belus." Neither of them reacted beyond extended anticipation for further information. "He says I'm traveling through time."

Both men immediately shook their heads at her. It wasn't a surprise since time travel, even from a fictional perspective, took great leaps of faith to accept. Nonetheless, she got the impression it was outside the scope of even the abnormal possibilities.

"What?" she asked, looking between them.

Both of them sat down in preparation for the discussion. She moved to the second chair and pulled it a good foot away from Belus before sitting. He noted the movement with deepening confusion, but said nothing. She didn't care. Until she knew what was going on, she was going to do her best to keep anyone from hurting her family, including herself.

"Cori, I'm not sure what just happened," Danato began, "but the time bubble is strictly monitored by us. Schisms in the fabric of time have a telltale energy signature. If you had traveled through one, you would be setting off a slew of alarms. We would know if you were jumping into a different time."

"But it's not..." She touched her cheek where she should have been feeling pain. "It's not my body. Each time I jump, I am in whatever condition I was at that time. It's more like my mind is jumping around. It's as if somebody mixed up the order of my memories."

Danato thought about that for a moment, exchanging a furtive glance with Belus. "When did this start?"

"I came in this morning—the first time. I went to the time bubble, did my work, came out, and got shocked by Efrat."

"Then what?" Danato murmured.

Cori sighed, not wanting to waste time going over the same information, but she supposed he wanted to double-check her memory. "Then I came in *this* morning, thinking that my yesterday was just a dream. That's when we went upstairs for the PET scan. I saw the vision of Belus shot. We came back here to discuss it, but I was sidetracked by another vision of Efrat. Who, by the way, is still an asshole in any timeline, thus the strangulation. Sorry about that." She shrank down, hoping the explanation would excuse her actions.

Danato nodded, brushing off her mortification as inconsequential to the moment. "And what time did you get in each morning?" Danato asked.

"Well..." Cori debated whether she should mention the discrepancy with the clock. "8:05." There was no reason to add to that confusion.

"So, you think that we have just gotten back from your PET scan that you took on your second round of the same morning?"

Cori looked between them and smiled like there was a joke she wasn't getting and should just pretend to get it until it fully dawned on her. "Yeah." She gulped, not wanting to know why that had to be clarified. "What am I missing?"

"Sweetheart, check the clock."

She looked at the clock. It read 8:09. If she counted back in the minutes, she could estimate that it read 8:05 right around the time her hands were clutching Danato's throat. She was in her third repetition of her early morning.

She stared at the clock hands as if they had betrayed her. "No, that can't be." She looked between them for the explanation she had yet to find in this mess.

"Cori." Danato stood and came around the desk to her. "Ethan left yesterday. You took the day off. Do you remember that?"

"Yes, of course I do," she snarled, feeling the microscope being positioned over her.

He put his hands up in surrender. "I'm just saying this is the day after that day. You walked into this office at 8:05. Immediately after that, you tried to strangle me."

"This is impossible. None of this makes sense. Why am I back here? Where's the rest of my morning? If I'm going to repeat my day, shouldn't I at least get to finish it before I start over? Isn't that the rule?" Cori threw her hands up, but couldn't decide on whether to slam them back on the chair or hide her face in them. She decided to tuck them under her arms for safekeeping.

Belus and Danato looked at her with concern, but neither of them seemed to know where to begin to ease her mind. They also appeared to be having a silent conversation about what they were going to do about the situation.

"I am not crazy. You two have to believe me. This is the third time I have arrived in this office at 8:05." She looked at the clock again and wondered if it had the power to cause her time shift. As if sensing her accusation, the clock volume increased, resonating three pejorative second-hand ticks before resuming as usual. She dismissed the theory, but not the suspect.

"You've never made it past the morning?" Belus asked.

"No," Cori answered. "I mean, if you count the time in the time bubble as *my* time and not outside time, I've had two, maybe three, hours each time."

"But you're not jumping before or beyond this day," Danato clarified.

Cori shook her head.

"Could it be possible the shock Efrat gave her triggered something, mentally or physically?" Belus asked Danato.

"That's assuming Efrat was really involved, and that isn't another issue altogether," Danato said.

"Excuse me." Cori raised her hand. "The PET scan came out fine. My amygdala is functioning at normal levels, so this isn't a dream feeder." Both Danato and Belus looked at her like she had just recited a verse of the hobgoblin lineage. "We've already been through that. Besides, if this morning is starting over again, I can prove that Efrat is involved. We can just go up to the time bubble and catch him when he sneaks in."

"What time will that be?"

"In about ten minutes. Actual time about 9:00."

"What?" Danato looked at the clock.

"Danato, you should really get that clock fixed. I've been 45 minutes late for work the last three mornings."

20

C ORI STOOD AT THE ready behind the double doors leading into the time bubble room. Her pistol was perched in her hand and pointed at the ceiling. Despite objections by both men, she'd asked that they stay as far back as possible. She knew Danato didn't like the use of guns, but when it came to a man that could electrocute you with his bare hands, the argument about gun safety was overruled.

On the 9 o'clock hour, Cori saw Efrat's hand reaching through the metal doors to touch the light switch. A shockwave traveled up to the control booth, and the poor unsuspecting guard that they hadn't warned fell unconscious against his station.

Cori took two silent steps forward. As the back of Efrat's head came into view, she jammed the nose of her gun into the base of his skull. "Don't move!" she said with more force than volume. "Come in, but keep your hands to yourself."

Efrat stepped into the room sideways, keeping his hands half raised in surrender. He was wearing the same blue flannel she remembered from earlier. His boot-cut jeans had seen better days. His belt buckle also looked worn and even a little melted around the edges. She wasn't sure why he wasn't in the uniformed gray like the other prisoners, but she didn't really care enough to ask about it.

"What's up, kitten?" he drawled. "Revenge at its coldest?"

She cringed at hearing the pet name again. It was such a condescending nickname. It was like 'cupcake.' Sexist, but with the added insult of observing her youth. She could tolerate the term "kid" from Belus because he was older, and he said it to Ethan too, so it wasn't sexist. However, Efrat wasn't that much older and hadn't earned the tenure to patronize to her in that way.

"Put your hands..." Cori realized that putting his hands anywhere wasn't going to help the situation. "Just kneel."

"I'd rather die standing," he said.

"I'll make a note of that, Mr. Drama," she said, pushing on his calves, which buckled his knees. He fell into position and folded his fingers in prayer before him. "I'm not here to kill you. I'm here to prove that I really have been seeing you out of your cage."

Danato and Belus joined them, circling around to face Efrat. He looked over both of them. "Cavalry's here. Is this your new sheriff?" he asked Danato, nodding back at her. "I thought Ethan was the big man behind the big man?"

"He is," Danato said. "Cori is his second."

"Ahh." Cori could see his cheek tense with his smile. "The little woman, behind the little man."

Belus didn't exhibit any ire at the statement. He was as much an observer at that point as anything. She wondered if she should make it a point to observe the way he handled himself in these situations. If she was going to be an asset to the prison, she needed to practice keeping her smartass remarks to herself.

"How long have you been jumping floors?" Danato asked.

"How long have I been here?" Efrat asked. "I like to visit the time bubble. Minutes away here and hours there is just the break I need."

"How do you get back out?" Danato asked.

"A bolt into the sky usually pops me right back out."

"Son of a bitch." Danato took a step at him like he wanted to punch him.

"Have you spoken with Cori before this moment?" Belus interjected, dispelling Danato's irritation.

"We did have the brief conversation during our battle last year." He looked back at her and winked. "Good times."

"We haven't spoken today, though, right?" she asked while he had his attention on her.

"Aside from this? No. Why?" He looked back to Belus. "Are you referring to our meeting on the transmorph level several weeks ago? I wasn't sure you remembered that." He looked back at her.

"Vaguely, but no, that's not what we are referring to." Cori pulled her gun back and distanced herself from him as she circled around to stand next to Belus. "Now what?" she mumbled as she looked down at him.

"We take him back," Belus said.

"No!" Efrat stood up and Cori realigned her gun with his heart.

"Get down!"

"Danato." Efrat turned his attention to him. "Let me go back on my own. If they find out I've been leaving whenever I want, they'll kill me."

"I doubt that." Danato rolled his eyes.

"You doubt it because that's what keeps your conscience clear. They will be out for another two hours if they aren't disturbed. Take me back, but don't inform them."

"Two hours?" Cori hadn't meant to say it out loud. Efrat and Danato looked at her. "Nothing, I just—never mind."

"And what is to stop you from roaming the halls?" Danato scolded.

Efrat paused. He had no answer for that. "They *will* kill me."

"Cori," Danato snapped. "Secure your prisoner. We're going to the top."

"Yes, sir." Cori repositioned herself behind Efrat. "Clasp your hands." With his hands secured in front of him, she prodded him with the gun. "Move."

Cori remembered leaving the room and entering the elevator, but she didn't remember anything that would have prompted Efrat to lift her into his arms, let alone be running frantically through the corridors of the transmorph level.

21

Cori whimpered as she felt the pain in her right arm. "What did you do to me, you bastard?" She turned to face Efrat. He was doing his best to run while he cradled her.

"You stupid girl! You did this to yourself!" he hissed quietly. She could feel static shocks hitting her where his hands were touching her leg and side, but the pain was minimal compared to her wound.

"What?" she groaned.

"You thought you were saving me," he grumbled.

"What?" she asked again because he still wasn't making sense.

"Stop saying *what* and keep your voice down. They will be looking for us. We need a place to hide."

"Why?"

"Because you just broke me out of captivity right under Danato's nose."

"I did?" Cori wasn't sure why she would have done that to Danato, and more importantly, why she would have done that for Efrat. "Why?"

"Because you knew the military would kill me if they found out I was gone."

Cori wasn't sure she had any sympathy for Efrat, but she did have a general reverence for life. She didn't like killing, even when it was self-defense. "The freight elevator," she mumbled, feeling obligated to stick with the path of events, even though it didn't currently make any sense to her. "No one ever uses it. It parks on the seducers' level in the north-west corner."

"One level up. Stairs, great."

Cori noticed he was panting. He wasn't prepared to carry her up a flight of stairs. No matter what his arm strength was, carrying another human being up a flight of stairs was no less than a 2K run. "I can walk. It's just my arm."

"I'm more concerned about blood loss."

"I'll make do. You can always ditch me if I get bad enough. Danato might be pissed at me, but he isn't going to let me die."

"Okay." Efrat put her down and jogged ahead to check the stairwell. As she caught up, he whispered, "It's clear for now. We have to go fast and quiet."

She nodded, and he darted up the stairs as quiet as a mouse. She bolstered her strength and pinched off the wound on her arm before beginning her ascent. She made it up to the seducers' level, where Efrat was surveying the floor through the rectangle window in the door.

Cori saw a drop of her blood hit the floor. She wiped it away with her shoe, just in case they could track her. Another one dropped in its place. Before she could bend down to wipe it away, Efrat wrapped his blue flannel over-shirt around her bicep to bandage the bleeding. He wiped up the extra drop and pulled her along by the tight grasp on her arm.

Sweeping along the west wall, they found the obscure freight elevator that they only used to transport big equipment and big prisoners like the rock man. Efrat pulled the doors open to avoid alerting anyone to its use and yanked her in behind him.

After the doors were shut, he sent a bolt into the controls to shut down its function. Cori shielded herself from the sparks. The lights, though too dim to be considered illuminating, went out. He reached up and pumped the metal frames holding the fluorescent lights with energy.

Cori watched in fascination as he charged the metal until the lights flickered on, as if he had just put batteries into the devices. There were probably a dozen reasons why that shouldn't have worked, but she imagined that his electric blue energy didn't abide by the same rules as natural electricity. He saw her watching him and gave her a look of loathing that she didn't understand, nor cared to.

"You, I take it," Efrat said, pointing to a first aid kit lying in the corner of the elevator.

Cori looked at the conveniently placed red-cross box. She shrugged. "I guess, I'm so freaking far behind on this day. It's not even funny."

Efrat unwrapped her arm and checked the front and back of it. "Bullets still in. We should get it out. Lie down."

Cori found what looked to be a semi-clean spot for emergency surgery and lay down. Efrat grabbed the first aid box and kneeled beside her. He neglected the contents and reached to his waist, unbuckling his belt.

Without a second wasted to rationalize, Cori crab-walked painfully away from him and cowered in the corner. She was suddenly aware that she was trapped in a small space with a prisoner who hadn't been alone with a woman in who knows how long. She scrambled for her gun and checked for the clip. It was in place.

Efrat stared at her with a hint of his brash smile. She brought her gun in line with his heart. "What's the matter, kitten? Boys make you shy?" A snap of static electricity from his poised hands made her jump. He finished pulling the belt out of his jean loops. He held the oval metal buckle in his hand. Blue webs of energy danced around the surface. His hand vibrated until he released it. The metal oval flung across the elevator and stuck to the wall.

Cori looked back between the belt and Efrat. "Electromagnetic?"

"Good, you get an A in science for the day. Now get over here." Efrat removed the buckle from the wall while Cori holstered her gun and positioned herself on the floor beside him. "This is going to hurt," he informed her without any note of sympathy in his voice.

"I know," she said, trying to sound tough.

"That's what they all say," Efrat muttered and clamped a hand over her mouth. Tiny stabs of electricity tickled her lips. She grabbed his wrist, but didn't really attempt to pull it away. He placed the metal near the wound and locked eyes with her. "Are you ready?" he asked. She nodded, even though she knew it wouldn't make any difference if she wasn't.

He recharged the magnetism, feeding it with ripples of blue. She could feel the bullet pulling out like a fingernail being ripped off her finger. She did her best to stay quiet, but she couldn't help but groan. "Almost out," he whispered.

Once she was free of the bullet, he cauterized the wound with his electricity and put a few feeble stitches in to close the wound. Dazed and sweating from the pain, she dared to look at the wound. "Those are the shittiest stitches ever, Efrat," she said, partially as a joke, but he took a good deal of pleasure in stabbing her with a needle full of morphine. "Why didn't you put that in before?" she said with a wince.

"I didn't see it," he murmured, sounding almost guilty about it.

She closed her eyes and took in a deep breath. She could feel the morphine miraculously remove her pain.

"Now what?" Cori asked.

"We take him back up to General Clark and report that he has been getting out of the level," Danato said. She opened her eyes and saw him looking at her from his position beside her in the elevator.

22

ORI FELT HER ARM, but the wound was gone. Efrat was ahead of her, beside Belus. They were riding up the east elevator to the top floor. She was thankful that she hadn't returned to 8:05 again, but there was new confusion being placed at her feet.

Cori wasn't sure what to do about the new information she had. Clearly, at one point in this day, she was willing to break Efrat free to help Belus. Was she supposed to save Efrat *now*? Was it really necessary? Couldn't she simply tell Danato what was going on? Where was the right and wrong in this situation?

She was pretty sure abstaining from the truth counted as lying in this case, but she didn't exactly want to admit to betraying Danato before she had actually done it. "What now?" she asked as casually as possible. "Do they have a punishment for this type of thing?"

"They will have to find a new way for him to stay contained," Danato answered.

"Maybe we could just slip him back in and post our own guards until they wake up."

"To what end, Cori?" Danato turned to her and gave her the darkened gaze of a man not willing to negotiate his orders.

She looked away, bolstering her strength for her duty. She could see Efrat's ear had been tipped to listen to her conversation, but nothing she was saying was making a difference and so far, she saw no motivation for the heroics that had apparently gotten her shot.

The elevator ride was quick, as it always tended to be when Danato was a passenger. It seemed even the elevator knew better than to waste his time. Cori pushed Efrat out and Danato punched in a code to open the secondary door to the elemental area. She steered Efrat into the big open space behind it.

Despite the fact that she had fought the elementals, she had never technically seen their cells. Unlike some of the other floors that allowed a little hint of sunshine through tiny crevice windows, this floor had none. An observatory lookout station sat on the wall adjacent to the corridor of a half-dozen large cells. The walls were scorched and the metal frames of the cells melted from the mini battles that took place any time someone got a bee in their bonnet.

Access out of the singular section was obstructed by brick walls. The two blocks of expansive space beyond the one section was unnecessary for four prisoners, and probably a nuisance as well. Despite that, though, they were still the only ones renting the top floor.

The half-dozen-plus military men inside the glass-windowed observatory that had buttons and doohickeys in spades were unconscious. The men stationed above the observatory in the lookout were also unconscious.

"How do they not know you left?" Cori whispered behind Efrat. "Don't they realize something is up when they wake up?"

"Hirem and the others attack once I am back. They are too busy defending themselves to realize the time lapse. Usually, I leave for a half hour or so. No one ever misses that amount of time," Efrat said. "They might have suspected, but since there aren't any reports of us leaving, they don't suspect anything."

Danato punched the code in for the observatory door and opened it. He shook a man awake inside and started explaining the situation to him. Cori could see movement to her right. Hirem, Garr, and Remi emerged from their cells, watching the unfolding situation.

"Will they attack?" Cori asked, taking a step closer to Efrat in case she needed a human shield.

"Doubtful. It's too late for me now, anyway."

"What do you mean?"

"Why were you asking if we had spoken before this?" He turned his head back to see her in his peripheral.

"I've been doing some time jumping. I keep meeting up with you in a different timeline, or maybe the same timeline, just a different part, I don't know."

"And we spoke in one of these timelines?" he asked, forgoing the usual look of WTF that she might have expected.

"Yeah, you are sort of helping me. I think you might have even just saved me in one of them," she admitted. She expected him to make a snide comment, but he just turned a little more to catch her eye. For once, he didn't look mad, bitter, or cocksure.

He looked forlorn.

"Well, maybe in the next timeline you can save me."

"Stand down!" A voice boomed on the other side of Efrat. Cori peeked around and saw an olive uniform with stars on the collar. The beret on his head didn't quite match the hard face. He glared at her over Efrat's shoulder and she suddenly realized he was talking to her.

"Stand down!"

She jumped from the second command and holstered her gun before backing away. She would have been annoyed by his imperious attitude—if she weren't too busy debating how many pushups it would take to appease him.

Danato came from behind the four-star general and swept her to the side of the room. She was relieved to be manhandled away from the scene, even if it made her look more like an underling.

The General had a beer-belly gut, something that was only acceptable for high-ranking military officers. He, no doubt, would claim that he was just as fit as his younger counterparts, but it would only be his intimidation that kept anyone from the challenge, not his physique.

"Cori." Danato pulled her along further, trying to leave the room.

"I warned you about escaping, Efrat. You just had to fight me to the very end, didn't you?" the General bellowed with a red face. "I told you not to push me. Looks like your risk has finally outweighed your potential." Without another word, the General pulled his handgun and shot Efrat in the face. The back of his head exploded in a shower of blood, brain, and skull.

Cori squealed and buried her head in Danato's shoulder. She had never seen anyone shot, let alone been close enough to feel the spray of blood. It didn't matter who it was. It was still a horrific sight and her tears were as much for her shattered vision of humanity as for Efrat.

"Shhh," was all she heard as a hand pushed her head from the warm shoulder. "Quiet," Efrat whispered from below her. He was still alive, for now.

23

"E FRAT?" A FEW TEARS of anguish spilled onto his t-shirt, soaking into the fabric. The prop room was dark, but she could see him clearly beneath her. Her fingers were wrapped around his neck, paused in strangulation.

She touched his face to see if it was real. His chin pulled down into his neck as if he was searching for the hidden weapon she was distracting him from.

"What's wrong with you?"

"They shot you," she whispered. His forehead was pinched so tight, he had developed a uni-brow.

It must have been a strange turn of events from his perspective. Moments earlier, in the heat of their argument and his assaulting slap, she had tried to shoot him. Now she was crying because someone else had shot him.

"Who shot me?"

"The General just shot you." She drifted her hand to the back of his head to search for damage. She knew she wouldn't find any, but she had to alleviate the pressure of the embedded memory in her mind. It was too real not to physically disprove.

"Oh," was all he said before laying his head back on the floor. She was aware her body was on top of him, but for the moment, she was too distracted to care.

"Why would he do that?" Her eyes watered and she pressed her forehead into his chest, trying to rid herself of the instant replay in her head. "How could he do that? Point blank..." She shivered.

He lifted her head to look at him. "You really do live in a fairytale world, don't you?"

Her eyes flickered over his. She was offended, but she soon realized that he might be right. "If a fairytale world means I don't ever have to see a man's brains explode, then yes, sign me up for more." She lost a few more tears, and he frowned before he pushed her to sit up with him. She was aware of the stinging from his hands, but it wasn't painful.

She wiped away her tears, seeing the futility of expressing emotion to this man. Her cheek felt bruised from his earlier slap, but the anger from that had since dampened. "I'm not a moron. I know bad things happen. I just assumed there was a protocol for stuff like this. Danato would never execute a prisoner." Cori knew of one time he had done so, but she also knew how mad he was at having to do it. Despite the occasional necessity, she knew Danato took the health and preservation of his prisoners very seriously, and as such, would never outright murder one of them.

"General Clark isn't interested in protocol. He has one job: keeping us contained. If he can't..." He ended his sentence with a hand gesture of a gun shooting. The innocent gesture roiled her stomach more than the actual shooting did. She covered her mouth in case she threw up. He watched her curiously, not attempting to comfort her.

She uncovered her mouth. "You're a complete bastard and I think I really do hate you, but I don't want you to die." She could feel his eyes on her. He was as suspicious of her as she was him. "I think I need your help to get me out of this. Unfortunately, my hero is somewhere in France, being seduced by my arch-enemy, so neither one of those positions is available. I was hoping you wouldn't mind taking the good-bad guy role. At least until I know Belus is safe and no one else is dead."

Efrat leaned back against a pile of junk that might have been a dining room table on its side. For the briefest of moments, Cori wondered what trouble a dining room table could get into.

Dinner couldn't have been *that* bad. *Ba-dum-dum-ching.*

"Would you have tried to stop it?" he mumbled. "If you knew he was going to kill me, would you have tried to stop him?"

"I've already helped you escape once so far. Got my arm shot doing it."

His brow dipped temporarily. "Someone shot at you?"

"I think they were aiming for you. I was apparently 'rescuing' you." She air quoted.

"I don't really need rescuing from bullets."

"Could have fooled me," Cori said, straight-faced. Efrat held her gaze for a moment before he looked away, as if he couldn't stand to continue this line of conversation. "Why have I relived this same morning three times?" she asked, happy to get back on track.

"I told you... you're jumping through time."

"Danato says that's impossible."

"Yeah, well, he doesn't know everything!" he barked at her, offering her a glare that made her pursue her gun. Her fingers dragged the floor until she felt the metal muzzle. When her hands latched on to it, she remembered that he still had her bullets. He took notice of her hand gripping the weapon again. "You should have killed me this morning when you had the chance." He grabbed her shoulders. The tingling, prickling pain of his power entered her body, making the muscles in her back arch uncontrollably. "I could still kill you with one bolt," he said through gritted teeth.

She wasn't entirely sure how the timeline was going, but she was almost sure that he couldn't kill her at this point. She took the risk and called his bluff. "Get on with it then, so I don't have to listen to you crow." His energy released enough to make talking easier. "I don't have time for this, Efrat. I need to know what you know. I'm operating blind here. Why did I bring you into this?"

He let her go, and she fell back against her pile of junk, which prompted something to fall in her lap. She raised her hands, not wanting to touch it. "Oh crap, what is it this time?"

"A snow globe," Efrat said disinterestedly after he peeked at it. Cori carefully placed the globe off to one side.

"Seriously, why do we keep this shit here?" Cori snarled. She intended to make a very serious argument for removal or organization of the props as soon as she wasn't saving Belus, Efrat, or herself from bullet holes. "Okay, Efrat, let's do the time warp again. When was the first time you saw me this morning?"

"When you jammed your gun in my back and threatened to *not* kill me, but sever my spinal cord." He glared as if she were directly to blame for that threat, which apparently she was.

"I got the drop on you when you came into the bubble room?"

"No, I bolted you. You got off a shot, but you missed. I thought you would be out for a good number of hours, but when I turned away, you jumped me."

"Interesting, you bolting me was part of my first morning memory, but I've had several memories of this morning since then. I can't tell what's real and what's been overwritten. What did I tell you?"

"You told me that we had two hours to save Belus, save me, and stop you from jumping through time."

"How do we do all that?"

"You weren't exactly forthcoming with all the information. Either you didn't know, or you didn't want me to know."

"Or I didn't want *me* to know," Cori mumbled as she scratched her fingers and twisted her gold rings to massage the blanched tissue beneath. They didn't seem to react well with Efrat's electricity. She couldn't remember whether gold conducted electricity or not. "So, what are we doing in here?" She motioned all around.

"Hiding. We sort of got caught together negotiating our alliance. By now Danato knows I'm out, and he knows that you are with me." Cori's mouth gaped as she tried to think of how Danato would react to finding out that she was harboring a fugitive. Why did this keep happening to her? The minute she started to earn points with anyone for good behavior, she was forced to do something stupid. "Despite what the guard saw, I'm sure Danato thinks I'm the one kidnapping you," Efrat added, as if he could sense her concern.

"It doesn't matter. He's going to be pissed no matter how this ends. My luck never allows for easy endings. Hell, I've already gotten shot, and I haven't even finished the morning. If I can stop Belus and you from being shot, it will likely be at the cost of me breaking an arm, or a leg, at least."

"Why do you do this job? Why don't you just leave?" His voice wasn't asking so much as accusing. The glare embedded in his face would not be satisfied by her love story with Ethan. He was too cynical to believe love could make someone become an indentured servant.

"I did once, but…" She trailed off, thinking about a hundred things at once, from the smell of Paris, to her last moments with Vince, and her first kiss with Ethan.

"But?" he urged with a softer tone.

"You can't hide from your family. Danato has given me so much. I know it sounds strange to you, but I feel more at home here with a family of no blood relation than I ever did with my father or my aunt."

Cori couldn't tell if he disapproved of what she said or was just disappointed. For a moment, he looked like he might make a biting comment about how pathetic she was. "What about your mother?"

She cringed, thinking of her mother. She was the exception. Her mother had been everything to her, but she was long since gone. "My mother isn't my home. She is my foundation. She's with me wherever I go."

He frowned and looked away. He apparently didn't much like this conversation either.

The air stilled, and she was aware of the vacuous silence. She wondered if she should ask more questions. Did he even know anymore? Part of her still wondered if he was the one who had shot Belus. Was she simply leading the event into fruition by dragging this elemental around with her?

"Efrat," she said when she felt the silence become claustrophobic. He looked at her with the same disapproval he had before. "I wish I knew—"

His hand flew over to her mouth and covered it. She couldn't move to get away from him, except to further push herself into whatever sharp object was making its home in the small of her back. He shook his head and pointed at the lamp.

A pair of ghostly eyes surrounded by mist appeared over the lamp. They looked around and caught sight of the two of them staring at it. The eyes widened and disappeared into oblivion.

Efrat leaned back, releasing her mouth. She shook her head. "Thanks. I don't need another entanglement." Cori shifted to feel what was bothering her back. Something fell between her legs.

She picked up the fallen object, a folded piece of white paper. She decided it must have been on the bottom of the snow globe that fell in her lap. She unfolded it and read it. She smiled, recognizing her own handwriting. It was strange to hear from one's future self, especially when the future self was here prior to the current self. Her future-past-self had horrible handwriting. She could barely make out the words.

"Hey." She stood up and held out her hand to Efrat. He looked at her outstretched palm like it was a snake that might bite him. "Get up. We need to go."

He didn't take her hand, but he stood up and made his way through the maze of clutter toward the door. "Where are we going?"

"You'll see." She caught up with him and yanked her bullet clip out of his back pocket. He turned around and watched her slip the clip in. "I'm going to need these."

"I told you, bullets aren't much good against me." He smiled. His disapproval had vanished, and he was back to calm, quiet, and cocky.

"They aren't for you." She weaved back into the junk piles. "They're for saving you." She winked and ducked down. The prop room door burst open just as she disappeared into the sea of crap-topia. She could see flashlight beams zigzagging the walls before merging on their target.

Shouts echoed through the room, demanding Efrat's slow surrender. Through all the ruckus, she heard him say, "You bitch." She had to bite her lip to keep from laughing. She was sure, at this point, he assumed she had thrown him to the wolves, but as soon as he calmed down, he would remember she had mentioned that she had broken him out once before. Her only concern was whether he would know better than to give her up.

She listened as the guards badgered him about her location, but he denied ever seeing her. It was an outright lie, but one he would likely stick with the whole way. She wasn't sure what time it was, but she figured she didn't have long before Danato decided to call in the military.

She knew Efrat wouldn't give a second thought to amping her into cardiac arrest, but she couldn't let him be executed like that. Not if she had the time to stop it.

She headed toward the door of the prop room to leave, but instead she arrived back where she'd begun.

24

C ORI HEARD THE FAMILIAR duet of "Gun!" She realized she was entering Danato's office instead of leaving the prop room. She placed her gun in the bin and checked the clock.

8:05.

She had started over again. She was sensing the pattern in the day. In general, it was just chaotic jumping, but it seemed her time would repeat after a set parameter, regardless of which timeline her clock was ticking in.

From what she'd gathered from Efrat, she knew that the origin of her timeline aberration started right after she got shocked on the wizard level. But, instead of starting over right at her point of entry, she was bouncing back to the beginning of her morning. She could only assume that there was an automatic reset spot. With the exception of the first repeated morning, when she ricocheted back to her first conscious moment in bed, she was always coming back to 8:05.

Not only was it a pain in the ass, but she was wearing down. Her body didn't know that it had been without a break for several hours, but her mind did. Between trying to keep track of where she was, when she was, and what needed to happen in order to keep things in some semblance of the functioning timeline, steam should have been coming out of her ears.

"Son of a bitch!" she griped through clamped teeth before falling in a depleted pile on the pleather chair in front of the desk.

Danato looked up at her over the rim of his glasses. "What's with you?"

Cori wasn't sure what she looked like to Danato and Belus, but she imagined her thoughts were making her eyes bug out. Their querying faces looked back at her with a mixture of worry and suspicion. It was fairly common for her to stroll into the office chagrined with the news of yet another mishap, but telling them the whole spiel seemed redundant and unnecessary at this point.

If she was right about the time fluctuations—which would be a miracle, since she was pulling her information straight out of her ass—her original timeline that led to Efrat shocking her had to be upheld. It was the origin of her actually entering this state of flux, and therefore, couldn't be overwritten.

The subsequent 8:05 mornings were merely a boomerang effect of piggybacking a linear mind onto the nonlinear time matrix of the time bubble. That meant this timeline, as well as all the preceding 8:05 mornings—save the first—would be trashed the minute she woke from Efrat's shock.

It made complete sense.

Sort of.

Despite her new understanding, she had an obligation to fill them in on what's been happening to her. If anything, she could claim later that she explained everything to them. However, since they wouldn't remember her explaining or not explaining, she could just as easily say that she told them without actually having to go through the tiresome effort of explaining it to them now. On the other hand, she kind of needed to say it out loud so she could get a better grip on things herself.

Danato and Belus were still staring at her, waiting for an answer. She rubbed her face with her hands and groaned. She straightened up and slapped her hands on the chair arms. If nothing else, she could consider this a measurement of how well Danato and Belus took foreknowledge of her screw-ups as opposed to after-knowledge.

"Okay, here goes." She looked at both of them to make sure they were prepared for the long-haul explanation. "At 8:05 this morning, I arrived for work. I went to the wizard's den to plant my crops. After which, I was electrocuted by Efrat. However," she added as the impending questions rounded on both of their lips, "I woke up again in the morning, which was incidentally the same morning, reported to work at 8:05, told you about the experience, after which, you two decided that I had been attacked by a dream feeder and proceeded to give me a PET scan. While in the infirmary, I had a future vision of Belus shot and dying on the floor." Cori touched her hand on Belus's for a moment of sympathy. "However, Efrat was there and helped revive him with his..." Cori wiggled her fingers. "...special skills."

Danato leaned back in his chair. She could see the veiled annoyance on his face.

"I know what you're thinking. Impossible, he's a douche, but what am I to think? So, we head back to the office to discuss the incident, and I have another vision. This time Efrat and I are in the prop room, and he tells me that I'm traveling through time. Which," Cori held up a finger to Danato before he could interject his rebuttal, "you inform me is impossible, even though I was then on my third morning arriving at work at 8:05. After a short discussion, we decide to catch Efrat as he enters the wizard level and get some answers.

"Since he hasn't technically interacted with me on his timeline yet, he has no answers for us. We return Efrat to General Ass-munch, who promptly executes him right in front of us. A conversation we are *so* getting into later." Danato's questions disappeared from his face, and he crossed his arms, allowing her to continue without interruption.

"I feel I should let you know that at some point in this day, I am going to break Efrat out of his imprisonment, so that he won't get shot. However, *I* might get shot in the course of this, so we should probably get some A-negative ready for me. After I free Efrat, I am going to utilize his skills to save Belus once *he* gets shot. And, before you start to lecture me, I already know that none of these events are appropriate or by the book," she glanced over at Belus, "but I will not stand by on the sidelines of my own timeline and watch anyone die." Cori crossed her arms, resolutely satisfied that all was explained.

"Oh," she quickly counted on her fingers. "By the way, this is my fourth morning of arriving at 8:05 for duty, so... yeah, I guess that's it." She returned to her resolute position, again satisfied that *all* was explained. She waited for the barrage of questions.

Danato and Belus looked at each other.

25

CORI WASN'T SURE WHAT she had expected them to do. The scenario up to that point had been the long discussions where they debated what creature or demon could be causing the dramatic changes in her life. She had anticipated a reproach for her abandonment of duties. Given Danato's concern for her well-being, she had hoped he would have shown sympathy for the hours of baffling jumps through time.

The one thing that had not occurred to her, and was likely to be penciled in for another heated discussion with him later, was him taking her up to the infirmary where he handed her off to the orderlies to be strapped to a bed like a demented lunatic.

Cori knew she wasn't doing herself any favors by kicking and screaming like a frenzied maniac when the nurses and orderlies took her from him, but she couldn't help but fight captivity. It was fully integrated into her survival mechanisms and was beyond her control.

"Danato!" she screamed as they dragged her into a small room with a high bed bracketed by metal bars like an adult baby crib. He watched them take her, but he didn't say a word. The stoic expression on his face was scarier than the determined orderlies gripping her. She couldn't believe he really thought she was insane. All she'd done was tell the truth... for once. "Let me go!"

She could feel the hoarse, ear-splitting screams coming from her mouth, but the more she yelled, the less anyone listened. Her legs were being held by two male orderlies, while the nurses held her arms. She was flailing, but they had no trouble carrying her to the bed.

The pressure they placed on her shoulders and legs only reminded her of one thing, and she couldn't distance herself from the fear. She could feel her eyes sting with tears and her lungs hyperventilate. She knew it was irrational, but fear always was. "No! Don't touch me! Get off me! Danato, please," she begged through tear-blurred eyes. He took a step forward, then surrendered the advancement and crossed his arms.

She ground out a horrific scream and kicked sharply at her male captors' genitalia. The men doubled over and released her long enough for her to get purchase with her feet. She pushed back against the mattress, getting her upper body away from the women. She elbowed one and punched the other. They both squealed in pain and surrendered, cradling their bloody noses.

She vaulted from the bed and elbowed one man in his back for good measure. She dashed for the door, feeling the security of the distance expanding between her and confinement.

A thick arm wrapped around her waist, picking her up like a stuffed toy, dashing her dreams of freedom. She shrieked and kicked, but Danato was not so easily wounded by her quick fists. He dropped her body on the bed and pressed her legs and chest down with two broad forearms. The weight that backed his strength was staggering. She could barely move, but the pressure still left her enough room to breathe.

She felt the others take control of her wrists and ankles. She was down for good. She was caught. She couldn't explain why that was such a painful prospect to her. Her screams shrank to whimpers, and she clenched her eyes, releasing the loitering tears.

She felt drops on her neck. It took a moment for her to realize they weren't her tears. She opened her eyes and saw Danato's eyes were red and fraught. He was holding her down with the strength of a bull, but his face was as fragile and pained as her own.

She had never seen Danato cry. His teddy bear heart was always willing to express his love and affection outwardly, but his iron will had kept this part of him hidden. The situation was just too much for him to watch without breaking him.

She knew he was doing this because it was the right protocol to take when your employee says she's traveling through time and planning to break out a prisoner, but she had no idea it would be so devastating for him to follow through with.

She stopped struggling and whimpering. She focused on him. She was no longer concerned about her own situation. She was mortified to have caused him this pain. She wanted to comfort him.

She lifted her hand to touch his cheek, but her restraint fell a few inches short. He looked at her hand and moved his face to meet it. He pinched his eyes and let her caress his face. She trailed her bent finger under his eyes to remove a tear, though it was replaced just as fast.

He opened his eyes and sat back with angry determination. "Remove the straps," he barked at the nurses, who were standing by with an arsenal of drugs to make her high as a kite. One nurse objected, pointing to her bloody nose, but Danato threw her a glare that stalled her complaint. "Remove them or I will."

The women unlashed the straps on her wrists and her ankles before leaving the room entirely. They had had enough trouble for one day. Danato was on his own.

Cori lay on the bed, not wanting to make any sudden movements, and not quite trusting that Danato intended to release her. He leaned back into her hand and kissed her palm. He pushed her hair back, that had matted to her tear-wetted cheeks. "I'm so sorry," he whispered before laying his forehead against her neck.

She wrapped her arms around him and rubbed his back. "I know." She knew Danato loved her more than anything. She wasn't sure how he had come to love her so much when all she did was cause him trouble, but somehow, this giant of a man had a weakness for her.

After a few minutes of calming and consoling each other, Belus joined them. He stood at the edge of the room and cleared his throat to get their attention. Danato looked over at him, seeming baffled by his presence.

"Do you need a minute?" Belus asked.

"I'm not doing this to her, Belus." Danato said it with the weight of his title backing him up, but he was still waiting for Belus's response.

"I can see that." Belus looked between the two of them, like he was assessing what damage had been created by this debacle. "I can't really say I expected you to follow through with it." Cori wasn't sure if that was meant as a statement or an accusation. He walked over to them and leaned against the railing on the bed. "We have a lot of tests we need to perform."

Cori sat up on her elbows. "It really doesn't matter. You aren't going to remember any of this. The only reason I even told you guys was so that when this is all over and you guys ask why I didn't tell you about it, I can honestly say that I did." She looked at Danato, smiling sympathetically at him. "It doesn't matter whether I'm honest, if you don't believe me." Cori turned back to Belus. "You told me once today to trust you, and I do, but that doesn't matter either, if you don't trust me."

Belus shook his head. "You just... make so many mistakes. I don't want you to end up..." He glanced at Danato and trailed off.

"Belus," Cori said firmly. "I am not going to let you die. Somehow, some-when today, you get shot. If I need to break Efrat out of his cell to get your heart pumping again, I will do it, even if that means defying a direct order from you."

Cori could see him trying to reconcile his desire to have control of the situation with his desire to be living at the end of the day. "Do you know why this is happening?" Belus asked, finally allowing for the possibility that she was telling the truth.

"I assume it had something to do with the time bubble since I was there when Efrat shocked me the first time. I haven't repeated that part of my day yet. I think it's my starting point. The latest memory I have is you dead and Efrat reviving you. I think that's my end point, but I haven't repeated that part of my day either, so I don't know how you get shot."

"It could also be that these are fixed points," Belus added. "You may not be able to change these points in time. Whatever happens will happen and you can't stop it because stopping it might be what causes it. It's best to follow your instincts. If Efrat does indeed save me, then there is no reason to interfere with that incident."

"I don't understand how she could be moving through time without the sensors detecting it," Danato told Belus.

Belus nodded introspectively. "Unless our time bubble has attached to her." Danato's eyes widened momentarily. "*Just* the bubble," he clarified. "The energy that creates the field and breaks the barrier of time and space."

"It wouldn't register as anything abnormal because it holds the same signature as the original," Danato added with further realization.

"Right," Belus agreed, and they both nodded with a thoughtful "hmm" silently passing between them.

Cori raised her hand. "Hello. Does anyone care to explain to the inept one?"

"Part of the time bubble may have broken off when Efrat attacked you the first time," Belus said. "If it's attached itself to you somehow, then you are an extension of the time bubble. Instead of your body going anywhere, though, your consciousness does." Belus gave Danato a furtive glance. "As long as you are staying within your own mind, and a confined timeline, I don't think you will incur any damage."

"So, how do I stop it?"

Belus raised his eyebrows and pulled an answer from his mind after he thought about it. "This skew should only be temporary. As soon as you make it to the end, you should be able to break out and continue with your normal day. I can't imagine that a time bubble fragment has a long lifespan."

Cori got the distinct impression that this was Belus's way of saying he had no idea. She leaned back in the bed and groaned. "Why does this stuff keep happening?"

"This was Efrat's fault, not yours," Danato said, putting his hand on hers.

"I know. I just wish you could have an employee that doesn't accidentally screw everything up." Cori clasped her hand over her mouth.

"What?" Danato said.

"I accidentally touched a lamp in the prop room."

Danato's mouth gaped. "Did you make a wish?"

"Not then, but just now I said..."

"I doubt the wish would transfer through different timelines," Belus pointed out. "But you may want to put a clamp on the wishing words, anyway."

"See!" Cori threw her hands up. "Even in the middle of an already messed up crisis, I can find another way to..." She broke off, feeling a lump in her throat.

Danato gave Belus a look, and Belus meandered out of the room, leaving them alone. Danato pressed a lever under the bed and pushed the bars on his side down. He scooted up on the bed closer to her. "I knew a woman a lot like you once upon a time. She was even more headstrong than you. She got herself into all sorts of trouble. I used to think it was her fault. We would have terrible arguments about it, but I came to realize, as you will, some people are just destined to be on the back end of a bucking bull. You can't stop it. Fighting it only makes it worse, trust me.

"You're doing the right thing. Belus and I can't help you when we don't understand. You're just going to have to do things your way until you can get out of this."

"I don't suppose you could write a note to your future self about that."

"You don't need a note, Cori. You've had a firm grip on my heartstrings for quite some time now. Just give a little tug."

Cori smiled and touched his cheek again. "I don't know how much longer I have."

"Do you want me to stay?"

She nodded, and he found a chair in the far corner to pull over. He sat down beside her and she closed her eyes. He rested his hand beside hers, and she took hold of it.

The hand felt softer and smaller than she expected. The slight tingle from it reminded her of when her foot woke from a pinched nerve.

26

"IS THERE SOME REASON you need to be holding my hand?" Efrat said from beside her.

She looked over at him from her prone position on the floor of the elevator. She could feel the pain in the arm that wasn't quite covered by the shot he had given her. He was sitting cross-legged beside her. She had a hold of his knobby-fingered hand. Tiny prickles of electricity came through his hand into hers.

"I was holding Danato's hand." She let go of his hand and pushed herself up so she could sit against the wall. She pushed with her good arm and rested against the cold metal.

"I'm surprised you can tolerate touching it," Efrat said.

"Danato is the gentlest man I've ever met," Cori said defensively. "You don't know anything about him."

Efrat looked her over, stone-faced. "I meant mine."

She met his eyes, but he looked away right away. "What do you mean?" She looked at his hands. As if he sensed her eyes on them, he crossed his forearms over his bent knees. He fisted his hands in anger or frustration. She wasn't sure which. A thin blue crackle of electricity shimmered over them as he did.

"I just mean my hands don't exactly have a shut-off switch," he said without looking at her. "I can't usually touch people with my hands." He looked at her with a glare of hatred. "You're the first person I've touched with my hands in... a long time." His sneer faded into something she might have assumed was sadness if his fist weren't shimmering with trickles of electricity. "I don't suppose you have an answer for that."

Cori could feel the hair on her arms stand on end as the energy feeding into the room rose with his temper. The lights above brightened with the proximity of the power, as well. Her fingers itched where her gold rings had singed her skin.

"Why are you so special?" His face still looked sad, but the radiating threat said otherwise. She didn't have an answer for why his touch was tolerable to her. She didn't know why her tolerance was building as the day went on.

"I don't know, Efrat. I really don't. Maybe traveling through time dulls the sensation. Maybe that first blast knocked out my nerve endings." She struggled to find any dimwitted theory that might appease him before her hair caught on fire. She knew she could reach for her gun, but she got the distinct impression this topic was just sensitive enough that she shouldn't risk it.

His eyes were still on her. She wasn't even sure if he knew how much energy he was putting out. Even his furry arm hair was starting to stand on end. She noticed a ring around his forearm. It was on both arms, in the same spot just below the elbow. His flannel had been covering it, but now that she saw it, she couldn't believe she hadn't noticed it earlier.

The ring was a pencil-thick line wrapped around the arm. The scars were puckered and pink. She tried to think of what could have caused two uniform scars like that.

The bulbs above burst, sending her thoughts elsewhere. She yelped and shielded herself from the raining glass. "Efrat stop! I don't know! I'm sorry. I just don't have any answers. I don't know why the hell any of this is happening to me!"

"Cori," Danato said from above her in the darkened room.

27

D ANATO SAT AT HIS desk, doing yet another batch of paperwork. It was standard paperwork involving requisitioned materials, specifically toiletries. He hated that he had to explain any change in the amount of toilet paper they used. If the cafeteria made chili more than twice a month, he was likely going to have to requisition more TP.

Belus sat across from him, sipping his coffee. His paperwork was already done for the week. He never procrastinated like Danato did. He also didn't have nearly as much as Danato.

If Danato wanted, he could delegate his paperwork to Belus, but they already had a precariously balanced relationship. Asking Belus to do more than his share would enrage his inferiority complex. Danato valued Belus too much to ever make him feel like an underling.

However, watching Belus sip his coffee so sedately made him wonder if he wasn't flaunting his procrastination-free work ethic.

Before he could ponder if that would count as a passive aggressive attack, he saw Cori come up to the office door.

Since she grabbed right for the handle, he knew she hadn't bothered to deposit her gun. As the doorknob turned, Belus's head perked. "Gun!" they both hollered.

He heard Cori grumble in frustration as she placed the gun in the bin. He afforded a glance to Belus, who was smiling at her antics, but shaking his head with frustration. Belus had struggled to find common ground with Cori. He very much wanted to train her to be the kind of second he was, but since Cori was erratic and compulsive by nature, his patience was wearing thin.

Unlike himself, Belus had managed to keep an emotional distance from Cori and Ethan. Mostly that was because he didn't live with them, but also because he preferred it that way. Unfortunately for him, Cori was a very emotional being. Her reasons for being at this prison were based on her love for Ethan, her need to belong, and her desire to please.

Belus expected he could treat her the same as Ethan and get the same result. Ethan had flourished in this place because he craved the structure he had missed in his former life. Ethan was a boy of clay ready to be molded into a man, and mold him they did. Between Belus's training and Danato's tutelage, Ethan was an easy transformation.

Cori, on the other hand—to put it as delicately as Belus—was a pain in the ass. She came from a life where she'd had love and attention, but it was consistently taken away from her. Her father effectively abandoned her. Her mother died before she made it to college. Her aunt, the last of her functioning family, died before she graduated. To top it all off, she was kidnapped, raped, and sold into slavery. It was no wonder Cori necessitated so much more than structure and expectation.

Cori was capable of doing great things. She was a forward-thinker, with creative and logical solutions. Despite some ill-conceived plans, she was a smart girl and had the potential to change the face of the prison for the better.

Danato learned early on with Cori that brandishing his anger and authority would produce the opposite result. If Belus wanted Cori to be the bright and winning student that Ethan was, he was going to have to release his heart to her. Danato wasn't sure if that was too much for him. Belus had his reasons for keeping his distance from Cori, and although Danato couldn't blame him, he knew it wasn't fair to Cori.

"Sorry I'm late," Cori apologized before sitting on the arm of her chair. He ignored that for the moment and looked up at the clock. She was notorious for being late, but the clock only read 8:05. That might have been objectionable to Belus, but he certainly wasn't going to fret over a few minutes.

"Five minutes? That's hardly worth apologizing for."

Cori double-checked the clock. She must have thought it was later than it was because her face muddled with confusion. She shrugged off the mistake and rubbed her hands together eagerly. "Are we going to the time bubble today?"

There was no hiding her excitement. Cori had been begging him to let her plant a garden in the wizard world for weeks. She had even recruited Belus to provide an objective perspective regarding the cost of garden-produced food over shipped food. Little did she know he thought it was a justifiable experiment, but he let her work for the privilege rather than hand her the reins immediately.

"No, sit on that chair right," he added gruffly when he realized she was still sitting on the arm of the chair instead of the seat.

"No?" she wailed, sitting down in the chair. He could see the panic in her eyes. She was seconds from rehashing every argument she had used to justify her plan. She took one look at Belus and clamped her mouth shut, waiting for him to explain. He wasn't quite sure how Belus had managed the magical feat of stilling her protests, but he appreciated it.

"*We* are not going. You are," he clarified.

"Me, by myself?" Cori stammered.

Cori had never officially been to the wizard world by herself, with the exception of a few minutes here and there. She was smart enough to still fear it, which was good, but if she intended to make weekly trips into the world, she needed to be prepared for the dangers it held. If having fresh vegetables wasn't worth risking *her* safety for, then whose safety did she expect to risk getting them?

"With your gun, of course," he added when he thought she might start hyperventilating. "I mean, that was the point of getting them, wasn't it? So I don't have to babysit you all the time."

"Babysit? I resent that," she said.

He was exaggerating, but it wasn't far from the truth. Cori was used to having Ethan and him around to be her security blankets. She obviously had training in self-defense. She took to her gun like a pro, and when push came to shove, she shoved. Her only issue was being too complacent. It was Belus's chief complaint.

When Ethan and Cori were together, she didn't concentrate on her actions. She also didn't take his authority seriously. If she knew how many times he and Belus had discussed keeping their duties separate, she would probably be appalled. However, it wasn't just her safety that was at risk. Ethan was the one risking his life to save her, and with that risk came the risk of losing Danato's successor. As painful as it would be to lose Ethan, he didn't know if he had the will to do this all over again.

"You know the risks of this, don't you? If a wizard gets the drop on you, that gun isn't going to do you any good." Danato offered the worst-case scenario to her just to see if she had really thought this project through.

He could see the dip in her brow. His unsympathetic tone was upsetting her, but he knew it would be short-lived. She looked over at Belus as if he might hold the answer to this particular question. She turned back to Danato, squaring her shoulders like Belus had just told her to stand at attention.

"I'll be very vigilant," she said meekly, as if he had just asked her to scrub toilets. "Do you have any preference as to the location of the garden?"

"I assumed you had a spot in mind," he said, officially passing the reins to her.

"Yes, sir, I have an ideal location picked out: moist, fertile, and rich with sun." Her eyes twinkled, on the verge of smiling. She was starting to realize how close she was to getting her own way, and that always pleased her.

"Well, have at it, you're the botanist. I wouldn't presume to know your job," he said dismissively. He wasn't about to dictate to her about growing plants. She clearly knew more than any of his manuals did.

"Thank you, sir." Her grin finally surfaced, and he felt his own mouth try to mimic it. He loved seeing her smile. Cori may have been a pain in Belus's ass, but as cliché and sappy as it was, she was the light in his life. When she was happy, he was at peace with his life, including his past.

"Get on with it then," he grumbled, trying not to let the moment turn sappy in front of Belus. The last thing he wanted was to have Belus lecturing him on work-appropriate behavior. "You'll need to if you're going to get the paperwork done for it by the end of the day," he added as she reached the door. It was probably a harsh reality to stick her with, but he certainly wasn't going to volunteer to do the paperwork for her project. He had enough to do.

She let out a groan at the door before turning around. "No, paperwork; paperwork for vegetables?"

"Paperwork for everything," he said.

He half expected her to jump up and down and whining, as disappointed as she looked. "Yes, sir," she mumbled.

He nearly laughed at her dismal concession. He hated paperwork, but Cori had enlisted Belus as her stand-in doctor on more than one occasion to avoid the paperwork of the infirmary.

On her way out, he and Belus both bellowed before the door shut, "Gun!" He heard her growl and the scrape of the pistol leaving the bin. When she was out of sight from the window, he let out a snort of laughter that Belus joined him in.

"That gun is going to get her into trouble one day," Belus said, still chuckling. "I don't know why you ever let either of them carry guns." He lost his smile as the humor started to fade from the subject.

"Ethan carried a weapon as a guard. There is no reason he shouldn't now."

"There are plenty of reasons," Belus said. "He isn't supposed to be putting himself in a situation that requires a gun. He is supposed to direct his men into those situations."

Danato agreed with that statement, but he also trusted Ethan to make good choices. "You know Ethan would never ask his men to risk their lives without being right beside them."

"I understand that and I respect it. That's why I didn't object more vehemently when he lobbied for it."

Danato sat back in his chair. This was going to be a conversation that he needed to look relaxed for, even if he wasn't. "But?" he proffered the conjunction on a platter for Belus.

"But Cori is not as disciplined as Ethan. You see that she can't even remember the gun. It's that kind of blasé attitude about gun safety that makes me nervous."

"Have you discussed this with her yet?" Danato asked, more out of curiosity than anything else.

"Not yet. I'm giving her a little space. For now," Belus added in case the statement left room for the appearance of surrender.

"I see." Danato arched a brow. "What prompted that? Don't tell me you were hurt by her Cactus Toad comment?" Danato smiled, still amused by the altercation. Belus didn't join him; either he hadn't reached the amusement stage, or he really had been offended by the jibe. "I think she got the hint when I made her walk the dragon."

"Yes, I imagine you would think that." Belus's condescension was almost too much for Danato to shake off, but he put his hands behind his head and leaned back in his chair even farther. Perhaps if he looked calm, cool, and collected, Belus wouldn't notice the restrained undertones of warning in his voice.

"Would you care to explain that statement?"

"I need Cori to respect me. I don't think I should need to ask your permission to punish her."

Danato could feel his anger piquing. He didn't like the word *punish* in reference to Cori. Especially off Belus's lips. "I think as warden of this prison, I should have the right to dictate how my people are being handled." He hoped that came off as diplomatic and not passive aggressive, even though he meant it that way.

"I understand your desire to control your prison." Belus seemed to be working the diplomatic angle as well. "I'm not trying to usurp your authority, but we both know Cori is different." Danato couldn't respond. Their locked eyes were now the eyes of wild animals prepared to attack. He knew what was coming. He knew how he would respond, and there was nothing he could do to stop it. "She is her replacement."

The words that spilled out of Belus's mouth were not meant with malice or accusation, but Danato couldn't help but feel like he had just been slapped across the face. The memories that he tried daily to suppress flowed back to him.

Danato didn't remember getting off his chair. He was grateful that the only thing he had thrown in Belus's face was his accusatory finger as he leaned over the desk. Belus was up as well, prepared for the battle. He had never truly had a brawl with Belus. The result was far too obvious to bother with, and he would never disrespect a man so much as to beat him to the ground with one punch. Belus was a strong man—he was familiar with the virility juice of the dragon—but his size was still too much of a hindrance for a fair fight.

"How dare you!" Danato could feel the shaking in his throat that matched the tremble in his hand. "I will not discuss her with you."

"Which one?" Belus said it with as much civility as he had the other comment, but Danato knew it was an inducement. He wanted him to say her name, and Danato wouldn't.

"I am not having this conversation." He was impressed at how quickly he shut off the shake in his voice. He removed his finger from Belus's face. "She has nothing to do with Cori."

Belus's mouth dropped open, and his calm exterior disappeared in a sea of disbelief. "She has *everything* to do with her!" he yelled. "Don't patronize me like I didn't know her!"

"I will not discuss her. Do you understand? She is gone. Cori is the issue here." Danato wanted to add a *please*, but he refused to beg for what he had just demanded. He needed to keep his authority intact to prevent Belus from bringing this topic up again.

"Yes... she is," Belus said somberly as he crossed his arms. Again, it was unclear which *she* was being referred to, or which statement he was agreeing with. "Will you allow me to reprimand Cori as I see fit?"

"No," Danato answered without thinking.

"And why is that?" Belus asked, no longer maintaining his civility. Danato didn't answer. "Why is that, Danato?"

"Because I don't want you to." He was seething with anger, but the response sounded petty.

Unbelievably, Belus continued to push the matter further. "Why can't I dictate to her, reprimand her...?"

"I don't want you near her."

"Why?"

"Because she's mine!" Danato slammed his fists down onto his desk, bending the flat center into a trench. He trembled, feeling the raw emotions at the tip of his tongue. He wasn't sure what he was even arguing for anymore, but he was sure about one thing. "Cori is my responsibility. You can train her. You can guide her, but you don't get to tell me how to deal with her. You have a problem with her attitude. You come to me. You have a problem with her obedience. You come to me."

Danato expected the disappointment on Belus's face, but it surprised him that his ruined desk still wasn't enough to silence the man. "How can I train her to be Ethan's second if you won't let her out from under your wing?" Belus looked down at his desk and shook his head.

"Danato, sooner or later they will find out. You can't hide your past forever. Cori has a right to know why she is here."

"She has nothing to do with her," Danato reiterated.

"I'm not blind, Danato! I knew it had something to do with her the second I saw her outside of that village. I let it go because I figured she would help you get over your grief, but it isn't working. If anything, she is making you worse."

"Shut up."

"How many sorrow demons do you have on that leg now?"

"Shut up!" Danato didn't want to hear any of this, not now, not ever.

"No, I won't shut up. I've shut up for the last five years. I'm your friend, Danato, or at least I was, once upon a time. I know you better than anyone in this prison and I think I have the right to say whatever I want to you, without risking my head being splattered like a watermelon."

Belus pointed at the desk. Danato looked at the paper-and-pencil-filled divot. He knew Belus had a point. His anger and violence should never be used as a defense against his friend, but how else could he have made him stop? This violent act hadn't ended the conversation. Would it stop if he walked away, or would Belus just follow him?

"What do you want from me, Belus?" Danato said, keeping his voice and head down.

"I want you to forgive yourself," Belus said. "I don't expect you to forgive me, but at least forgive yourself."

Danato looked up at his friend, his partner, and the man that had lived through the pain of his wife's death right alongside of him. "You know I can't do that."

"Then tell them. Unpack all those horrible memories."

"Why? So I can relive it all again?"

"No, so that when someone does bring up the topic, you don't kill the furniture. You've spent too many years garnering this temper to keep your sorrow under wraps, but clearly it's still there." Belus nodded to the wall where his cane was leaning.

Danato knew it was too much to ask, but he also knew Belus was right. Cori had already expressed an interest in the story of his wife. Her curious nature would eventually drive her to find the answers he wouldn't readily give her.

"I'm sorry, Belus." He didn't know what to apologize for first. "I'm sorry for the past five years. I'm sorry I haven't been the friend to you I once was. I'm sorry I'm holding on to Cori too tightly. I'm sorry that..." He couldn't help but laugh. When he looked up at Belus, he could see the confusion on his face.

"Ethan came to me the other day, and asked permission to have a poker night, and a BBQ. You would have thought the poor boy was asking me if he could go to Acapulco for the winter." Danato shook his head, thinking of how Ethan had simply accepted it when he thought the answer was no. "I've been terribly selfish in my sorrow, Belus, and I am ashamed most of all for that. Please forgive me."

"I've never withheld my forgiveness from you, Danato, for anything." Danato felt the impact of those words like a stake in the heart. He took a deep breath, hoping the desire to weep would pass. He knew that might be the exception to Belus's forgiveness. "So, how do I get an invitation to this poker night?"

Danato laughed, thankful for the levity. "I'm not sure Ethan had a chance to get it in order before he left, but I'll make sure your name makes the cut."

Belus nodded his appreciation. "You do realize this desk was already the ugliest desk there was?"

"Yeah, I know," Danato said, looking down at the disgraceful evidence of his temper. "I'll be lucky if I don't get a card table next."

28

ELUS MADE UP SOME excuse to leave the office. They both knew it was purely for the purpose of separating themselves from the uncomfortable after-argument small talk, but Danato was also glad to have some time to think.

He managed to bend his desk back up, but it still left a crack in the center that he would have to cover to keep himself from getting cut. He made a mental note to requisition some duct tape from supply and continued to organize his desk again.

He spent the better part of an hour trying not to think about what he thought he had wanted time to think about. He was relieved, albeit temporarily, when Duke burst into his office. "Warden, sir," Duke stammered as he gave Danato a salute that was neither necessary nor part of any protocol that he had instigated. "I'm sorry to barge in, but I think I need your advice."

"On what?"

"Well, I was going to relieve Chuck from his post on the time bubble, and I found Cori in there with that electric elemental guy."

"What?" Danato stood up so fast his chair fell over.

"She had her gun on him," Duke added with waving hands. "She said she had everything under control and not to worry."

"Not to worry? Why didn't she report this?"

"She said it was very important that I don't tell the guys upstairs. She said she knew I was probably going to go straight to you, but she wanted me to tell you not to tell the military anything until she had a chance to explain things. She said if anyone sounded the alarms, they'd have hell to pay."

"I don't understand this. Efrat is dangerous. If he's out, we need to get the military to suppress him immediately." Danato grabbed for the phone, but Duke ripped the receiver from his hand and smashed it against the side of the desk. The plastic shattered, leaving its guts hanging by wires. For good measure, Duke ripped the metal listening device out and stomped on it with his foot.

Danato stared at him in awe of his audacity. Duke looked back at him with horrified eyes, like he couldn't believe what he had just done, either.

"I beg your pardon, Warden, sir, but she made me swear on Grammy's grave that if you tried to call upstairs, I would do anything in my power to stop you."

Danato could see the abject fear in Duke's eyes. He knew how loyal Duke was to Ethan. Consequently, he had shared that loyalty with Cori, but he had no idea he would take on Danato's wrath for her. Either he and Cori were better friends than he thought, or his Grammy was a *very* dear woman to him.

"Okay, Duke, start from the beginning. Is Cori hurt?"

"No, sir, she said she's fine. She said she just needed to babysit Efrat for a little while, and that it was all for the best, she hoped."

"What the hell is she thinking?"

"I said something similar to that myself, and then I tried to get close to her." Duke paused, licking his lips. "She then turned her weapon on me."

"She threatened you?" Danato couldn't believe his ears. There had to be more to this situation than what Duke was seeing.

"She said that she didn't want to hurt me, but that a wounded man would rest better on her conscience than a dead one."

"What does that mean?"

"I was going to ask that myself, but Efrat said he had had enough, and he gave me a ripe old zap in my butt, and told me to get the hell out of there. I hightailed it right down here."

"Alright, I need to get up there and see what's going on." Danato grabbed his cane and stormed from the office with Duke right on his trail.

29

THE ELEVATOR *PONKED* ON the fifth floor and Danato stepped out, along with Duke and three other guards he had lassoed on his way up. He pushed through the double doors and found the room empty. He observed the glimmering globe before him, but no one was inside. Above, on the lookout, the guard Chuck was passed out.

"Wake him." Danato pointed up at him. While two of them checked on Chuck, a winded Belus came into the room behind them, followed by the guard Danato had sent to fetch him.

"What's going on?" Belus asked, panting. "He said it was an emergency."

"It is," Danato said. "Duke saw Cori with Efrat. She seems to have taken him hostage for some reason, but now I don't know where she is."

"We need to sound the alarm and get the military down here to subdue him."

"No, sir." Duke nearly jumped into Danato's face. "My Grammy will haunt me from now to eternity if I break my word."

"Yes, yes, Duke," Danato calmed him before gently shoving him away. "For now, Belus, we need to find her. She has some explaining to do. I'm not entirely sure she's not off her rocker or under the influence of something."

"All the more reason to get more people involved."

"No!" Duke said urgently.

"Duke, shut up." Danato threw a fretful hand over his shoulder at the irate guard. "We will find Cori, and determine her reasons for making Duke swear on his Grammy's grave not to let us call in the military, and then we will determine what course of action to take. For the time being, I would like to give her a little leeway, at least for the sake of potential poltergeists." Danato rolled his eyes as Duke thanked him profusely and made the sign of the cross.

"Are you sure *you're* not under the influence of anything?" Belus asked.

"No more than usual." Danato turned away from Belus as the guard Chuck joined them. "What happened to you?" he asked him.

"I don't remember, sir. I got Cori out of the bubble, and then I went back up to my post. I don't remember anything more until now."

"He must have knocked you out. We need to find them now. I want all of you to do a silent search down from here. When you find them, corner them and report to us before you take them into custody." The guards filed away for their assignment. Belus hung back with Danato.

He waited for the impending questions about why they weren't following protocol.

"She doesn't want us to tell the military that Efrat is out?"

"Yes, I'm trying to give her a little trust here, rather than jump to conclusions about her motives."

"That's not what I'm getting at," Belus said with consternation etched on his face. "Why don't they already know he's out?"

30

DANATO ENTERED HIS CODE for the elemental entrance. The military rented the entire top floor, but like the transmorph level, it was mostly dead space. Since they only housed the four prisoners, they had bricked off the remainder to minimize their movement. Trying to keep from alarming the floor, he opened the door just enough to peek in.

On the wall, catty-corner to the door, was a lookout tower similar to the one for the time bubble, only bigger. The guards posted in and above it were bent over their stations, passed out like Chuck had been.

Danato slipped the door shut and looked back at Belus. "They're all out cold," he whispered.

"What about the other elementals?" Belus asked.

"Do you want to poke your head in to see if they're awake?"

Belus glared, but didn't volunteer to do it. "There is no way that Efrat got the drop on all the guards *and* all of them. They must be in there."

"If they are, then why? With all the guards passed out, why aren't they trying to escape?" Danato asked rhetorically.

"You don't suppose they are working together on this?" Belus asked, moving away from the door and back to the waiting elevator. They stepped in and Danato thought about the ramifications of the elementals working side by side in a civil plot to escape.

"What if Cori did see Efrat that day she got caught by the transmorph? He could have been in and out of his cage dozens of times since then."

"Someone would have seen," Belus said, but he didn't sound convinced.

"The transmorph level is nearly empty. He could jump in a cell, pretend to be locked in, and who would question him if they assumed he was impersonating himself. The time bubble only has one guard posted. He could have knocked them out like Chuck."

"They would report that," Belus said, certain this time.

"Not if they thought they had fallen asleep on the job," Danato argued. "Come on, Belus, do you really think anyone is going to admit that to either of us?"

"What about the men upstairs? There's got to be eight of them passed out. They aren't all going to wake up at the same time."

Danato thought about that. "If the elementals are working together, they might just start up a fight when he gets back. All they need to do is to have enough hail of fire to wake them into a firefight. Anyone questioning the lost time would assume they were rendered unconscious by the attack. As long as they make the final battle last long enough, the men won't realize how much time has actually passed between when they went out and when they finally subdued the inmates. You know how long their fights can last. I've heard of them doing a two-hour shift rotation on the worst of days."

"Shit!" Belus said, seeing where Danato's thought process had taken them. "He could have been running around this prison willy-nilly for the past year. That is assuming this cooperation is a recent development since their last engagement."

"Let's hope. Right now, I think it's more important than ever to find Efrat. Maybe he has already told her all of this, and she is keeping him down here to interrogate him without the military involvement," Danato said with hope backing his statement more than belief. Belus threw him a look that said he didn't agree, but he wasn't going to argue.

When the doors popped back open on level five, Chuck jumped inside and pushed the button for the main floor. "They are hiding out in the prop room. We've got guns trained on the door and are waiting for your order."

31

As soon as Danato gave the order, the men were in fine form, announcing their demands with flashlights and guns trained on Efrat. His face fell as he turned around to face them. He cursed and did as the men requested.

He placed his hands behind his back and strolled over to them. The men placed handcuffs on him, despite the shocks it gave them to do so. They shook the painful, numbing sensation away and dragged him by his elbows out of the room with four guns aligned with his movement. "Take him to the part-time level. We need some privacy," Danato said as he headed into the darkened prop room.

"Danato," Belus said quietly. He looked back at him. "She's armed."

Danato nodded. He knew Cori had a weapon. On any other day of the week, it may not have been necessary to mention, but for some reason today it was worthy of noting.

He stepped soundlessly through the rubble and found Cori crouched behind a pile, with her gun holstered and her head shielded from an unseen attack. "Efrat stop! I don't know! I'm sorry! I just don't have any answers. I don't know why the hell any of this is happening to me."

"Cori," he said. He hadn't spoken it loud or abrasively, but he could see her jump at the sound of his voice. She looked up at him, baffled by his sudden appearance. "What's going on?"

"Danato." She looked around the prop room as if she couldn't remember why she was there. He didn't like that. He hadn't liked the idea of her taking Efrat to do her own investigation of his Houdini escapes, but he liked her confusion even less. "Why did I come here? I should have gone back to 8:05." She looked up at him as if he could answer this question, but he couldn't since he had no idea what she was talking about.

"Cori, do you know where you are?"

She looked around again and stood up. "Yes, I am in a shit-hole storage closet, with the dangerous artifacts that no one has taken the time to catalogue, let alone organize. I can't believe this festooned fire hazard made it past Belus's radar for this long."

Danato took a deep breath, trying to decide if this was the side of her he'd wanted to see. "We can discuss that later. Why have you kidnapped Efrat?"

Cori looked back at the entrance. As if remembering something, she whipped her head back to him. "Where are they taking him?"

"To the part-time level."

"You haven't told the military about him, have you?"

"No, not yet." He added the last part to assure her it was still a possibility.

She pressed her hands to his chest. "Please don't, Danato. I know this doesn't make any sense right now, but I can't afford to screw up on this track. This is the only one that matters. Promise me you won't involve the military."

"You told Duke that this morning. Why?"

"I did?"

"Yes." Danato could see the confusion return to her eyes and he didn't like it even more the second time. "Do you not remember holding a gun to Efrat this morning and telling Duke not to tell the military he was out?"

Cori smiled. It was a fake smile. He knew what her smiles were. He looked forward to them too much not to memorize their meaning. "Of course I do. I just forgot that was his name." That was a lie. She didn't want him to know she didn't remember.

"I think we should go up and talk to Efrat now," he said.

He could see her trying to figure something out. She looked like she was trying to calculate a mathematical equation in her head. "Yes, I think we should do that."

He let her lead the way out so he could watch her. He gave Belus a look over her head that he hoped conveyed, "*I have no freaking clue what's going on with her.*"

Belus looked Cori over as she came out. "Cori, has he been hurting you?"

"What?" Danato pulled her around and he saw what he had missed in the darkened prop room. Her cheek was red from an impact. Danato could only assume it was from a hand or a fist. "Did he hit you?"

Cori touched her cheek. A look of confusion and then anger crossed her face. "Oh, yeah, don't worry about that. He's probably already gotten his payback for that. If not, I'll get it in later." She turned to go down the hall, but Danato grabbed her by the arms and pulled her back.

"Sweetheart, do you know that you aren't making any sense to us?"

She looked between him and Belus. She nodded her head and scrunched up her face. "I know, but I can't just jump you guys up to speed in the middle of a race. I've tried explaining, but there just isn't enough time. We should go talk to Efrat. I think it will help."

Belus gave Danato a look that said *no*. Cori pushed away from him and kneeled before Belus, as she always did, to allow their conversations to take place with him as the dominant figure. It was one of the few things she ever did consistently to respect Belus. Danato wasn't sure what had initially prompted the action, but he was certain it wasn't at Belus's request.

"I need you to trust me," she pleaded.

"This is Danato's call," he said, taking a step back.

"Belus." She grabbed his hand. Danato could see his discomfort at the affection, but he tolerated it rather than ripping it from her grasp. "I need *you* to trust me." Danato could see Belus's eyes trying to read her, trying to find the screw that was loose in her head, but when his eyes finally settled on hers, he saw the weakness that Belus usually saw on Danato's face when Cori needed something he didn't want to offer.

Belus pulled his hand away and nodded to her. He looked at Danato with the concern of a man who may have just accidentally sold his soul to the devil for cab fare.

"Let's go talk to Efrat," Danato instructed.

Danato let her lead the way to the elevator so he could watch her. Once they were all inside the lift, Belus stayed on the back wall with her, while Danato stood in front, near the controls. He turned back to her, checking if her gun was still holstered. "We know that Efrat has been getting out. We don't doubt that you saw him that night you got taken by the transmorph."

She chuckled and gave him a smile. "That ship sailed a few mornings ago for me, but thanks for the acknowledgement. *I told you so* always sounded catty coming from me."

Danato looked over the coy smile on her face. She was amused by this whole situation, or maybe just at the baffled look on his face. "What do you find so amusing?"

"You, I like for once not being the one asking all the questions."

"I don't," he said with threat in his voice. Her smile disappeared, along with the sparkle in her eye. He hated how easily he could rip the joy from her, but he didn't like being toyed with. His patience was wearing thin. "Perhaps you could help me with that?"

"To what end, Danato?" she said, almost smugly. "If you don't mind, I'm just going to let this play out a little longer to see where it goes. We just need to get to Efrat."

"This cryptic shit will have consequences later, Cori. I hope you have a damn good explanation for it." He turned away, not wanting to look at her anymore. She was putting him in an impossible situation.

Before the doors opened, he felt her hand slip into his. She squeezed it gently, but he refused to squeeze it back. He didn't want to do anything that might give her the impression that what she was doing was okay. When he didn't respond, her hand slipped slowly away.

The doors *ponked* and this time he led the way to where the men had stashed Efrat. They'd chosen a wolf-sized cage, so they had full access to shoot him if he tried to electrify anyone or anything.

Danato wasn't concerned about Efrat trying to escape. The military used the elemental weapons to keep him in line because they wanted to keep the elementals alive. With real guns and real bullets facing him, he was sure Efrat would stay content in his cage.

He stopped in front of the cage and crossed his arms. "We took a peek upstairs, Efrat. Your babysitters are fast asleep. I wonder what the General would say if he knew you'd been sneaking in and out of your cage."

"He wouldn't say anything," Cori said, taking a spot next to Danato in front of the cell. Efrat leaned on the bars and watched her. "He would just pull out a gun and shoot him in the face."

Danato balked at her statement, losing his commanding facade. "And why do you think he would do that, Cori? Did Efrat tell you that?" Danato knew the General was a hard-ass, but he knew the military took great lengths to keep these prisoners alive and contained.

"I watched him do it," she said so matter-of-factly that he thought he had misunderstood. However, the sympathetic look she directed at Efrat made him realize that she'd not only said it, but she believed it.

"Cori, Efrat is right here, very clearly alive." Danato glanced at Efrat, who was eying Cori just as dubiously as he was. That, at least, was some comfort.

"Yes, and I plan to keep it that way. For all involved, it's just better we stick to the way things have played out before." Danato assumed she was responding to him, but she was still looking at Efrat when she spoke. He could see Efrat drinking in her words, and he gave her a subtle nod, as if he understood everything she had just said.

That was the final straw. Something was wrong with Cori. She hated this man with every fiber of her being. She wasn't going to communicate with him at all, let alone in this subtextual manner. "Enough." Danato grabbed her arm just above the wrist and pulled her along. "We're getting you checked out."

"No, Danato, not again," she said, dragging her feet behind him. He didn't understand what she meant by *again*, but he didn't care to ask. He knew she couldn't get free from his grasp, and her weight was no challenge for him, so he didn't falter when she tried to pry his fingers loose and yank her arm away. "Danato, let me go."

He could tell she was trying to remain civil to appeal to his logic, but he was beyond appeals. Her behavior was downright sketchy, and he wouldn't let her get away with keeping secrets from him.

"No!" she finally yelled.

Danato felt a shock in his hand that traveled up his arm through the bone. The loud *crack* that came with the pain echoed off the high ceilings. He pulled his hand from Cori where the pain emanated from.

He turned around with the intention of threatening Efrat to leave them be, but the wide eyes from the room, including Efrat's, told him that the elemental had not been the source of the shock. The fear on Cori's face registered as high as Duke's had when he'd smashed the phone.

Danato let the many questions regarding her static acquisition pass, and he reached to take her arm again. He needed to get her out of here and away from Efrat.

She yanked her arm back before he could grip it again. She pulled her pistol from her holster and aimed it low on his body. He stopped. The look on her face was still fearful, but there was no mistaking the determined eyes that were begging him to stay away.

"Cori." He had tried to sound calm before, but that was gone now. "Put down the gun."

She shook her head. "I'm sorry," she whispered. "I'm so incredibly sorry. There just isn't enough time." She frowned. "I can't screw this up. It's life or death." She backed away slowly.

He took a step forward, and she stopped. "You won't kill me," he said, certain that he was right.

"No, but do you really want to see if I'm accurate enough to maim?"

She continued to back away and he let her, even though he was feeling sick to his stomach with rage. As she passed Belus, he spoke with the quiet, calm voice that Danato was no longer capable of. "Cori, you asked us to trust you."

Her gun stayed true, but her gaze moved to Belus. "No, I asked *you* to trust me."

"Kid, you need to put down that gun before you make this worse for yourself."

"I don't care about myself right now. Everything I'm doing right now is for you. I know you don't understand, but I've already been given permission to break the rules. I'm going to fix this. I've failed you once; I'm not going to do it again." She could see his brow dip slightly, but he didn't bother asking what she meant.

She backed into the bars behind her and handed Efrat her keys to unlock his door.

"I'm not letting him leave with you," Danato said. "I will give the order to shoot him." Danato gave a nod to the men to be on the ready for his command. They were all excellent marksmen. He had no doubt they could hit him and miss Cori.

For a moment, Cori looked panicked, but when Efrat emerged from the cage, she simply stood in front of him. Given that Efrat was still a head taller than her, he still wasn't concerned about his men's aim, but he couldn't trust that a sudden movement wouldn't cause her to be in the path. To save her life, he may have to risk wounding her.

The decision wasn't long on the docket for voting, though. Efrat pressed his hand against the bars behind him and a bright blue current twisted over the bars. Guns ripped from the guards' hands and clanked against the metal: one, two, five.

Cori's gun, along with her hand, slammed against the cell too, but as the energy dissipated, she pulled it back and held it trained on the men. She backpedaled down the corridor, half-pushing Efrat, and half being pulled by him. One guard, understanding the danger, ran after his gun.

He dove to the ground, plucked up the gun, and aimed his weapon. "No!" Cori yelled and pushed in front of Efrat as he prepared to strike the man before he could fire.

Danato didn't have enough time to yell before the gun went off. Efrat gave up his shot and shoved Cori back out of the path. His shoulder was thrown back from the impact. The other guards joined the fight and went for their guns, but Efrat swung around and bolted all of them. Three men flew through the air, while the other two got the privilege of catching them.

Cori holstered her gun and pulled on Efrat. He tried to throw another bolt out, but she screamed, "Stop!" and pushed his arms down. She nearly dragged him away from the fight, and Danato could only watch her go.

What the hell had happened between 8:05 that morning and now to cause such a shift in character? What madness had prompted her to side with the elemental who had tried to kill her?

32

C ORI TRAVERSED THE EAST stairs and tried to remember how Efrat had taken her. They were on the wrong side of the building for the freight elevator. They had already climbed two flights of stairs to the seducers' level. Luckily, Efrat was doing well enough with his wound not to require her assistance.

"The blood, they'll track us," Efrat said, wiping a drop away with his shoe. "We don't have much time. They'll fan out and find us."

"Shut up. This is all wrong." Cori pulled his flannel over-shirt off his back and wrapped it around his arm, just as he had for her. She could tell she was hurting him, but she couldn't slow down. "I was the one who was supposed to get shot. What happened?"

"You said you got shot helping me escape," he said.

"I did? You remember that? That must have been part of the real timeline... but we changed the outcome. Belus said the endpoints might be fixed, but if I didn't get shot in the arm, that means they are negotiable. I don't know if that's good or not. I didn't return to a new 8:05 morning, so this is all real. Which means Danato will remember this.

Shit! Come on, the freight elevator is still the only safe place to hide out."

She grabbed his hand and tugged him along behind by his good arm while she continued to babble. "I'm starting to lose the tenuous grasp I had on my reality. I think my ricochet just lost momentum. I don't have my 8:05 safe zone to clear my head. I may need your help to figure out where and when I am."

"How is this possible?" he gasped in awe.

"I don't freaking know. It has something to do with you bolting me right in front of the time bubble." She could see the elevator ahead and ran for it. Efrat stayed with her, keeping up a pace she hadn't been capable of when she was the one with the gunshot wound.

She pried at the doors, but in the end, Efrat reached above her and helped her open them. They slipped inside, letting the door clamp shut again. Efrat fell to the floor of the elevator, exhausted from the effort of running. "I meant your hands." He panted.

"What?" Cori asked, confused by his words as much as the situation. She reached for the first aid kit that was conveniently in the corner. She was mad that she was now in the position of helping him. She should have been grateful not to have a bullet hole in her arm, but any deviation in the timeline might mean they wouldn't make it in time to save Belus. She just didn't have enough information to start making adjustments.

At least some things were starting to come together. She understood why Danato had a gun on her when she found Belus. She also knew how hard it was for him to let Efrat save Belus. Neither of them were doing their best at making friends this morning.

"My hands!" Efrat grouched at her lack of understanding. "You never told me how you're able to touch my hands?"

"Damn your hands! Shut up about your hands!" Cori threw down the kit and grabbed his hands. She slapped them against her face. "No, it doesn't hurt. No, I don't know why, but I'm starting to suspect that I've absorbed enough voltage in the last few hours to be immune. Just shut up, Efrat, please! My brain is already fried, and I don't have time to coddle *your* sense of reality." She shoved his hands away, not wanting to be touched anymore. He winced from the pain of being manhandled, but said nothing.

She took a few breaths and put on the gloves from the kit. "When did you manage to get that in here?" he asked, nodding to the little metal box.

"I have no idea." Cori reached to unbuckle his belt. He grabbed her wrists. He didn't bother asking what she was doing. He just craned his neck to stare at her, wide-eyed. She laughed, even though it made her sound manic. She liked the turn of the tables. "What's the matter, pup? Don't you like girls?" She winked at him and proceeded to unbuckle his belt with his hands still affixed to her wrists.

She was curious at what point, or any point, would he actually stop her? He released her wrists as she tugged the belt from the loops. He lifted, allowing the belt to release. She put the buckle in his hand and closed his fingers around it. "I need a magnet."

As he electrified the belt, she removed his shirt from his arm. It was bleeding a lot more than hers ever did. She wondered if this was too much for him to cover up when he returned to his floor. "Is this what I did for you?" he asked.

"Yes, but you're bleeding a lot more than I was. I'm not sure if I can stop the hemorrhaging."

"I can cauterize it. Just get the bullet out."

"It's going to hurt," she said, more singsong than was probably appropriate given that she had been on the other side of this once today.

"It won't be the first," he said without a hint of the bravado that the statement suggested.

Even though it took the fun out of her reciprocated torture, she withheld the smartass retort he had used on her. She pressed her knee against his shoulder and held the magnet against the wound in his bicep. He reached over, touching the buckle to amplify the energy until it made him grit his teeth.

She held his hand in place, surprised that she only felt tiny pinpricks from this concentration of energy. She wasn't really serving any purpose other than making sure the buckle was over the wound. She caressed her thumb over his hand, mostly to feel useful, but also because she remembered how much this part hurt her.

Somewhere between Efrat's muted groans and the view of warm sticky blood flooding from the bullet hole, she closed her eyes. When she opened them, Efrat looked white as a sheet, but the bullet was hanging from his buckle. "You okay?" he asked her.

She wasn't sure if he was being sarcastic or not, but she grabbed his hand and directed it to the seeping bullet hole. "You need to burn it." She gagged a little and tried to remember a time when vampires drinking blood sounded romantic. "You're losing too much blood." She held his hand in place while he burned the wound.

Cori smelled burned skin as the tissue sizzled. She coughed and turned her head so she wouldn't vomit on her patient. When she heard the sizzling stop, she looked back at Efrat. He was shaking from blood loss or shock. "It's always easier when it's your own blood," he said, giving her a weak smile.

She hadn't thought of it, but he was right. She had no trouble dealing with her own injuries. Seeing herself bleeding all over the floor never bothered her. "It also didn't help that you were bleeding like a stuck hog." She gagged again over the mental image she had created. "I'm sorry." She wiped away the moisture that formed in her eyes. "You were a much better nurse for me than I'm being for you." She grabbed the first aid kit and pulled out the morphine that she wished she had remembered sooner.

"It's alright." He laid his head back and stared up at the ceiling. The lights were still on inside. He hadn't zapped out the electrical system like he had when she was shot. "War tends to harden your heart and iron-line your stomach."

Cori wanted to ask about that, but she wasn't sure how far casual conversation should go. It was better to stick to pertinent questions. "Why did you save me?" She tapped the syringe before injecting him.

He turned his head and looked her over with exhausted eyes. "I'm not sure. Maybe a piece of my heart hasn't been devoured by my black soul." He said it contemptuously, seemingly responding to an accusation she didn't remember making.

She wasn't sure what would have prompted her to say it, but it was clear it offended him. "I just meant I know why I was trying to save you, but it might have been just as well for me to get shot. You're the one who has to save Belus. What difference did it make?" She pulled out a suture to close his wound further, so it didn't leave a gaping scar.

"No, I suppose it didn't make a difference who was shot. You are the only one keeping me alive, though. Danato knows I'm out. He won't keep that secret long."

"He will, as long as I explain why."

"He won't believe you."

She shook her head. He didn't understand the relationship she had with Danato. "He's like a father to me. If I explain everything, he will listen."

Efrat chuckled. "Still living in that fairytale world, aren't you?"

"Don't condescend to me, Efrat," she snapped, feeling her peevishness come back. "I'm trying to save two lives here today. One of which, if you haven't been keeping up, is yours. Trashing my friends is not going to raise my enthusiasm for the task."

"Oh." Efrat drew out the word like he was receiving a back massage from a talented masseuse. "I almost want to tell you. I would just love to blow the legs out from under the pedestal you've put him on."

"Tell me what?" she said, overlapping his monologue debate.

"In the end, the pleasure would be too short-lived. As much as I want to see that horrified look on your face, I hate to see women cry."

"You're bluffing, and it's pointless. I'm already helping you, despite my personal feelings for you. That should be enough of a feat for you to trust my intentions."

She snapped the thread and leaned back just as Efrat sat up. He grabbed her arm. The tingling prickles she had felt before were gone. It was only his bare hand on her bare flesh. He was about to speak, but the contact distracted him. He stared at her arm for a moment, before tracing his fingers down her skin.

From the change in his breathing and the gaze in his eyes, she got the distinct feeling that he wanted to feel more than the skin on her arm. It may not have even been sexually motivated, but either way, it was not consensual.

"What do you want to tell me about Danato?" she asked, to break his concentration. He looked up at her, remembering once again that she was in the elevator with him. A flicker of sadness crossed his face before his smug smile returned.

"No," he said pointedly. "I don't want to be the one to disillusion you. If I do, then you will only have me to hate."

"I already hate you," she scoffed and shrugged.

"No, you don't." She lost her amused smile, and he lost his smirk. "I know what hate looks like. I've seen it growing in my reflection for the last five years. This irritation you have with me isn't hate. You don't hate me any more than you hate that transmorph that sucked you in. You feel superior to me because I'm your prisoner, but if you knew the man I was before I came here, you would feel anguish for me."

He raised his hand and caressed her cheek. His blue eyes were full of more raw emotion than she could translate. She didn't know if he was grief-stricken, infuriated, or if... "I'll give you the key, but you have to seek out the answers yourself." He gripped the back of her head and pulled her forward as he leaned into her.

It took a few too many brain synapses for her to realize that he intended to kiss her. Although her first instinct was to pull away, she could feel his grip on her neck charge with prickling heat. He intended to kiss her whether she cooperated or not.

A flurry of things crammed into her head simultaneously. *What will Ethan do? Should I pull my gun? Are his lips electrified? Did I brush this morning?*

A *clunk* sound shattered her thoughts along with his intentions. She backed away, pulling from his grip. He looked around. The elevator was moving; down, according to the numbers. He looked at her. "Is this right? Is this what happens?"

"I guess. I never knew what led up to Belus being shot. I assumed they either find us or we find them. One way or another, we are going to be surrounded by a room full of guards, a pissed-off Danato, and a dying Belus."

"Okay, how do we do this?"

Cori didn't want to admit that she had no freaking clue what was about to happen, but she hoped it turned out better than her future had alluded to. "Just don't shock anyone. No sudden movements. Maybe Belus gets shot in a hail of premature gunfire." She stood up and helped him up. He looked wistfully at her, probably regretting his lost opportunity. "Look, maybe I don't hate you... anymore," she added for good measure, since she was pretty sure she'd hated him a year ago. "But let's not get too cozy with our resolve to be friends."

He smirked. "We'll never be friends, Cori."

Cori couldn't help but frown at that statement. He was inches from kissing her only a minute ago. How had he gone back to being her enemy so fast? And people thought *she* was hot and cold.

33

T HE ELEVATOR DOORS OPENED to the part-time level. They were back to where they had started before the botched escape. Cori calculated that they couldn't have escaped more than half an hour ago. Her morning, thus far, had amounted to about three hours. She had been stupid to think she could hide out from Danato in his own prison.

There was no flurry of movement outside the doors except to adjust the aim of the pistols and elemental weapons being wielded before them. A short line of three kneeling men stood before a back row of three standing ones. Their guerilla warfare tactics were now useless against the British line-up—especially, when they were stuck in a box.

Cori could feel the hair on her arms and neck stand on end as Efrat's defenses rose behind her. He was up, but he was leaning against the rear doors. He looked ready to pass out at any moment. She didn't have to guess how dangerous it was to be stuck in a metal box with him, especially when he was wounded and cornered by his enemies.

She raised her hands slightly to the guards and turned her head so Efrat knew she was talking to him. "Don't. Please." She added the *please*, even though she knew it wouldn't make a difference. If he chose not to fry her and the guards in an effort to escape, it would be out of a precarious balance of trust, and not because she was polite.

She could feel the tangible energy wane enough for her to move without creating static electricity with her pants. That was all she could hope for at this point.

Danato and Belus were nowhere to be seen, but she knew that wouldn't last. This scene was going to play out just as her memory had, and she hoped knowing that future would give her an opportunity to change it.

"Ma'am." She heard the gentlemanly address and looked at one of the back guards. Duke, one of Ethan's better friends among the guards, was holding on to his manners as tightly as his gun. "I'm going to need you and the gentleman to come out of the elevator."

Cori wondered if he would ever use her name, or if he would eventually switch to calling her "sugar." She nodded. "Sure, Duke. We can do that. Can't we, Efrat?" She said the last part a little loudly.

"Yep," was all he said.

"Ma'am, you just need to place your hands high where we can see them. Sir, you can just place your hands behind your back," Duke instructed prior to signaling the men to back up.

Cori did as he asked, and Efrat did as well. They stepped forward from the elevator and, as instructed, moved into the hall of the part-time level. There were a few more guards as backup, already blocking the hall. Duke and his group surrounded them, keeping them from attempting any escape.

With the guards now armed with elemental weapons, Cori knew Efrat had no chance of escape. He couldn't magnetize anything without them deflecting the energy. As much as she wanted to believe that they wouldn't shoot either of them with their pistols, she wasn't sure. They had already tried once, and now they were even further on edge. There would be no room for sudden movements or mistakes here.

"Ma'am," Duke said almost apologetically, "I'm gonna need you to slide that pistol over to me."

"I'm afraid I can't comply with that just yet." Duke's face melted as if he knew what that might mean for her. "I know I seem crazy to you, Duke. To all of you." She scanned the room. "I wish that—"

"Cori!" Efrat snapped behind her.

"Shit," she said, realizing how close she had come again to making a wish. Although she wasn't within earshot of the genie, it wasn't wise to get in a habit of making that statement with an unused triple-wish pack lying around just two floors down. "If Ethan were here, he would give me the benefit of the doubt. I know I'm not him, but I'm concerned that someone is going to be hurt, and I need to protect them. Until I'm sure they are safe, I'm just going to keep this pistol with me."

Duke looked like he was about to object or plead with her, but Danato and Belus came around from the west elevators. "Cori!" Danato snapped. "What the fuck is wrong with you?"

Cori took in a deep breath. Any fleeting thought she might have had about explaining things to Danato was gone. His face was already pink with rage. His knuckles were white from gripping his cane like it was a substitution for her neck. He was walking so fast, Belus was barely keeping up behind him.

"I..." She opened her mouth, but she scrambled for an explanation. What could she tell him that wouldn't make him madder? "I love you."

The words just rolled out of her mouth like a dog dropping a fresh kill at his owner's feet, but it worked. His face momentarily blanked and after a stunned silence that included a few furtive glances to his men, he spoke with a calmer, albeit overwrought, tone. "Why are you helping him?"

"I need him to save Belus."

"Belus is fine!" He lost his composure again.

"I only know what I saw, Danato. I'm sorry I don't have time to explain this, but I don't want anyone to die today. I'm just trying to make it through three hours without anyone dying!"

"What you saw?"

"I'm jumping through time, Danato."

Danato's face froze for a moment. Cori already knew the thoughts that were going through his head. Demon parasites, dream feeders, brain tumors: it was anything but what she just said. "That's not possible."

Cori lowered her face, not wanting to explain this all again. "It's true," Efrat said behind her. It probably wasn't helping Danato's temper for him to be speaking directly to him, but she appreciated being backed up. "I've been with her all morning. At first, I thought she was just going nuts, but she's not, she's just out of order. Her memories got scrambled. Probably my fault, we're guessing. She's lucid one moment and has no freaking clue what's happening the next."

Cori gave Efrat a look that hopefully showed her gratitude. She knew he was probably only saying it to keep things civil. He knew as well as she did that they were officially at the end of the line and it was time to start kissing ass to recover from this fiasco.

"You should have come to me with this," Danato said in an even tone that expressed his anger as equally as his disappointment.

"To what end?" Cori yelled, happy to use that turn of phrase back on him again. "The ending where you poke and prod me in the lab, or the one where you hold me down on a gurney kicking and screaming while nurses strap down my arms and legs?" Cori could feel her voice strain with the emotion of that memory. Although it wasn't a real memory for him anymore, she was sure that it would need to be answered for before she could trust him again. "Maybe we should just go straight to putting Efrat in front of a firing squad. Those are about the only outcomes I've gotten from explaining things up front to you, Danato! You demand so much from me: my respect, my obedience, my trust."

"I think I've earned those by this point." He was quiet, but something in the tone told her she had hurt him with the statement.

"When do I earn mine?" She paused. This was probably the worst time ever to bring up the subject. It was like asking your boss for a raise right after you trash the office. "If Ethan had walked into your office and said he was jumping through time, I kind of get the feeling he might have been taken seriously. Since it's me... I get analyzed and questioned. Even now, you're not really listening to me. You're just trying to figure out how to get me sequestered so you can get my gun and get me away from Efrat. You're protecting me, but you're not *helping* me!"

His chin rose, expressing his defiance to the statement, but it lowered again, acknowledging the little hint of shame that came with being called out on your mistakes.

"It's not you, Cori," Belus said. Cori turned to him. He stepped through the guards, but kept his distance. She glanced behind her at the guards, trying to see where their weapons were aimed. She didn't want to do anything to incite gunfire. "He's too afraid of losing you to treat you any differently." Belus glanced at Danato. She followed his gaze and saw the distant misery in Danato's eyes. "He loves you to a fault. It doesn't mean we don't trust you. It just means more precautions will be taken to protect you. That kind of cloistering can have its benefits at first, but you're probably just starting to see the downsides."

"Do you believe me, Belus? Do you believe I'm jumping through time?"

"I have no competing theories, but I did just find out about it." Cori gave him a thin smile. She should have known better than to expect a simple "yes."

"Before... in a fractured timeline, you told me that I might need to just let things play out as they had the first time. You said I might not be able to stop you from getting hurt, but I disagree." She looked around again for antsy body language. Itchy trigger fingers were a threat as far as she was concerned. "A change in the timeline has taken place. I think I can do it again. I think I might be able to stop you from being hurt."

Belus shrugged. "Well, you know how I feel about you going against my express orders." He smiled. She wondered if he was just playing the part of a sympathetic policeman talking a jumper down from the ledge. "But I'm not a proud man. I don't mind being saved by the damsel." He chuckled a bit, and she knew he was playing her. She didn't really mind, though. She felt compelled to tell him she loved him, just as she had Danato, but she wasn't sure he would appreciate such an admission before this particular audience.

Somewhere between her compulsion to declare affection at inappropriate times, and her intent to suggest that Belus leave the room for his own safety, she found herself on her back on the floor, with her gun in hand.

34

ORI COULD FEEL THE stuffiness in her ears, similar to the time bubble exit, but not quite as bad. Her eyes were closed, and she kept them that way. The burning pain where her rings had superheated and the ache permeating her spine told her this was the beginning.

She was actually mad that she had jumped this time. She finally had a chance to see if she could save Belus, and now she still didn't know. How was a damsel to save the day when she couldn't even stick around long enough to find out who she was supposed to be fighting?

She couldn't hear Efrat's footsteps; his damned expensive leather shoes were too quiet to hear. She did, however, feel the air move on his approach. He pushed his foot into her side, but she remained still. She could hear his knees crack as he crouched down to her.

He stayed there a moment, examining her. She heard him scoff. She assumed that he just recognized her and found the humor in this situation. He pressed his fingers to her throat, and she hoped that the slight race in her heart was justifiable after being electrocuted.

"I'll be damned," he mumbled. "Energizer fucking bunny." With another creak in his joints, he stood, and the air wisped as he walked away. Cori opened her eyes and slowly moved to see where he was.

He stood below the guard station, examining the guard Chuck from below. Cori didn't bother waiting since he would likely turn to head into the time bubble soon. She was glad her joints weren't as vocal as his. She was also glad that the boots she had traded her sneakers in for were very flexible and quiet.

It was only a few feet to stalk before she reached him, but she ducked low and took long, soft, intentional steps to him. He was not her friend, and according to him, never would be, but at this particular point in his timeline, they weren't even tenuous allies.

She jammed the gun into his back and prepared her monologue of haughty dribble that would ultimately prove to be what started this trainwreck of a day. She'd expected to get the drop on him, as Efrat had suggested. She hadn't expected to get an elbow swinging back in her face.

As she recovered, she could see the shock in his eyes. She had surprised him, but he was apparently the type that hit first and asked questions later. She raised her gun, but he dropkicked it out of her hand like a black-belt, or at least a kickboxing enthusiast.

The gun skidded across the room, and she mentally cursed herself for not keeping a hold on it. She lunged at him. It was a last-ditch effort, but she needed to try. He easily maneuvered around her and kidney-punched her as she lurched past him.

She was barely able to catch her breath from the spasm of pain overtaking her lower back when he grabbed her from behind. His hands slipped under her arms and behind her neck in a full nelson. She couldn't even feel a tingle in her neck from his contact. She wondered why he hadn't used his power on her instead of teasing her in this cat-and-mouse game, especially when he was clearly the cat.

Or was that his purpose to begin with?

She kicked back his knee, and he grunted from the pain. She let her body weight drop down to the ground, and her arms slipped from his slackened grip. She slammed her fist into his crotch and pulled on the bend in his knees.

He fell back. She had hoped for his head to hit the floor and knock him out, but no such luck. His back smacked firmly and she dove on him. She wasn't sure why she'd thought her body weight would be enough force to hold him down, but it wasn't.

He thrust her off as if she were a child playing airplane on Daddy's legs. It wasn't without effort as it might have been for Ethan, but she was still no challenge to him.

When she landed, she expected to stand and begin again, but his body weight pressed down on her before she even opened her eyes from her hissing cringe. His wiry legs wrapped around her thighs like some high school wrestling champion. His hands pinched her wrists and pressed them against her chest, as he had done before when she'd attacked him over Belus.

She didn't like the constraint, but she refused to let the dominant position keep her from doing what needed to be done. "You're good," she panted as she stared up at those baby blues. It was probably the strangest thing to say in this particular moment, but she was on a roll for disarming men with blatant honesty. Not to mention he could kill her with one misplaced power surge. If there was a time for kissing ass, it was now.

His eyes narrowed as he tried to figure her out. He looked down at his hands touching her and she could see the gears grinding. She could feel him increase his energy output, but it only gave her prickling pain. "Yeah, I can feel that. Not like you want me to, though."

His eyes narrowed further, as if she had baited him into a challenge. She felt a sudden spike in pain, but it was short-lived when a loud snap forced him to pull his hands away. He released his leg lock, but remained on top of her while he rubbed his wrists. "Efrat, I need your help."

"How did you do that?"

"I didn't, you did. I got enough static electricity from you over the past few hours to light a Christmas tree. Just stop trying to kill me for a second so I can explain what's going on." He didn't move, nor did he contest her request. "I know you've been getting out of the upper level without the military knowing. I know that if they find out, General Douche is going to outright shoot you."

"That's why they need to not find out." Efrat wrapped his hands around her throat and pressed his fingers into her windpipe.

"No!" she screamed, but it sounded like more of a whimper. She gripped his hands, but there was not enough strength in her to get him off. She wondered what went wrong. What had she done differently to get the drop on him? As her eyes watered and blurred, she thought how wrong she had been to even begin to trust this man with Belus's life.

Even as she started to black out, she could sense the shift in lighting and location.

35

C ORI FELT THE GUN in her hand again and the weight released from her body. She was still on the floor. Efrat was standing on her left. She aimed her gun at him. "You son of a bitch! You tried to strangle me!"

A strong hand reached down and ripped the gun from her hand. Her trigger finger stuck, and she felt the pain of a sprain as it was yanked along with the gun. She looked back and saw Danato staring at her in horrified shock. "What is wrong with you? How could you do that?" He wasn't so much angry as appalled.

Cori shook her head and looked around the room, remembering where and when she was. It was getting harder and harder to stay caught up with her movements. She was already frayed, but now a fresh headache was setting in, and a feeling of déjà vu was making concentration near impossible.

She was on the part-time level. The guards were surrounding her. Efrat to her left. Danato to her right. Belus... dead on the floor.

"No!" She sat up fully. "What the hell happened?" She looked around for the offending shooter, but no one looked guilty. They all looked the same: fearful and baffled. She looked back at Danato as he slowly backed away from her. With each step, he raised her gun against her.

She looked down at her hand. Her trigger finger looked off; it was dislocated. It was starting to swell. Behind that pain, she could feel the dull ache of impact on her palm. The feeling one gets after the buck from a discharged weapon.

She looked at Efrat. She couldn't quite place his emotion, but he looked like a new boyfriend enduring the discomfort of his girlfriend's family reunion. Only, at this family reunion, his girlfriend had decided to shoot her uncle.

She shook her head. "Me?"

He nodded. "Yeah, kitten, you did it." He seemed for once earnestly sympathetic. Somewhere in those beautiful blues was a man who she could trust with the duty of saving her friend's life. It was such a shame that he wanted to kill her so badly.

It was all gone. Just as quickly as it came, but at least she knew who she had to stop.

36

C ORI WASN'T SURE WHO decided where she would leap to and when, but she was thankful that she hadn't returned to Efrat strangling her. She was all for a fair fight, but she was beginning to understand that Efrat was not purely an elemental. He was trained in fighting.

She regretted not working harder on her fighting skills with Belus. She regretted not doing a lot of things for Belus now. She was fairly good at self-defense when she needed to survive, but there was no hope against an enemy that actually listened to his trainer.

She felt the pain in her fingers and back. The cold, glossy white floor that made the prison seem sterile was just the welcome she wanted. She kept her eyes shut and waited for Efrat to do his bemused assessment of her before he moved on. Just like her 8:05 morning starts, it happened the same way. Of course, this time it wasn't going to end the same way.

She crept behind him exactly as she did before, since that wasn't where she'd screwed up. She didn't jam the gun into his back. This time, she tapped him. He swung around to elbow her, but she ducked and jumped back.

She raised the gun, but once again, he kicked it away with surprising agility.

It skidded away, and she made a mental note of how far it had gone. She didn't attack him. She took a defensive stance. His face flickered amusement, and he charged. She barely wheeled out of his grasp and slammed her elbow into his kidney.

He tripped her on the way by. She landed in a roll and jumped back up just in time for his return charge. Since she was already barely balanced, she ducked just as he reached her for the tackle. The quick drop kneecapped him, and her forceful rise just after flipped him over.

She would have celebrated her victory if he hadn't tripped her on her escape. She landed within reach of the gun and grabbed it. She whipped back just as he sat up, grabbing for her. They sat on the floor with her gun jammed in his throat and his hand clenched on her throat, dangerously tingling on the verge of electrocution.

This time, he mirrored her panting. At least she had made him work for it in this round. She couldn't help smiling at the stalemate. It wasn't a checkmate, but at least she could breathe.

His eyes narrowed, observing a number of things about her he didn't like, no doubt including the fact that she was still breathing. "Where did you learn to fight like that?" she asked, distracting him from yet another conversation about his damned hands.

"Special ops," he answered ingloriously. "Where did *you* learn to fight like that?"

Her smile grew bigger than she probably should have let it, considering he was still likely to kill her if she pissed him off. "From you, five minutes ago." His eyes narrowed and she could see him formulating a smart quip to lead up to his attack. "You aren't going to kill me, Efrat. I already know how this day ends. I, on the other hand, could empty this whole clip into your skull and save myself the pain of the next three hours, but I'm not going to do that either."

"Why is that?" She could see his eyes transfixed on her throat. His fingers were loosening, but only so they could feel the delicate skin there. She didn't care as long as he didn't choke her.

"Because unlike you, my heart hasn't been devoured by my black soul," she seethed. His eyes locked on hers with a glare that was more annoyance than anger. "Besides that, I've already seen you die once today, and I don't want to relive it." She held his gaze, making sure she had his full attention. "And watching you bleed kind of makes me queasy."

She drew the gun away from his chin just enough to offer peace, but not enough to leave room for stupidity. "I know General Dumbass will kill you if he finds out you've been getting out of your cage. He doesn't have to find out."

"Why doesn't he?"

"Because I'm trying to save lives today. So far, I've gotten me shot once, you shot twice, and Belus shot once, which makes for a shit-ass job of heroism, if you ask me." Cori wondered if she could just let him go and toss her gun to make this all end. *Was it as simple as all that?*

"I'm not sure what my blast did to your brain, but it seems to me that the best way to save me from the General is to remove the witness of my escape."

Never simple.

Cori sighed and shook her head. It would be easier to put Efrat back upstairs, ditch her gun, and hide out until she knew she was safe to be around, but clearly he was intending to kill her either way. The only way to protect herself from Efrat was with Danato's support. He had to find out about this. That meant she still had to protect Efrat from Danato until she could convince him not to rat him out. That also meant she couldn't ditch her gun... yet.

"Something you did with that bolt has sent me spiraling through my own timeline. This is the first time you've seen me this morning, but I've been hanging out with you all day. Let me tell you, it hasn't been that fun, but I've suffered through it to save your life and Belus's."

"Belus?"

"Yeah, I... have to save him." She wasn't sure how much he should know. In order to keep control of the timeline, she thought it best if only she made changes, lest another variable be added to the mix. "You are going to help me."

"Why would I do that?"

"Because of this gun."

"I'm not exactly unarmed." He ran his finger down her throat.

"Oh, what, these?" She grabbed his hand with her free hand and shook it. "If you haven't noticed, I'm kind of getting immune to them. You might be able to pull that crap on my earlier self, but right now, you're a fish on dry land, and I'm a fisherman... *with a gun*." She poked the barrel into his chest and threw his hand away.

She stood up and put some distance between them in case he didn't fall for her bluff.

"Get up," she said it herself, but she heard his voice instead.

The transportation through her timeline was starting to muddy. The sounds and sights weren't matching up anymore. It took a few seconds for the backdrop of the time bubble to disappear and the elevator to come into view.

37

"SHIT, I CAN'T TAKE this anymore." She sat back against the wall of the freight elevator. "Where are we?"

"The freight elevator," he answered.

"*When* are we, you jackass?"

"Apparently going down to level 2, to be captured by Danato again," Efrat sneered right back.

"Already, damn it." She looked at the dial above the door. "Well at least this time I can get it right."

"Get what right?" he asked suspiciously.

"Never mind, just don't blow a fuse, okay? Stay calm. I don't want to get fried in here. Just trust me."

"Famous last words," he mumbled.

The elevator doors *ponked* and everything happened much like before. Duke was polite in his requesting that they leave the elevator and Efrat reluctantly obliged. They stepped into the center of the surrounding guards and Duke asked for her weapon. "Ma'am," Duke said with the same apologetic tone, "I'm gonna need you to slide that pistol over to me."

"I understand." Cori took the pistol from its holster and bent down to place it on the floor.

"What are you doing?" Efrat mumbled behind her.

"Saving lives," she mumbled back before sliding the pistol over to Duke. He picked up the gun and placed it in his empty holster, while keeping his gun on her.

"Can you come toward me now?" Duke held out his hand to her. It was a strange gesture in light of the fact that she had just broken Efrat out of captivity and helped him flee. "Boss would be real unhappy if I let anything bad happen to you on my watch." His eyes were pleading with her. She was again the jumper on the ledge of the building, but this time, Duke was her soothing negotiator.

"Duke, this isn't that simple. I'm not being held against my will. I'm holding him against his."

"Cori!" Danato snapped. "What the fuck is wrong with you?" Danato stormed in, with Belus trailing behind. She was relieved to see him alive again.

"Danato..." she started to explain.

"We have her weapon, sir," Duke reported.

"Good. Grab her and take Efrat back to the upper level."

"What? No!" she objected as the guards came at her. "I told you they'll kill him!"

She wanted to protest more, but an arm wrapped around her from behind. She struggled to pull away, but the grip tightened across her chest. It wasn't until the sparking hand stretched out in front of her that she realized it wasn't a guard manhandling her.

"Stay back or I'll kill her," Efrat threatened. The men backed off instantly. Efrat whispered close to her ear, "I told you he wouldn't believe you."

"Shoot him now!" Danato yelled.

"Let me explain!" Cori pleaded to Danato.

"That time is over!" Danato yelled.

Efrat released an encompassing bolt. Unable to risk using the elemental weapons with her in the way, the blast resulted in three men being punished with electricity. She screamed and bit Efrat's hand. He threw her to one side.

She felt a spike in electricity as the guards fired on him. A wave of tangible but barely visible energy deflected the bullets. She felt her chest explode in pain and then she could barely breathe.

Time slowed and for a moment she thought she might be transporting again, but the image before her stayed the same. The guards stopped shooting as they saw her double over. Efrat looked at her with a look of subdued shame. She was sure he was already trying to convince himself this was the way it had to be. No shame for veterans, only guilt.

He didn't see Danato approach until it was too late. His face was red with anger, but his expression was blank, like he was no longer present inside of himself. His newly gained pistol pressed into Efrat's stomach and shot again and again until all that was left was an empty cartridge to click at an empty body on the floor.

Danato stared down at Efrat's motionless body, and Cori felt her legs slip beneath her. She felt hands on her neck and back, easing her down the rest of the way. Belus was beside her. She had saved him. Three or more guards were dead, Efrat was dead, and apparently so was she, if the look on Belus's face was telling her the truth.

He was saying something to console her—something that anyone should say to anyone when they were about to die. She was sure that if she died in his arms, he would find some way to blame himself. She was also sure Danato would not recover from this. She was mortified to leave Ethan a widower. She hated herself for that, as much as he would hate her for it.

"I killed you, Belus," she finally said when she tasted blood. "I went back and forth through time to save you, but now I've killed myself, and everyone. I'm sorry. I tried."

He looked confused, but he pretended to understand. There was really no point in arguing with a dying woman. "You tried to change my future? Why would you do a stupid thing like that? You know that never works out." He chuckled and she could hear a tremble in his voice that she knew would never translate to his face.

"I might still have a chance."

"Okay, kid. You give it a go. But next time, don't get yourself killed over me. I'm an old man and nobody will miss me."

"I'll miss you!" she scolded, croaking over the blood pooling in her throat. His face cringed and she could see two tears drip from his hard eyes as he touched her cheek. It was the rarest of visions, but she wasn't sure it was worth dying for.

She thought her tears were blurring her vision, but it was the time jump. She had another chance to undo what she had tried to undo. If at first you don't succeed... die trying.

38

E FRAT'S FACE WAS PROBABLY the last image she wanted to see at that point, but he was at least alive to feel her wrath. With her gun in hand, she backhanded Efrat with more strength than she knew she possessed. Despite the rage-induced effort, he didn't fly across the room as she had hoped. He did back away, rubbing his cheek.

"You stupid son of a bitch!" she screamed as loud as she could, letting her voice echo over the hollowness that surrounded the time bubble. "You killed me! How hard is it to just not kill me? Is it hardwired into your DNA?"

She was following him with stalking steps and he was obliging her wrathful fit by keeping his mouth shut. "Electrocution, strangulation, and finally shot dead! I am not your enemy! Can you understand that, you arrogant ass? Just so you know, Danato unloaded an entire clip in you after you killed me. In case you needed to know how that went on your end."

His face took on some understanding of her words, at least the part where Danato killed him for killing her. "What happened?"

Cori shook her head. She still wasn't sure how many factors she wanted to introduce into this mess. "I tried to save Belus, and in saving him, you started a gunfight, which killed me and a few others."

"Sounds about right for me."

"Don't." She held the gun in his face. "Don't get clever with me, like death is no big deal. I was serious when I said my morning would go a hell of a lot easier if I just killed you. Without me, you're dead, no matter what. Either Danato kills you or the General does. So don't mess with me. I will do what I can to keep you and Belus *and* me alive, but you will do what I say, when I say it, or this is over and I accept the repercussions for killing you in self-defense. Do you understand?"

She set her teeth and wondered if she could actually do it. Could she gun him down just to make this day go away? But would it go away? Even though the timeline was cinching in, she was still repeating and she didn't really believe that if she made things right, that everything would magically go back to normal. Something had propelled her to go in and out of her timeline, but whether it wore off or stopped suddenly, she needed it to stop at some point. Preferably right after she fixed this hellish mess Efrat had created.

Efrat must have sensed her internal debate because he took another step away from her as he nodded. "Okay, kitten, don't get your morals in a twist over me. I'll play along. I still think you're nuts, but this might be entertaining. Just so you know, though, my people upstairs won't be asleep forever. If you can't get me back upstairs in a couple of hours, your use to me will expire."

"Don't worry, you only have to do this morning once. It should be a quick ride for you. I, on the other hand, have to figure out how to save Belus from... his attacker, save you from Danato, and save me from you. Maybe I can..."

"What in tarnation is this?" Duke howled from the double doors as he pulled his weapon.

"Oh crap," Cori said, exasperated. "I forgot about that."

After several minutes of assuring Duke that she was okay, and several more spent convincing him that the military were not to be involved, she sent Duke on his way to tell Danato of their whereabouts. She couldn't stop him from doing it, and since she already knew when and where Efrat gets taken, there wasn't much point in trying to prevent the truth from getting out.

Her timeline was already hopelessly bent out of shape. Adding new dimensions to her past engagements with Efrat was pointless. Not to mention she didn't want to spend any more time in this morning with him than she had to.

She took Efrat down to the main level via the stairs. She caught a glimpse of Danato taking the elevator up with Duke through the window on the door to the stairwell. She waited until she was sure the doors were closed and headed down to the freight elevator.

With Efrat as a lookout, she placed a first aid kit on the elevator and sent it back up to the seducers' level. They sneaked through the cafeteria, where she grabbed a grocery pad and a pen to write with. She wrote herself a sloppy note and took it into the prop room to place under the snow globe, so she would know that Efrat was supposed to be taken and not to stop it.

When she slipped back out into the hall, she looked over Efrat. She wondered how much she could truly trust him at this point. She should have known based on the outcomes that she had seen, but one screw-up could change so much.

"Listen to me," she said gently. He stopped scanning the hall and brought his attention to her. "You must have made a good soldier, but this isn't a war. Not with me. Not today, anyhow. I know you don't trust me, but at some point I think you'll realize I'm one of the good guys, and not just because I wear the uniform."

She pulled her gun and released the clip. She shoved the magazine at him. He stared at the proffered bullets. He must have thought it was a test. A test he wasn't sure how to pass. "If you think I'm nuts now, things are about to get a hell of a lot crazier. You know more than I will in a few minutes. You will have to explain to me what's happening to me. I'm not going to trust you either and you really need to take this because I *will* try to shoot you."

He took the magazine and slipped it into his back pocket. "What should I tell you?"

"Just make sure I understand that you are going to help me with Belus, whether you believe it or not yourself. Just say it to me. I already know you'll do the right thing in the end." She stared into his eyes. He shouldn't have had blue eyes like that. He should have had cold, hard, dead brown eyes with no luster or highlights.

She wished she could tell him something that would make him understand how many lives were in her hands, and consequently, his. Even if she could convey that, he wasn't likely to care. His survival instincts were stuck in overdrive and probably had been for years. There was barely room for civility, let alone compassion.

"Try not to kill me, okay?" she said.

"I'll do my best."

"Cori." She let her eyes fall away from his as she holstered her gun. "My name is Corinthia Ellen Reiger. In case you need my *full* attention."

She paused, waiting for him to offer his full name, but he didn't. He just stared at her with that same annoyed, cocky—*you are a bug to me*—look. At some point, she was going to have to stop having expectations for him. Simple social mores were clearly beyond his capability.

She stepped into the prop room and motioned for him to follow. "Alston."

"What?"

"Lieutenant Sergeant Efrat Alston. In case you need *my* full attention."

She nodded and headed into the prop room. She could already feel time and space warp around her.

39

CORI ARRIVED IN THE freight elevator in much the same place she had the first time around on her redo. It seemed to be her new reset point. The time between her beginning and end was getting shorter. She needed to make the necessary changes while the time bubble fragment was still functional. The last thing she wanted was for the juice to run out before she had her ducks in a row.

Efrat was panicking about being caught. "Don't freak out," she said from the floor. "I got it under control this time."

"This time?" he wailed.

Cori took the clip out of her gun and stuffed it in one of her many pockets in her cargo pants. She didn't want to give up her gun, but that didn't mean that she couldn't give up her bullets. Pleased with her plan, she gave Efrat another round of calming speech before the doors opened.

This time, she didn't even wait for Duke to ask politely. She instigated her surrender with Efrat in tow. They stepped into the room and allowed the guards to surround them. Duke, of course, asked for her gun. She said she would surrender it after Belus and Danato were present. He agreed and didn't press the matter.

Danato arrived, cussing her out about her behavior, and demanded her to give up her gun. She agreed to give it up as long as Efrat was allowed to return to the upper level unharmed, and without the involvement of the military.

Danato grumbled for nearly a minute about protocol before he looked at Belus. Belus gave a small shrug that said, "What choice do we have?"

"Fine, Efrat can return to the upper level after you give up your gun," Danato conceded.

Cori was out of time and back in before she even recognized the change. Her hand held her gun. Belus and several guards were ducking, and she was on the floor again.

"What the hell are you doing?" Danato ripped the gun from her hand, this time without dislocating her finger. She started laughing when she saw Belus standing alive before her, unharmed. No one was attacking. No one was yelling, aside from Danato, and that was just normal.

"Oh, thank God." Cori repositioned onto her knees with relief. "I'm so glad this is over. I will explain everything. I promise."

Danato eyed her up and down. "We need to get you checked out."

"Fine, anything, poke and prod all you want. Belus is alive. I'm alive. Efrat's alive." She exhaled, feeling the stress lift.

"Go with Belus to the infirmary. I'm taking Efrat back to the military."

Cori looked up at him. She sensed the determination in his tone. "You agreed not to tell them, Danato. You remember?"

"I'm sorry, sweetheart, he is a prisoner." His voice was apologetic, but his eyes were not. "He can't just be roaming the halls."

"I knew it," Efrat said as two guards flanked him with elemental weapons. "Fairytale fucking world, kitten." He shook his head at her, disappointed, but for once she was in agreement with him.

"Danato, the General will kill him."

"I doubt that."

"I don't." She stared earnestly at him, but he didn't understand how much trial and error it took to get to this point. "I've been trying to get this day to end with everyone alive. I promised him that you would do the same."

"Cori." Danato stepped closer as if to spare Efrat the details of his demise. "There isn't a redeemable bone in his body. It's a waste of time and energy to get wrapped up in protecting him. The General will figure out what is best for him. He is not our responsibility."

Cori watched as they dragged Efrat away, with Danato following. She couldn't believe Efrat was still going to die after all. She'd hoped that this future would turn out differently, but that was unlikely.

"Danato..." Cori pleaded once again, but he waved her off.

"Enough. Report to my office after the infirmary."

Danato headed around to the passenger elevators with them. Belus approached to take her with him to the infirmary, to get poked and prodded, while the remaining guards scattered to return to their normal posts. "Are you all right?"

"No, I'm trying to do the right thing and every time I've got it right, it's wrong."

"What's going on?"

"The short version?" Cori raised her brow at him. "I've been changing the timeline to save your life. I've done it, but it always ends with someone else getting killed."

He looked her over, trying to decide how serious she was. She gave him a stern look that normally might have been reserved for a child, but his query vanished and he nodded. "I'm not sure what you've gone through, but it seems to me you're fighting an unwinnable battle."

"Possibly." She looked him over. It was a cruel fate for Efrat, but Danato was right. She couldn't rationalize losing Belus for him. "But my mentor taught me to fight even when the odds were against me."

A smile perked at the corner of his mouth. "He must be a very wise man."

"He is." She smiled, content that the right choices had been made.

As with any contentment in life, it was short-lived. Yelling and gunfire hailed from around the corner. She could feel the tangible static in the air. Belus ran to help, but a bolt threw him across the room.

Cori closed her eyes and cursed. When she opened them, Efrat was coming around the corner. He walked the few steps to put her in range of the pistols at high-noon duel and stopped. For a moment, all she could do was stare at him.

She knew Belus was probably dead. Danato was probably dead, along with the guards. It wasn't a guess based on Efrat's power, but more of a Murphy's Law hypothesis. Save Belus: she dies. Save Belus again: everyone dies. That seemed to be the natural order of time travel. Maybe Belus was right after all. Some events are just meant to happen.

"You said you were going to save me," Efrat began when she didn't plead for her life or chastise him for killing her family. She was too tired to play that game, but at least she finally understood the rules.

"I tried. I've been trying. In fact, you are the only reason any of this has happened. You started my time jumps by electrocuting me while I was entering the time bubble. I shot at you just as I dipped in, but it fractured my timeline and sent me momentarily out of time and space. Belus was the unfortunate recipient of my attempt to defend myself. He just got caught in front of me when my body linked into the latter part of my day. You should've been shot, not him. I tried to save Belus, and you got me killed. I tried to save him again, and you killed everyone."

His eyes stared back at her as coldly as she stared at him. "You do realize you'll die, anyway?" she continued. "You've accomplished nothing. I hope I have another time jump left because now there is nothing to stop me from shooting you in the face."

"Nothing but your freedom from your time jump."

"What?"

"I thought of it as Danato's goons were taking me away. You said you've been jumping between this morning and now. That means this is the end of your time loop. You're stuck on a record, replaying the same few hours, albeit in the wrong order." He came forward to conversational distance. "I think if I electrocute you again at the exact time that you shoot Belus, which will technically be your first schism into this time flux, it will stunt it. Complete the circuit, if you care for the electrician lingo."

Cori narrowed her eyes. "You want me to shoot Belus?"

Efrat looked back at Belus's unmoving body. "You're right that I am the cause of everything, but I am also the solution. If you kill me, you don't stop jumping through time. If you don't find a way to protect me from the General, I will fight and I will kill. I'm not going to die for Belus, Cori."

"I don't imagine that you would scuff a shoe for Belus."

He moved forward, slowly at first, but increased at the last second to grab her throat. She didn't do her best to hide her fear, but his hand shifted up, leaving the pressure to pull her chin up rather than block her air. "You don't know me. You don't know what I've been through. Forgive me if I've lost my sympathy for the people taking money for my unlawful incarceration." He pulled her forward. She gripped his wrists so tightly she thought she might at least be bruising him. "It may not look like it now, but this is me being sympathetic to your cause. Fix this for all of us and we all get to walk away."

"What about Belus?"

"That's between you and your bullets."

40

DANATO CLENCHED HIS TEETH as the elevator took him and Belus back up to the part-time level, where he asked the men to unload Cori and Efrat. He didn't know how things could go so wrong so fast. Cori had been fine that morning, but somewhere between her being giddy over planting her crops and when Duke found her with Efrat, she had gone off the deep end.

He wanted to trust that what she was doing had some purpose, but how could she team up with Efrat for anything? He was a cold-blooded killer and nothing more. Danato was honestly surprised that Efrat hadn't just electrocuted her when he came upon her in the first place.

It wasn't long after they had broken out when he got the confirmation of their location. Cori should have known better than to think she could hide from him in his own prison. He knew all the little nooks and crannies. It was only a matter of time before his men found her in one of them.

When the elevator doors *ponked* and opened, he jumped out, barely using his cane. His leg hurt like hell, but he was far too angry to pay attention to that now. Belus even struggled to keep up with him, and not for a lack of trying.

When he rounded the corner from the elevators into the back hall of the part-time section, he saw his men surrounding her. He noted that she was still armed. Efrat was standing not far behind her, his hands dangerously sparking with static blue. "Cori, what the fuck is going on?" He probably should have approached her like a hostage negotiator, but he wasn't interested in discussion. He was about a heartbeat away from telling his men to shoot them both in the leg and be done with this whole thing.

"I..." she stammered, before catching sight of Belus. She didn't bring her gaze back to Danato until he spoke to her.

"Cori, why are you helping him escape?"

"It's a long story. One which I will explain when we are all through with it, but unfortunately, it's not over."

"What is that supposed to mean?" He ground out the words.

"It means you need to shut up, calm down, and listen up," she announced as if she were... him. He wasn't nearly as taken aback by her words as he was by the look on her face. Less than an hour ago, she'd seemed disoriented and worried, but now she had found her grit. Even her stance matched the sturdiness of her guard captors. With the black cargo pants and boots, only her white t-shirt and long blond hair separated her from his men. "I met up with

Efrat this morning. We had a very short interaction which has led me to be tangled up in my timeline. Apparently, his electricity and the time bubble don't mix. We should probably note that somewhere in the handbook.

"I've been jumping in and out of the last three hours, trying to make sense of things."

"That's not possible," Danato interjected, prepared to explain the many reasons it was indeed not possible, but she didn't let him finish.

"It is possible when the original time bubble is what is actually causing my shift. My movement doesn't alarm the system because I am essentially still in it. Or at least, my consciousness has attached to a fragment of it." His previous objection was overruled. If she was correct, the system would not be alarmed by the same time signature, no matter where it occurred.

"I've been through the wringer: PET scans, straight-jackets, your overprotective bullshit, Efrat's psychopathic need to create chaos." Cori looked back at Efrat, giving him a firm glare, which oddly enough made him look away and place his hands behind his back. "I'm sick of it." She turned back to Danato, her face no softer than his was. "The only person in this chaos who has made any sense is Belus."

Belus perked up at hearing his name. He glanced over at Danato as if he might know what he had said to get through to her. Cori's face softened as he looked at him. "I'm taking his advice and letting this play out as it was originally intended." Her eyes lingered on Belus another second before she turned back to Danato.

The hard stare she put on him was surprising. He had already forgotten about his anger. Maybe it was the shock of her audacity, or maybe he was just impressed by her fortitude. No matter what it was, he could see the stress that had been weighing on her. A stress that, for some reason, she had not been able to share with him.

"This is my last round of time jumps. Efrat will ensure that." She nodded back to the elemental. Danato caught his eye, but he saw nothing more in him than he ever did. Why did Cori want him here? If he could stop her time jump, why hadn't he done it already? "No one in this room is to shoot anyone!" She turned, pointing at each and every guard. She did a full spin. "No one," she said quietly to Efrat. He held her gaze this time and nodded.

"What is this all about?" Danato asked, wanting mostly to break the connection between them.

She turned back. "This is about me watching Efrat die; me watching you and Belus die; me feeling myself die. This is about me having yet another unpredictably bad day on the job. But mostly it is about you trusting me, which is going to be really hard for you in another thirty seconds."

"Why?"

"Danato, trust me. Don't let them shoot me or Efrat." Her voice was soft and pleading, but her eyes were still scolding him.

She turned to Belus and gave him a frown. "Belus..." He tilted his head, signaling that he was listening. "I love you." The sweet words would have melted any man's heart. Danato wasn't sure if they were enough to melt his, but there wasn't a lot of time to discern Belus's reaction, because Cori pulled her pistol and shot him.

41

D ANATO WASN'T SURE WHAT came first: the gunshot to Belus's torso or the electrifying blue that lit up Cori's body. She fell to the ground in a heap and Belus fell to his knees before keeling to his side and rolling onto his back.

There were no other gunshots. He didn't order any either. He wasn't sure if it was at her request or if he was simply too shocked to move. Cori had just shot Belus. Why would she do that?

Danato looked across at Efrat, who was looking down at Cori as if waiting for her to magically jump up from the attack. He approached her to check her pulse. If Efrat had killed her, there would be a hail of gunfire, no matter what Cori had wanted from Danato. He reached down to touch her neck, but she stirred. She raised her weapon either with the intention of aiming it or just repositioning it, but he didn't take any chances.

He ripped the gun from her hand, catching her finger on the way. She hissed in pain, but didn't try to keep the gun. "Belus?" she whispered.

"You shot him!" Danato yelled, pointing the gun back at her as he retreated. He didn't want to point it at her, but he had no choice. She looked at Efrat and he nodded. Efrat moved toward Belus. "Don't touch him!" Danato seethed at him.

Efrat raised his hands defensively, which for him was not a comforting gesture. Instead, Efrat moved back to Cori and helped her off the floor. He wanted to yell at him not to touch her either, but he could see the elemental was not trying to hurt her.

Cori immediately went to Belus and checked his pulse. "We need to get him to the infirmary," Danato said to his men.

"Not yet!" Cori gave a generalized bark, not really directed at anyone. "I can't feel anything," she said to Efrat, who kneeled down on the other side of Belus.

"I can get him back on track. Stand back so I don't get you again. You're already amped enough to charge batteries."

"I haven't jumped. This future is being overwritten. Whatever happens from here on out is permanent."

"I know."

Cori leaned back away from Belus and Efrat jolted his body. She checked his pulse again. "I think so." She looked over Belus. "There's so much blood. I don't remember there being so much."

"Blood can be replaced." Efrat double-checked the pulse. "They can move him now. He's stable."

Cori looked around the room for someone. "Duke, we need Belus in the infirmary now. He'll need a transfusion right away."

"Yes, ma'am." Duke didn't hesitate to follow her orders. He grabbed three other men, and they carried Belus away on a linked-arm stretcher. Several men accompanied them to fetch the elevator and to take the stairs ahead of them to warn the doctor of an incoming gunshot wound.

Danato's men were in fine form, even if he wasn't.

When he finally took his eyes off his friend being carried away, he looked at Cori as she approached him slowly. She looked to be herself again; her transformation into hard-ass had worn off. All that was left was an after-midnight Cinderella, a plain-Jane little girl in a woman's body. She looked fearful now.

It wasn't until she reached him and pressed her hand on the muzzle of the gun that he realized he still had it pointed at her heart. He inhaled and dropped the threat to his side. She seemed to relax a little, but she still looked concerned that he might reach over and snap her neck in a fit of anger. "What the hell just happened?"

"When Efrat shocked me, the first time, I was in the process of shooting him. What I didn't know was that I was actually here when I did that. My consciousness, anyway."

"Why didn't you just ditch your gun?""For a number of reasons, I can explain later. Right now, I need you to listen again. What I'm about to ask you is vital."

"What now?" He didn't like any of this, but somehow he knew this was going to be the worst of it.

"Efrat was here to save Belus's life. The only way this morning could end well was with Belus being shot, but I also needed to give him his best chance of survival. I know what you think of Efrat, and believe me, you are right, but I've made a promise to him."

Danato shook his head even before she spoke the debt.

"You need to let him go back up to the upper level without telling the military about his escape."

"That's impossible. He's been walking free for months now."

"Maybe, but until today, we didn't know that. His purpose is a little sketchy, but so far he hasn't exactly been killing people or letting out prisoners, so I'm inclined to assume that he isn't a threat to us unless we become a threat to him."

"Cori..." She placed her finger over his mouth and lowered her voice even further.

"And telling the military is a threat to him. They will kill him if they know he can leave at will." She let her hand slide down to his chest. "I've been through this again and again. Please Danato, I'm not asking as your friend, I'm asking as your employee: please don't ask me to knowingly send a man to his execution."

Finally, it clicked. Danato understood why she was protecting the elemental. "Do you know for certain General Clark will kill him?"

"In cold blood, without so much as a villainous catchphrase."

Danato glanced behind Cori at Efrat. He was observing their conversation with great interest. If Cori was right, Danato was either the man to stay his execution or hammer the first nail in his coffin.

He looked down at Cori. "You're asking me to save a man that I would gladly be rid of. He's a killer."

"I know. I'm not denying his character and believe me, I came close to taking him out of the equation myself, but we aren't a death row prison."

"What's the verdict, kitten?" Efrat hollered over when he couldn't take it any longer. Cori flinched from his voice, but she waved her hand dismissively, not turning to him. Efrat took a few intemperate steps forward, and Danato spun Cori behind his back. He didn't have to give the remaining guards any commands. They were already surveying Efrat like vultures. His movement spurred a united advance that was as striking to Danato as a ballet.

"One word, Efrat," he threatened.

Efrat scoffed. "I've been with her all morning. If I haven't killed her by now, I don't think I will." Cori scoffed behind Danato, peeking around to glare at Efrat. They both looked at her for the meaning of that, but she shook her head and ducked back behind him. "I saved your man's life. You owe me."

"You've got to be kidding me." Danato couldn't believe that was his argument for saving his life. "Do you know how many of my men you've killed? You've killed dozens, and you expect me to thank you for saving one."

"And Cori," Efrat added.

"She wouldn't be in this mess if it weren't for you!" He stepped forward, prepared to take this fight into a shoving match, but Cori jumped between them.

"Please!" Her hands were shaking, and she was looking pale. "I can't watch anyone else die. Please Danato, just post guards outside the upper level until we can figure out what to do with him."

"Cori, we can't just put a bandage on this and walk away."

"Told you he wouldn't listen to you," Efrat mumbled.

Cori whipped around so fast her ponytail smacked Danato in the face. "Shut up, shut up, shut *up*! Do you think you are helping your case? Do you think anyone wants to help a sardonic, psychopathic sadist?" She shoved Efrat back, and he took it without defense, despite the grimace of pain he showed with each impact. He reached for her to ease her back, but she sloughed his hands away. "I have been shocked, strangled, slapped, and punched by you today, and I am still standing here defending you!"

Danato kept up with her forward movements, in case Efrat decided to put her down. He should have tried to stop her, but he had never seen her so mad before. He had seen her irritated and offended to the point of tantrums, but this was unlike anything he had witnessed. Either the day had been too much for her, or Efrat had.

She shoved the elemental again. His jaw clenched, but he took it. "Do you know why he's having trouble deciding if he should save you? Because deep down inside, he wants you dead!" She shoved him again, and a crack of electricity echoed the room. The men closed in, but Efrat placed his hands farther away from Cori. "No one here gives a crap about you! They hate you!" She pushed again, but this time, the only crack was in her voice. "I did all this to save you. I could have shot you in the face like the General and been done with it. I should have!"

Her head sunk and Efrat examined her, as if he was unfamiliar with this emotion. Danato pulled her away from him and embraced her as she wept. He observed Efrat as he stared at the ground.

"I hate him," Cori mumbled into his shoulder. Efrat looked up at that comment, infuriation filling his face, but it faded as he met Danato's steely gaze. For a moment, Danato just cradled her, scolding Efrat with a glare for causing her so much pain. He didn't understand Cori's reaction entirely, but something about this man put her on polar opposites of herself.

"She speaks very highly of you," Efrat said, breaking the silent backdrop to Cori's sniffles. "She said that you wouldn't knowingly send me to my death. I, of course, told her that she was a fool. I told her that you weren't the man she made you out to be."

Danato tightened his grip on Cori. "Why should I help you? Give me one reason to think you are a decent enough human being to keep alive."

Efrat eyed Cori in his arms. "How about the bullet in my arm?" Cori looked up at him. "It was meant for her, but I took it. As I understand, the timeline that it did end up in her, I was the one who removed it and stitched her up." Danato looked down at Cori, and she nodded in confirmation. "Saving your friend's life might not be reason enough, but I wonder if protecting that beautiful treasure is."

Danato didn't like the choices that were in front of them, mainly because there was only one to choose. Clearly, Cori had had the moral choice in mind when she started this. She may have been regretting it now in light of Efrat's uncanny ability to be a pain in the ass, but placing Efrat in a position that would certainly get him killed was morally bereft. Logically, financially, and emotionally, he would have been happy to pull the trigger himself, but as Cori said, this was not a death row prison, and Danato was not an advocate of capital punishment.

"Fine, I'll post the guards." Cori pulled away and turned to wipe her tears as if she hadn't already left the evidence of her meltdown on his shirt. "I'm only doing this for her. I know she'll blame herself if you're killed."

"She does seem a bit heavy on the ethics," Efrat said.

"My men will escort you to—"

"I want Corinthia to take me back." Cori looked back at him distrustfully. "I'd like to express my gratitude properly, without an audience."

"I'm not leaving her alone with you."

"Then chaperon, if you must, but I won't cooperate unless she takes me back up herself." He looked at Cori, but she just shrugged and rolled her eyes. Her tears had dried, and she was back to being annoyed. She was likely to agree to anything just to get the rest of this morning over with.

"I'll be chaperoning with this." Danato waved Cori's pistol to remind him that he still considered execution an option for him, even if Cori did not.

42

CORI COULDN'T HAVE FELT more unease if she were standing on the edge of a cliff holding an anvil. Belus was probably fighting for his life because of her... hopefully fighting, and not already lost. She was stuck in an elevator with Danato and Efrat, which was like being stuck in an elevator with a grizzly bear and a mountain lion. Sure, when push came to shove, the grizzly bear would probably win, but she would have been collateral damage either way.

She stayed against the back wall with Danato and pressed as close to him as possible. She hadn't been afraid of Efrat most of the day, but for some reason, now, in the presence of others, he didn't seem to be the same person. She told herself she had just been trying to see the good in him because it made it easier to put her trust in him.

He wasn't good.

At all.

But why had he put himself in the way of the bullet? Was it instinct implanted by special ops training, or had he really been saving her? And why did he save Belus? Because she'd asked him to? Was that really the answer?

She didn't want to think about it anymore, but as Efrat leaned against the side wall watching her, she felt like something in a petri dish. The only reason she agreed to bring him up was to stave off any last-second attempts at escape.

She caught his eyes, and she tried to look stoic, but all she wanted to do was bury her head in Danato's shoulder and beg him to send the bad, bad man away. She cleared her throat and decided that silence was the incendiary device in this scenario.

"How long were you in special ops?" she asked, giving voice to a question she had never gotten around to asking. Time travel leaves so little room for chitchat, especially when your conversational partner is trying to kill you.

Danato looked at Efrat, but looked away as if pretending not to care what his answer was. Efrat eyed him and turned his attention back to her. "I'm still in it," he said. "At least, they haven't court-martialed me yet."

Danato looked back at him, perplexed either by his honesty or his answer.

"Is that how you got your scars, or was that an off-duty incident?"

Efrat held up his hands and looked at the banded scar on each arm. He looked at Danato, but he only glanced at the scars before pretending not to be a part of the conversation.

"Oh, kitten, I really wish I could explain, but of course there's just not enough time." He smiled. "Unless you think we can ditch the chaperon again."

"Try it and you'll have two bullet holes to hide from the General," Danato growled without looking at him.

Efrat gave him a muted glare that may have passed for mere vexation if it wasn't for the static raising the hair on the back of Cori's head. She could feel Danato tense as he prepared to raise the gun.

"Please, don't." She whispered the words through clenched teeth and layers of stressed emotions. She hadn't technically directed it at either of them, but it was meant for both.

She felt the static charge in the air abate, and Danato slowly released the tension in his arms and shoulders. The elevator thankfully sounded their arrival. It was the most relieving *ponk* ever, and that counted some of her uncomfortable silent rides with Belus.

Danato stepped forward and held his finger to the door-open button like a liftman at an expensive hotel. "This is where you get off. I assume you don't need a code to get back in."

Efrat stepped into the door's path and looked back at her. He held out his hand to her. "Care to walk me to my door, kitten?"

Cori looked at his hand, debating whether to go with him. She looked at Danato. He wasn't giving her any instruction. He was leaving it up to her. His overprotective side was apparently on a break. She had a feeling he wanted to be done with this whole situation as much as her. So far, Efrat was still being compliant, so he probably wasn't that worried about her safety. If he knew how frightened she was, he probably wouldn't be letting her make this decision. After all, she couldn't just go back in time to undo whatever he did now.

"I don't have much time, Cori," Efrat said. Without the "kitten" in place of her name, he didn't sound quite as cocky.

She stepped forward and reached for his hand. At the last second, she pulled her hand back. The extended hand was like a two-for-one deal at the grocery store that made you buy two when you didn't even need one. She stepped forward to follow him, and he lowered his hand and led the way.

Not far from the heavy metal door that needed a code to get through, Efrat stopped and turned around. He made a quick assessment of Danato's position. He was now in the elevator doorway, keeping his options open with Cori's gun clenched by his hip.

When Efrat finally met her eyes, she wavered under his scrutiny. He smiled at that. "Careful, I think your courage is running low."

"I can't undo any of this. Kind of takes the puff out of my blustering." He took a step closer to her, making his beautiful blues a little more unavoidable. "What do you want, Efrat? You have no idea how much I want to get home."

His eyes narrowed, and he lost all hope of a smile. "I actually know a lot about that desire." He glanced around at the prison.

She huffed out an exhaled breath. "Don't keep throwing your incarceration in my face like it's my fault. I didn't put you here. If you're here, you must have done something to cause it."

"You think that, kitten? If it helps you sleep at night."

She shrugged and shook her head and rolled her eyes as if it took all three to deflect what he was saying. "Yeah, okay, another obscure reference. I'll put some thought into that and get back to you when I've decided whether or not I should trust an imprisoned man who says he's innocent; because inmates never say that," she whisper-yelled.

Efrat nodded. "You're right, I'm being too vague, but I don't have time to explain." He glanced back at Danato again and took a step forward. "I owe you an apology."

"Yes," she scoffed, "but for which part? There are so many to choose from."

"Let's start with the first shock. The one that killed you."

Cori could feel herself shake just thinking about that day. How close had she come to dying... all the way? She never thought he would apologize for that, and as much as it probably killed his pompous ass to say it, she really didn't feel better about it.

"I assumed you were like all the rest, a mindless drone following Danato's will, but you aren't, are you? You aren't even a hired-out prisoner."

"Ethan and I are kind of indentured servants." Efrat arched a brow at that. "We are here by choice, though."

"Right. Ethan, your partner. Haven't had the pleasure yet."

It surprised Cori that he hadn't met Ethan yet, or perhaps he just hadn't picked him out from the forest of black uniforms. Efrat hadn't escaped on his watch yet, so Ethan hadn't had the opportunity to distinguish himself.

"My husband," she clarified. She expected an acknowledgment along the lines of a nod, but she didn't expect the return of his cocky smile.

"That's too bad. You're the only woman I've been able to touch with my hands in six years." To accentuate the point, he dragged his finger on the bare skin of her arm. The tickle wasn't electrified, but the shiver he caused activated her goose bumps. "At least not with my hands." He licked his lips, and she backed away, feeling an unwanted reaction that made her feel as sick as it did anxious.

"Stop it. I don't know what you want from me, but I can't give it. I don't even know the codes. I'm not even allowed up here without Ethan or Danato." She looked a number of places before she returned her gaze to him.

"I figured as much." Realizing it wouldn't work, he put aside his seductive tactics. "As for the remainder of my apology, I'm sorry I doubted your influence over Danato. Clearly, for you, he is a good man. I'm also sorry that I slapped you. That should have been beneath me. There was a time when I never would have raised my hand to a woman, let alone kidney punches and kicks."

Cori nodded to speed up the list of apologies and get it over with. "Fine, I forgive you if you're sincere—except the first one. I'm still not over being fried to death yet."

"Fair enough."

"So, why did you want me up here? You need to get back in there or it will all be for naught." Cori motioned to the heavy door behind him.

He nodded and glanced back at Danato. "I still need to thank you for saving me, and I need to give you something," he whispered even quieter. He wiggled his finger for her to come closer. She stared at the hand, but it hadn't transformed into a snake. "It's a secret. I can't just hand it to you, kitten. You're going to have to put your wedding vows on hold for just a second and come and get it."

Cori could feel her heart racing. She wasn't entirely sure what he was asking from her, but the sick, anxious feeling from before returned. "I don't want it."

"It's the answers to my obscurity. You'll want it. Just step to me so Danato knows you trust me enough to accept a thank you kiss." She wanted to run away, but her feet were planted. She had no idea what the protocol was for a situation like this. What did her marriage vows say about situations like this? Thou shalt not kiss another man unless he wants to secretly pass you something via saliva.

Efrat reached forward around her neck and pulled her forward. "Cori?" Danato drawled from behind.

"I'm okay," she lied.

Efrat gave Danato a wink before caressing her cheek and pushing his lips down onto hers. She put her hands on his chest in preparation for her withdrawal from his repugnant advance.

As horrible as she felt having another man's lips on her mouth, she was surprised at how gentle the first part of his kiss was. If she hadn't been married, and if he hadn't tried to kill her, and if he wasn't in prison, and a long line of other ifs, she might have actually enjoyed the kiss.

As it was, she was worried about what Danato was thinking. She was worried about what Ethan would do when he found out. She tasted blood in the kiss and she tried to pull away, concerned that he had bitten her. An irrational thought of him being a vampire on top of an elemental popped in and out of her mind.

He gripped her neck tighter and pushed a small, flat, oddly shaped object against her lips. Without a backup plan, she parted her lips to allow the object to enter her mouth. His tongue was more than happy to usher it through along with itself.

She managed to get the object into her cheek even as he continued to take advantage of her distraction. The sensuous kiss turned hungry. She tried to push him away, but he wouldn't budge.

She whimpered, and hated that it sounded as if she was enjoying this. She pushed on his neck, but it didn't stop him. It wasn't until Danato cocked the gun that he stopped and allowed her to push him away. She nearly fell trying to unravel herself from his arms.

She walk-jogged back to the elevator and tucked in behind Danato, who had the gun trained on Efrat at the door. "Go, Efrat," Danato said more evenly than she'd expected. The day's shocks were piling too high for anyone to get excited about any one in particular.

"I'll see you later, Cori," Efrat said before zapping the code panel to break back into his cage. The sounds of a raging firefight started shortly after he entered: the diversion he and his cohorts would create to disguise his three-hour absence, rationalize his gunshot wound, and obscure the specifics of the soldiers' blackouts.

"The hell he will." Danato slammed his fist into the button for the main floor. The doors closed, and he glared at her. "You shouldn't have let him touch you."

She nodded. "I just thought it was a gesture of thanks. I didn't know he was going to mouth-rape me." She hated the feeling of another man on her. She scrubbed away the taste on her lips. She suddenly felt horrifically guilty. She had been so worried about Ethan with a French woman, and here she was Frenching a prisoner.

She wanted to spit whatever it was he had shoved into her mouth out, but she wanted to look at it before she showed it to anyone else. At least that was the current rationale. She also wanted to wash her mouth out. She tasted blood, so she assumed that he'd had the object sutured on his cheek to hide it.

"Are you going to explain this all to me or not?" Danato said by the panel. He was still clenching the pistol. She wondered if he would ever give it back to her. Right now, she wasn't sure she wanted him to have it, either. He must have noticed her observation because he pulled the clip from it and placed the bullets in his front shirt pocket before handing it back to her.

She flinched at the black handle before she took it in her hands. She couldn't remember what series of conversations had led to her having a pistol. As she recalled, Belus was against it altogether. Danato didn't like the idea of either of them having guns, something about being a target, but since Cori was already a target most of the time, they decided to arm them.

Oh, how she wished she had listened to Belus. Why did she never listen to Belus?

"I need to find out how he is or I'm going to crawl out of my skin."

Danato pushed the button for the animal level and the elevator *ponked* within a few seconds, as it always seemed to when Danato was a passenger. It wouldn't dare expect the big man to wait on it.

"Wait here and hold the elevator."

She did as he asked and stood in the door while the doors insisted on trying to close. She thought about moving inside and pushing the door open button, but she enjoyed the steady push the doors were giving, like a bully shoving her in the back to pick a fight. She deserved it.

When Danato returned, he looked grim, but not upset. She nearly screamed when he didn't give her an answer instantly, but she let him usher her into the elevator and they continued their ride to the main floor. "He's in surgery."

She paused, waiting for more. "That's it?"

"Yes, that's it. It means he's alive and they are fixing him. They know their jobs, and they are bribed very well to do it. I don't think we have any reason to worry, but we will know more in a few hours. Just enough time for you to tell me your story."

Cori wondered if she could tell her story with this object in her mouth. She also wondered if she could take another round of explanation. She had relived this morning around three times. What had been three hours for them was gaining on eight for her. "Danato," she whispered. He narrowed his eyes, already sensing her evasion. "I don't suppose I could shower first?" She held up her hands, which still had remnants of Belus's blood on them.

Danato's face softened, and he nodded. "Of course." He looked her over. He must have seen the stress hiding behind her tired eyes. "If you promise to tell me everything, we can probably hold off discussing this until later."

She nodded somberly, but she was more than relieved. "Will you come tell me the minute you know about Belus?"

"Of course."

"The minute," she emphasized.

"Yes, sweetheart."

Her eyes grew wet and her face crumpled in preparation for further moisture. "I love you." She wanted to hear him say it back, but he just nodded.

"I know, sweetheart. Go get showered up; eat something and try to rest. I'll come home as soon as I hear anything." The elevator *ponked*, the doors opened, and she was thusly dismissed.

43

CORI TOOK A SHORT walk to clear her mind before returning to the house. After a few minutes of fresh air, she was certain that there was no hope of clearing her mind or making sense of the day. She went over the twisted, convoluted timeline in her mind and still came back to the same conclusion. She hoped Danato felt the same way when she explained it all to him.

When she finally made it home, she was greeted by dim lights and the late morning sunlight streaming through the kitchen windows. The natural light should have made the house seem airy and warm, but it only looked lonely and cold. She checked the front door again. She thought perhaps she would be locked in, but she wasn't.

No punishment yet.

She moved to the island and sat down on a stool. She missed Ethan so much. She hadn't fully realized how much of her life circled around him. His presence made this world make sense to her. When life gave you transmorphs, elementals, and possessed props, she had Ethan to make it all worth it.

A matter of weeks ago, she might have turned to Cleos for comfort. Nothing was stopping her now; the ban against him had theoretically been lifted, but she didn't want Cleos. Despite how attached she was or thought she was to him, he was not her family. It had taken time to learn that, and she was grateful she had.

Cori looked around, just to be sure that no one was home. She kept her eye on the door as she fished the object from her mouth. The flat, silver key had a square on one half to grip, and pronounced jagged teeth, rather than the long narrow bumps usually required for door locks. She could only surmise what it belonged to—a safety deposit box, a cabinet, a jewelry box.

"Great," she said aloud to herself. "What the hell do I do with this?" For all his pandering about giving her the truth, he had told her nothing. This key was just another piece of a puzzle she didn't have any desire to put together.

Efrat no doubt had secrets; secrets that, for whatever reason, he wanted her to know, but why? What did he think she would do once she knew them? What was his greater purpose?

That was the short list of questions to take on for the evening, and it was already too much. She slipped the key into one of her many cargo pockets and made a mental note to take it out before she washed them—lest the key in her dirty laundry become the key to her dirty laundry.

She undid her hair and slipped upstairs to her apartment. The house had been pretty stingy with the bathroom since Ethan had his blow-up while she was under the influence of a transmorph, but they had a nice roomy standup shower. Baths had to be taken in the downstairs bathroom until the house forgave him. Apparently, part of being married means you get to endure the same castigations as your spouse.

She undressed and slipped into the shower with only her gold rings on. She hadn't removed the delicate bands since her wedding, but with so many electrocutions, her fingers were too swollen to remove them, anyway.

She washed away Belus's blood. She gargled away the taste of another man's mouth. She scrubbed every inch of her body as if the time bubble might have left residual markers.

When humanity returned to her via cherry blossom shampoo and sandalwood soap, she wrapped herself in her fluffy white hotel robe and went downstairs, intending to eat. She grabbed a quick snack, but as soon as she settled into the couch to wait for Danato, her cheese and crackers were left to dehydrate on the coffee table while she napped.

44

DANATO DIDN'T COME STRAIGHT to the house when he got word about Belus. He waited outside the door for nearly ten minutes. He let himself take in what was left of the afternoon sun. He knew he needed to be tough with Cori, but he didn't want to scare her.

He was still confused about why the time bubble would attach itself to her. Granted, an electrical charge could easily have initiated her leap into the future, but why did she keep going? Why had it been necessary to shut her off with another bolt? The time bubble was created and maintained by an entity. There was no reason for it to feed the energy that was creating her time shift, so it should have worn off on its own.

The bottom line was Cori just shot Belus, and Danato needed answers.

He shoved open the door and stepped inside. He slammed it behind him. He didn't need to slam it and he shouldn't have, but he needed to start with anger so he could make his demands for information clear.

Cori's head popped up from the couch. She jumped up, nearly stumbling over the coffee table before rounding the couch. She stood in the center of the room in her white robe and pink bunny slippers. Her hair had dried in an array of directions while she was sleeping, and he was pretty sure she had a piece of cheese stuck to her neck.

He resisted the urge to laugh at her and stood his ground at the door, not voicing or emoting any information to her. The standoff rapidly disintegrated as Cori made her own assumptions about his lack of response.

"Oh, God." The back of her hand flew up to her mouth, and she started hyperventilating. She sucked in stuttered breaths and starting shaking her head. He could see her legs shaking and he knew she would drop at any moment.

"He's alright," he said when it finally occurred to him that she thought Belus was dead. He thought the news would relieve her anxiety, but the only change was her hand flipped to cover her mouth with the palm instead of the back.

She closed her eyes and cried, smothering her whimpers as much as one could do without a pillow. He wanted to go to her, but he waited.

"Cori, we need to talk about this."

She took in a severe inhalation and walked to him. "I tried to find another way. I swear. I didn't know at first that I was the one who shot him. I came to save him, and I shot him. I tried to give up my gun. I tried to take the bullets out. It just kept getting worse."

Her hands pressed against his chest and pinched at his buttons, tugging on the fabric. If he had been wearing a tie, she might have gripped it enough to bruise his neck. When he didn't answer or offer any pity, she crumpled against him, pushing her face into his chest.

"Please don't hate me. I didn't know what else to do."

His heart wrenched, and he begged his ego to give in. "You could have come to me right away."

"I did!" she screeched and pulled away like he had suddenly turned into a demon. "You held me down in the infirmary so the nurses could tie me to the bed." She pointed vaguely in the direction of the prison with a shaking hand. The pain in her voice was only a shadow to the anger. "I told you the truth three times. I *did* tell you! You didn't believe me or trust me. Efrat was the only person who knew what was happening to me because my future self told him. I had no choice but to trust him. I had to trust myself, even if no one else did."

Danato could see the disappointment from his betrayal etched on her face. Though he had no memory of most of the encounters, she had lived them. She knew what his reflex reaction to her situation would be, and she didn't like it. He had been coming here to discuss how badly she had handled this situation, but apparently he had also handled it badly.

"Ethan would have believed me," she said quietly. It wasn't intended as an accusation, but more a point to be considered when he balanced his judgment.

"The doctors said that Belus was probably in cardiac arrest. If Efrat hadn't stabilized him, he would have crashed. Crashing with a gunshot wound isn't good."

Cori nodded. If she was happy to hear that, she didn't show it. She turned away to face the couch. She wiped away another few tears and sniffed before she mumbled something he couldn't understand.

"What was that, sweetheart? I didn't hear you."

"What are you going to do with me?"

He stepped closer since she barely raised her voice the second time. "What do mean?"

"What's my punishment?"

He turned her gently to look her over, but she wouldn't look him in the eye. She thought he had come to drag her off to a cell with the rest of the inmates. Or put her on shit duties for the next month. He hated that. He hated that she saw him as a boss before anything else.

That was the way it was supposed to be, but he didn't want it that way. As much as it pained him to admit it, Belus may have had a point. Danato didn't want Belus dictating to Cori, but at what point did he really want to be the bad guy, when all he really wanted was to be the good guy?

He brushed her hair back over her ear. She glanced at him, trying to determine what was coming next. "I love you," he said, returning her sentiment from the elevator far too late to make sense. She looked up at him, baffled. Her eyes finally rested on his. He petted her head, pulling the unkempt hair back as he did. "I'm not going to punish you, sweetheart. I can see how much you've been through. I've failed as your boss. I'm not going to fail you as your... guardian." He caught himself before he said what he'd wanted to. It was a wholly presumptive connection, symbolically or otherwise.

Her eyes widened, and she turned to face him. He now broke the eye contact. Her hand came under his chin. Though he technically didn't need to raise his head to look down at her, he got the hint and looked at her. "...as my father?" she finished the sentence as he'd intended it.

He shook his head. "I'm sorry, I didn't mean to displace your birth father. I just think of our relationship in terms of family."

"He was never an attentive father to me, even when he was around. You've earned that title more than he ever did."

Danato took in a deep breath. He reached out to her, not sure what more he could do to her hair to satisfy his need to connect with her. She slipped into his arms and buried her face in his chest. "I love you too," she mumbled into his chest and he wrapped his arms around her, probably a little too tight, but she didn't complain.

So much for holding his ground and not letting his emotions get the better of him.

45

E THAN SAT IN A rental car two blocks down from the house he had been staking out for the last day and a half. He was normally impulsive when it came to acts of heroism, but with a baby involved, he didn't feel he could risk it. Not to mention he had seen four werewolves coming and going from this house in the last day and he didn't exactly want to take them on without a plan.

His throwaway cell phone sang out the tune to "Wipe Out" before he scrambled to dig it from his pants pocket. "What?" he grumbled into the phone. Between little to no sleep, convenience foods, and suffering the indignity of gas station coffee, he was starting to fray.

"How much longer do I have to wait?" Leona's voice hissed over the cell phone. It was only her third phone call in the last hour. She had expected to wait a full day, but when he insisted on waiting until all four men were in for the night, she'd started getting antsy.

Antsy was not an accurate word for a fem-wolf, though. It wasn't an accurate word for a pregnant woman, either. *Irascible* was a better word for her mood, or maybe *unhinged*. At any rate, she wasn't happy that his mission requirements were interfering with her preconceived time schedule.

"When you see number four come back with the pizza and beer, then you can start your distraction." He ground out the words, hoping that the third time would be the charm for this conversation.

"I still don't see why I should be the distraction," she muttered. Ethan couldn't help wonder how Cori thought this woman would be attractive to him. To Cori she must have seemed mysterious and sexy, but to Ethan she was pompous and spoiled.

At every turn, she had questioned his motives, without any suggestions as to a better plan. Even after he explained his reasoning for everything, she tried to find a flaw in it. He got the distinct impression that aside from her so-called sex appeal and her inhuman strength, she might have been dumber than a stick.

"Callin will not be surprised to see you on his doorstep. Me, however, he will be immediately suspicious of. Not to mention he can smell my emotions. I can't hide anxiety from a werewolf. He won't smell you beyond your perfume and musk."

He heard her huff on the other end and she hung up. She was back on board. At least until she forgot everything he'd said and called him back for the fourth time that hour.

He tossed the phone beside him on the passenger seat. He rummaged through the wrappers on the floor and found his leftover hamburger. He looked it over and decided it was not too noxious to continue noshing on.

He couldn't help but be amused by Danato's concerns for him as well. He thought perhaps the thrill of the chase would seduce him as easily as Cori thought Leona would. They were both wrong. The last two days had only reassured him that he was in the right place, with the right people, and he couldn't wait to get back to them.

Headlights blinded him for a moment as a vehicle pulled into the drive of the house he was watching. It was number four, returning with pizza and beer. Even as he reached for the phone, it rang.

Just for fun, he let it ring several more times while he finished his burger. When he finally answered it, he put on his best fake cheerful voice. "You must really like the sound of my voice."

"Number four is back," she said, ignoring his quip. She paused, waiting for him to say something. "That's what we are waiting for, right?"

"Yes, but I thought I would wait for him to get into the house before we approached. How does that sound?"

"Fine, whatever."

"Don't get too far ahead of me, Leona. I'm still the one with my butt on the line here."

"I just want my son back," she said brusquely.

Ethan took a mental slap to his forehead. She had to be the most annoying woman in the world to him right now, but she had a good reason to be petulant. Better than most, in fact. "I know. I'll get him back. I promise. My backup is already in place. If all goes well, you'll never see these men again, let alone have to lose your son."

"Good. He's inside. Can we go now?"

"Yeah, let's go." He hung up and slipped out of the car. He was in his usual black-on-black outfit, minus the jacket. It was a warm night outside of the arctic ring. He had considered bringing his pistol with him, but bullets were virtually useless on werewolves in their human form. They had little impact on them in their wolf form either, but at least they made it into the tissue. In their human form, their muscle fibers were so compacted that it was not unheard of for them to be downright impervious to bullets.

The only weapon he had on him was his speed, agility, and a small trinket that, for lack of a better name, he called a dog whistle. It was rather insulting, he supposed, to call it that, but nevertheless that was essentially what it was. The tiny cylinder hung from a chain on his neck, beneath his shirt.

He was happy to get out of the car and stretch his legs. It was only a short walk down the street to the house, but the romance of a long stakeout had worn off long ago, and he was thankful for any movement beyond adjusting the seat of his pants.

Before he slipped behind the house, he saw Leona jump from the roof across the street and land with catlike grace on the concrete. It was always disconcerting to see the human form land from a two-story jump with little more trouble than jumping off a tall fence. Yet another benefit of being a werewolf: joints like gelatin.

He slipped through the backyard, which was little more than a two-seat patio set on burgundy cement tiles. He skipped the back door and went straight for a triangular antenna pole. He climbed up to the second-floor window that was reflecting floating stars from a motorized lampshade.

He could see the baby, but he could also see Callin, the father. He was sitting in a rocking chair beside the baby crib, deep in contemplation. For a moment, Ethan wondered if it was right to be stealing a child away from his own father. The only counter he had was that it hadn't been right for Callin to steal him from his mother in the first place.

The doorbell rang downstairs, but Callin ignored it. As soon as his lackey came in to let him know who it was, he was off his rocker and out the door. Ethan pulled off the flimsy screen and tossed it away from the house. He pushed the window open and slipped inside.

The nursery was plush with stuffed animals—mostly dogs. It was furnished with several *can't live without* baby accouterments: crib, changing table, and an antique dresser that was much too big for baby clothes. Callin was at least providing his son with a good home.

He peeked over the railing of the crib and found a little baby boy asleep in the center of the mattress. "Hey there...

you." Ethan made a mental note to ask what the child's name was when he met back up with Leona.

This was it. All he had to do was grab the baby and slip out the window. Get in the car, and drive as fast and safe as he could to the meeting spot.

He knew it wouldn't be that easy. His plan had included the not-so-easy scenario and he would have been disappointed if he didn't get to use plan B. On the other hand, plan A did sound less painful.

The two sets of meaty hands that grabbed him from behind were far from gentle. They hit him in the face hard, but he didn't fully pass out. A lesser-advertised side-effect to dragon juice was being less susceptible to concussions.

The meatheads dragged him from the child's room and he let them. *Let* was probably not the right word either. Werewolves were far stronger than humans, so it was arrogant to assume that he had any choice. However, he wasn't an ordinary human anymore. His strength was worthy of at least a tiresome struggle with a werewolf, but there was no need for arrogance with his plan.

Technically, it was probably Danato's plan. He wouldn't let Ethan go into a wolf pack without the proper backup. Although Leona had bought and paid for his services to get the baby back, that wasn't why Danato had sent him.

The werewolf underworld, or the Council of the Moon, as they officially called themselves—despite the mockery they got for the title—did not approve of werewolf packs. For one, packs promoted hunting on full moons, which was against the treaty Danato had spoken of, as well as the prison rules when it involved human kills.

The other reason they didn't like packs was because it directly opposed their power. The Council was essentially the judge and jury for all werewolf-related matters. They were always quick to enforce their rules, and as part of the agreement with them, Danato was responsible for containing any known packs or potential packs. Normally, hunters would not be assigned to detain a werewolf pack, but since there was an infant involved, they could hardly endanger the child with their usual method.

Ethan was dropped on the sofa downstairs next to a woman he assumed was Leona. His left eye was blurring from the swelling, but he was sure it was her, from her scent. Callin stood in front of them both. Something about how he held himself reminded Ethan of Vince. He supposed all werewolves held themselves with the same swaggering, amused composure.

Callin was about as tall as Ethan. His khaki pleated pants and thin cashmere olive summer sweater were the only things intimidating about him. However, since this wasn't a business meeting to determine if their assets were mutually engaging, Ethan wasn't exactly quaking in his boots.

Callin had chocolate brown hair with dense waves and curls that gave him the look of a well-manicured model or a sloppy sleeper, depending on what light you saw him in. His heart-shaped face made him look younger than he was. He was growing his facial hair out, probably to appear older, but it looked patchy—an odd problem for a werewolf. Ethan thought he and Leona would have made a cute couple, if werewolves weren't repellent to each other.

"So, you must be Leona's new lover," Callin said with a high English accent not too dissimilar to Ethan's own. Callin looked him over without judgment or jealousy. Ethan raised his chin, not wanting to object to or confirm that statement until he knew what the man's opinion on the subject was. "I hope she didn't convince you that the child she is pregnant with is yours."

"It's mine." One of Callin's lackeys jumped forward to make his claim before Ethan could answer. He was a short redhead with enough facial hair to put Belus to shame, let alone his alpha male leader.

Callin gently pushed him back. "The baby upstairs is mine. The one in her belly is Randal's, and we shall see who she chooses next."

"You son of a bitch!" Leona charged him. It took all three lackeys to push her back down, but the effort seemed to exhaust her. "How dare you treat me this way? When I am not pregnant..."

"When you are not pregnant, you will be nursing, and when you are not nursing, you will be mating. You'll hardly be interested in revenge when you are begging for cock."

Ethan wanted to defend her out of some inner call to chivalry, but there wasn't much to defend. The females of the species were stronger, but the many facets of female reproduction countered that fact. The only time Leona would be at full strength was when she was in heat. Callin was probably already planning to take her second child and put her within reach of the remaining two men when she came back into estrus. It was no wonder that the prison never housed female werewolves. They were rarely a risk.

"I want my son back. You have no right to raise him."

"I always found that to be a strange edict for our people. Why would a father not be allowed to raise his own son?"

"Because you might eat him," Ethan said flatly.

Callin must not have liked the statement because he stared Ethan down like he was debating how best to kill him. "I would never hurt my son."

"I believe you," Ethan said, even though he really had no opinion on the subject. "I can see the control in you that Randal here missed out on. I can see how much of an effort you've made to care for your son. But... you asked why the Council doesn't let werewolf men raise their young, and the answer is infanticide. It's rare in modern days with the availability of food, but the Council is still concerned that the primal instinct to remove competition will cause an epidemic of child deaths. Not to mention that the female is supposed to nurse for the first year, so after that, shared custody would be the only thing she would allow, and frankly I just don't see a male and female werewolf coming up with an applicable custody agreement."

Callin's face had become increasingly cold as Ethan spoke. "You're not her lover."

Ethan couldn't hide his smile. "No. I've been assigned to return the child to his rightful parent."

"You're a hunter?"

"Close enough," Ethan said, not wanting to get into titles.

"And you think that I should be denied the right to raise my son because of a hundred-year-old edict that doesn't take into consideration modern conveniences?"

Ethan hissed and frowned. "I'm not going to begin to tell you that, but it is within my jurisdiction to take the child... and I will."

Randal and the others chuckled. Callin smiled. "I respect your tenacity, but how did you plan on accomplishing that?"

Ethan cleared his throat. "I'm hoping to avoid any violence here."

"Are you?" Callin crossed his arms. Ethan could see the smirk just on the edge of his mouth.

"I'm not opposed to it personally, but I have to protect Leona."

"Oh, don't worry about her. She can still kick my ass pregnant." Ethan caught a look between them that almost looked like respect. "She nearly ripped my head off when I took Lynnius."

"I'm surprised she failed." Ethan watched Leona sizing up Callin.

"I was as surprised as you." Callin's attention was locked on to her, and vice versa. They were either on the verge of attacking each other, or... *attacking* each other. "I think it might have been a small gesture on her part. A kindness not often extended to werewolves of the opposite sex."

Ethan looked between them. The tension was as much violent as it was sexual, but he was pretty sure that might have been normal for werewolves.

"Kindness is a weakness," Leona said, jutting out her jaw.

"It's not a weakness when you are kind to our son. Why would it be a weakness when you are kind to me?"

Leona's face fell from the copulatory gaze. "Let me see my son," she said, changing the subject. Callin said nothing, but he shook his head slowly. "I will not offer you any more leniencies."

"And I will not offer you a home here after tonight," Callin retorted. She promptly spat on his feet, which were covered in the finest leather. His other two lackeys, which Ethan now noticed were twins, used all of their strength to press her shoulders back into the couch.

"Home?" Ethan asked, to interrupt any further escalation. "What home?"

The twins eyed him from behind long, floppy auburn hair. It fell in their faces the way Ethan's used to before he discovered that vision was useful. They were not nearly as young as the other two, and, in fact, if Ethan had to guess, they were probably already into old age for werewolves.

Most male werewolves didn't make it past thirty. The few that did were considered elderly, and as such weren't usually well respected. In fact, they were generally pitied. Werewolves tended to die early because they lived with reckless disregard for their health and safety. It wasn't always viewed as a feat to make it over the age of thirty. It just meant you were a coward.

"I have requested that Leona live here and help raise our son." Callin bestowed his explanation on Ethan as he put his foot up on the couch to lean over Leona. He looked like he wanted to touch her, but the sneer on her face would have kept any man distant. Ethan was surprised he had even made the effort to get closer to begin with. The twins looked like they were straining even harder to hold her down.

"With your pack?" Ethan asked glancing at Randal, who had apparently been staring him down the whole time, but he hadn't noticed until now.

"As part of my pack."

"As your harem!" She lunged forward and bit his forearm before the twins could get her back. Callin gritted his teeth and gave an inhuman snarl as he clutched the bleeding wound.

"Hardly," he said with evenness forced into his voice. He lifted his hand to check the wound. It looked deep to Ethan, but he was hardly bleeding. "We would be your harem, you twit."

"That's new." Ethan put his elbow over the back of the couch to get more comfortable for the revealing soap opera. Callin looked him over. Ethan shrugged. "My research never discussed pack lifestyle. How exactly would that work?"

Callin moved away from Leona and pulled a chair up to sit in front of Ethan. Randal swung around the couch behind him. Ethan made a note of his position from the corner of his eye and leaned in toward Callin to make him flinch in defense of his alpha. Callin held up his hand to prevent him from attacking. Ethan was pleased to see that Randal was a good boy.

A good, good boy.

"Werewolf history has been skewed by movies and books," Callin began. Ethan was pleased that he was so forthcoming, but part of him wondered if this was a trap. Was Callin mesmerizing him the way Leona did to Cori? One thing was for sure—there would be no hypnotic kisses.

"The vague verbal history we have of our ancestors is of a matriarchal society of werewolves. They were nomadic peoples that interacted with humans through their travels, but always returned to the safety of forests, mountains, and deserts during the full moon.

"Our ancestors believed that the change was a spiritual journey. They believed that during the change, we could communicate with God. It was a blessing.

"Over the years, as man took away more of the barren lands, we became hunters of man out of a misfortunate convenience of overcrowding. We, in return, were hunted and killed into near extinction. I don't blame humans for this. If I were human and saw an eight-foot bipedal wolf, I think I would kill it to protect my family." Ethan smiled at his slight levity.

"The Council of the Moon," Callin continued, "was established in the mid-1800s as a way of finding unpopulated grounds where my people could roam and hunt during their change. The systematic distribution of werewolves took the spirituality from the change. They assigned locations to us that held absolutely no meaning to us and often had little sizeable prey."

Callin took in a deep breath and glanced at Leona before continuing. "There was a time during this period when offspring were eaten by werewolves. The Council didn't take into account the distance that a werewolf might travel during the change if proper prey wasn't available. I'm sure you're aware of how little control we have in our animal state."

"If by little you mean absolutely none," Ethan said.

"Yes," Callin said, looking back at Leona. He watched her for a moment and she lost the glare on her face. She leaned back on the couch and allowed the twins a break from their efforts. "Before the Council changed the rules and stripped the male rights away in punishment for their own stupidity, females were queens of packs. A strong female werewolf such as Leona would bear the children of her subjects. Much like in patriarchal animal groups, the female children would stay with the pack until they were old enough to form their own, or, when the time came, a daughter might challenge her mother and displace her from the position. The displaced queen would be allowed to stay in the pack if she remained submissive to the new queen.

"Leona doesn't like the idea of being the queen of my pack because she thinks that I'm asking her to be a breeder for us."

"You are," she said, pointing to her full belly.

"What she doesn't understand is that we would be her loyal subjects. We would serve her, provide for her, and obey her every command."

"I thought male and female werewolves couldn't stand each other?" Ethan questioned.

"One-on-one it becomes a competition for leadership. A pack must have a male leader to keep the peace, so to speak. That male chooses his queen."

"But you are still asking her to give birth to all of your children."

"Despite what Leona tells you, she still chooses who she wants to breed with. That decision is based on proof of strength and fitness, just like it would be for a human female. She would not breed with a sickly werewolf. As for the harem comment," Callin arched a brow at Leona. "She also decides what recreational activities she wants to have and with whom. I imagine a queen werewolf might have a variety of lovers, human and werewolf, but in essence we would be her harem, if she wished it."

"It's a ludicrous suggestion," Leona scolded. "Packs are banned. No female werewolf is going to pander to males for any amount of devotion they might claim to have to her."

Callin rolled his eyes at her, then turned back to Ethan. "What about you? I don't think I got your name."

"Ethan. Ethan Pierce." Ethan shot out his hand partially on instinct, but partially because this man deserved a proper introduction before he arrested him.

Callin looked over his hand, but shook it. "Callin Caldwell." Ethan could feel the grip on his hand tighten slightly, and he resisted the urge to grip harder. Their hands dropped and after a second of evaluation, Callin spoke again. "What do you think about werewolves going back to their traditional ways?"

Ethan looked over at Leona. She gave him a biting sneer before huffing and looking away. "It all sounds well and good to me, but she's right, the Council is still the policing factor in this situation, and they say no packs and no baby daddies."

"What would you do if your wife wouldn't let you see your son or daughter?"

Ethan furrowed his brow at hearing Callin reference his wife when he had only just gotten his name. Callin wiggled the ring finger on his left hand. Ethan looked down at the ring on his own left finger. The gold band that he often forgot about was still society's best indicator of marital status.

He smiled, thinking of Cori. He didn't have a child yet, and until right now, he hadn't really imagined it. The idea of a ballooned-up Cori complaining about swollen ankles and a sore back amused him. The idea of them both contributing to a human life was profoundly appealing. To have that grand creation and never be a part of it seemed cruel.

"Callin, what's your angle?" Ethan finally said, shaking away the opinions that were forming in his head and threatening to cloud his judgment.

"How do you mean?"

"What do you want? Did you steal Lynnius to be with him, or did you do it to lure Leona into your pack?"

"I want to be with my son," he said without the calm demeanor that he had been showing. He looked at Leona with the harshness that she had been showing him thus far. "I don't want to hurt you. I love you, Leona. I want you to raise our son, but not at the expense of me deserting him."

Leona stood up and walked away from them before the twins could even react to pull her back down. She wanted no part of this topic. She had probably heard it all before.

The twins followed her, but Callin waved them off. He looked disappointed, as any man would when his confession of love was rejected. "I don't know her well," Ethan waded into the water, hoping not to hit a deep spot. "If she likes her independence, as most women do, she might consider attaching herself to one man, a shackle. Four men..." Ethan glanced around to pinpoint Randal again, "...might feel like wearing concrete shoes to her."

Callin didn't seem to find what he said a revelation, but he didn't ridicule him for pointing out the obvious. "I'm not sure I'm reading you right, Ethan. You seem to understand how dangerous we are and yet you're in a room with four of us—not that more than one of us would be needed to rip your arms off—but you're not afraid. What kind of hunter is brave enough to kidnap a baby from four werewolves, smart enough to know how stupid it is, but not smart enough to blow that whistle for your backup?"

Ethan smiled and looked down at the tiny bulge under his tight black shirt. "It seemed rude to interrupt the conversation. Besides, I liked your history lesson. Illuminating, to say the least."

"Are you sure that was all you were waiting for?"

"What do you mean?" Ethan asked, playing dumb.

"Come on, Ethan," Callin smirked. "I know when a man is flirting with me."

46

"ARE YOU SURE YOU want to do this?" Callin said as he removed his olive summer sweater. His chest bore the same feeble attempt at hair growth as his face. He wore a leather strap necklace with a white tooth pendulum that he kissed before removing. Ethan assumed that it might have been the tooth of a passed relative.

"I'm afraid so. I've had a chip on my shoulder about this for a while," Ethan said. He saw no reason to remove his shirt. He expected Callin only did it because it was expensive.

Randal and the twins had cleared away the living room furniture, so they had an open space to brawl in. Ethan couldn't rationalize any of this, but that didn't matter at the moment. Callin had been dead on about Ethan flirting with his ego. He hadn't intended to make his intentions so obvious, but when he found out Callin was going to be civil about the whole taking his baby back thing, he was dejected. He came here for a number of obligatory reasons, but frankly, the idea of fighting a werewolf was the most appealing prospect of the assignment.

"You know you won't win?"

When Ethan arched his brow at him, Callin shrugged apologetically.

"I don't think winning is my goal. I just have to be rid of this desire."

"What desire?" Leona returned from the kitchen where she had been sulking. She had pizza sauce on her lips. Apparently, she wasn't above emotional eating. "What are you doing?"

"Sorry Leona, we got a little sidetracked," Ethan said.

She was on his throat faster than he could have predicted. "You promised me," she yelled in his ear as she squeezed his neck.

It took both the twins and Randal to get her off of him. "I know." He coughed and rubbed his neck. "We will get your baby back."

"Not if he kills you!"

"I've never killed a man, Leona," Callin griped. "I'm not going to start now."

Ethan was pleased to hear that. "I don't suppose you could give her that concession so she doesn't do it herself," Ethan asked.

"Are we negotiating now?" Callin asked.

Ethan shrugged. "She hasn't held her baby in months. You at least have to have sympathy for that."

"What's to stop her from bolting with him?" Callin asked.

Ethan couldn't answer that. Aside from Tweedle Dee, Tweedle Dum, and Tweedle Dumber, there really was nothing to stop her.

"Please Callin! I will not run! Let me hold him!" She prostrated herself before him. The submission left something to be desired since she took all three werewolves down to the floor with her.

Ethan wondered how many werewolves it would take to hold her if she weren't pregnant. It was no wonder their society was a matriarchal one; what man would take opposition to a woman that strong? No man except Callin.

The man Ethan had inadvertently baited into a fight.

"Let her hold her child, Callin," Ethan said. "We both know this could have been over a half hour ago. Let's just make this transition a little easier for Lynnius."

Ethan wasn't sure if his threat made the werewolf change his mind or the mention of Lynnius, but Callin went upstairs and brought down the baby in a bundle of blankets. Leona nearly dragged her capturers to their feet as she rushed over to her baby.

Her face showed a mixture of pain and joy. Callin placed the bundle in her arms and she wept. As she sniffled over her sleeping baby, she thanked him, despite the fact that he caused the grief to begin with. Callin brushed away a tear from her face before cradling her head to lean in for a kiss.

Ethan averted his eyes as the gentle kiss turned sultry and steamy. When they finally broke, it was Leona that pulled her lips from his. Ethan could see the panic in her eyes. She had liked that kiss more than she wanted to.

Ethan had thought Callin was lying, or at least exaggerating his affection for her. He couldn't see the foundation for the allure, but clearly Callin loved her. He didn't doubt that Callin fully intended to let her be with her son if she would only stay with him. Shared custody was a lot easier when Mom and Dad were still hot for each other.

"Stay with me," Callin whispered almost inaudibly. "If you take him from me, I will hunt him down again. I will never rest until you agree to share him."

"I will stay for your childish battle," she said loudly, looking at Ethan. He snapped out of his quiet observation to acknowledge her. "If you want to be paid, I expect you to finish this before he finishes you."

"Yes, oh patient one," Ethan mumbled as she sauntered to a chair to watch the events. Her bodyguards took position beside her and Callin took position across the room. "This is going to be one of those things I look back on and say, 'What the fuck was I thinking?' isn't it?"

"No," Callin said. "I imagine others would, but I think you will look back on this with pride."

"Even though I'm going to lose?" Ethan said, rolling his shoulders.

"Especially because you are going to lose. Any man can fight and win. Any man can fight and lose. Not many men can fight, knowing that they are going to lose."

Ethan smiled at his compliment. Despite being at odds with this man, he liked him. He was looking forward to trying to kick his ass. It was a chance to get in some legitimate male bonding time with someone his own age. It was going to be a shame to see Callin's face when he realized Ethan wasn't just taking the baby back.

Callin lunged at him. Ethan had expected to be allowed the first punch, but he could already tell that Callin wasn't as accommodating in his fighting as his hosting.

Ethan ducked and flipped him over his back. Despite his understanding of werewolf anatomy, the weight of the man was still surprising.

He jumped back and turned to prepare for the next attack, which he had anticipated correctly. Callin's fist swiped past him with a force that might have broken his jaw. Despite the near miss, Ethan was not concerned about his strength or speed. He was more concerned with his determination and stamina.

In human form, werewolves were as strong as a bear, but with the temperament of a dog. That explanation called to mind a number of images of dogs fearlessly snarling at grizzly bears and mountain lions. Even if Ethan was a match to his strength, the ferocity of fighting a man with animal instincts would still be a challenge.

Ethan blocked another punch with his forearm. He could only defend so long before the purpose of this fight became moot. At some point, he was going to wear out. If he wanted the glory of having fought and lost to a great competitor, he was going to have to actually fight.

Ethan took a chance and dove his shoulder under one of Callin's punches. While Callin doubled over, Ethan swung back with his opposing elbow and hit him firmly in the face. The crack was satisfying, but the low growl that followed was not.

Callin picked him up and tossed him across the room. There was no catching himself or landing well. He simply skidded across the shag carpet and gathered a rug burn on his arm on the way.

He jumped up before Callin could get the drop on him. Ethan could see blood dripping from his nose. He hadn't broken it, but he had definitely gotten a nice shot in, which Callin was likely to make him pay for.

Ethan shut off the part of his brain that was designated to self-preservation. It wasn't hard. A good swift finger-flick to the white angel on his right shoulder usually did the trick. The remaining red devil on his left shoulder cheered and jeered him to kick some ass. It was the same red devil that had sent him jumping off buildings and tearing through shards of broken glass without thinking about the consequences. There was a strong chance that little bastard was going to get him killed some day, but some day wasn't going to be today.

Ethan sprang back at Callin before he was even ready. He must have expected him to be taken aback by his grand show of temper because he didn't have time to stop Ethan's throat punch. That gave him enough time to kick his kneecap, bringing him to one knee. Taking life and liberty for granted, Ethan smashed his fist into Callin's face. The pain in his knuckles was enough to warrant not repeating the offense, but it was the low, long growl coming from Callin that urged him to surrender.

However, since the red devil was the only one running the show at that point, Ethan went for another and another while the getting was good. His fist started to bleed—or maybe Callin's face had—he wasn't entirely sure which.

Callin's anger finally reached its limit. Not unlike the moment a dog goes from growling to biting, he whipped his arm around Ethan's legs and knocked him down. Snarling and bloody-faced, Callin jumped on to him and took several shots to Ethan's face before he managed to roll him off, which was not an easy task.

They rolled a few times, trying to find the upper hand in a pointless wrestling match. When Ethan finally got on top, Callin flipped him over his head, letting him land on his back. What was left of his air was gone, but Ethan flipped up and faced off with Callin crouched as low as he could get.

With his eye swelling more than it had already, Ethan decided that keeping the werewolf at his front might save him in the end. Callin charged and picked Ethan up before he impacted. He body-slammed him into the living room floor, shaking every mobile object in the room.

Ethan sputtered from the pain. He wanted to curse, but his voice was gone. Callin grabbed his neck. His deadly vice-gripped fingers wrapped around Ethan's throat and strangled him.

Ethan wasn't sure if he intended to truly kill him or simply knock him out. Either way, it would give them enough time to grab Lynnius and run before he could call in the cavalry. Not that it mattered. Their scent was marked. Even if they chose to give up the baby, this was not over. The crime was committed. They would all pay for it with time in prison.

Ethan grabbed the man's wrists and pushed him back. Though Callin clearly had the upper hand and the body weight, Ethan managed to pry his hands off. Callin's hard fingernails left gouges in his neck that would need attention later, but at least he could breathe.

Callin clearly didn't like that Ethan's strength was comparable. He had no doubt presumed that Ethan was a cocky hunter, looking to get his merit badge in hand-to-hand combat. Little did he know Ethan was the poster child for dragon protein and he was only appeasing his ego by getting in the fight he never got to have.

Callin gritted his teeth and leaned forward to push more of his body weight into his strangulation reach.

Ethan knew that was too much to counter. As Callin's hands moved closer to Ethan's neck, so did his face.

The civil, edifying host was gone, replaced by the animal within. His eyes reflected the vacant determination of a simple task: kill. This fight was not personal to Callin, no matter what his composure was during the fight. He had feral instinct, without pride or personal gain, lording over his emotions. He was one mind and one task. It was Zen, just the opposite spectrum of its traditional form.

Ethan waited for his head to be in range and decided to challenge his lesser-known skill. He wasn't sure *not* passing out could be viewed as a beneficial talent when his migraine kicked in later, but for now, it might save his life. He rammed his head into Callin's face. When he didn't recede, Ethan did it again, and again. Finally, Callin backed off, but only to recover enough to throw Ethan from the floor to the adjacent wall.

Ethan met the wall with the same joyous expulsion of air as he had on the floor. He could see Callin was still shaking off the impact to his face. That had gotten to him. There was no pride lost in a man taking a pause after a triple head butt. The fact that he was still standing was enough of an accomplishment.

Ethan slid up the wall to stand. He was certain that the wall was the only thing holding him up. This was far from the worst injury he had ever received, but it was not the end of the battle. Even now, he could see Callin turning around to examine him with predatory hesitation. He would stand there and catch his breath while he waited for Ethan to run like a scared rabbit.

This was why Ethan couldn't win. His strength was a match, or at least in the ballpark. His speed and agility were attuned enough to keep his head from getting ripped off. Endurance was the issue. A bear will eventually tire of the game and retreat. A mountain lion doesn't waste its energy on prey that actually fights back.

But a dog?

Man's best friend was bestowed that exalted title because of his relentless bravery in the face of insurmountable odds. What dog would not throw themselves between their master and his attacker? What dog would not lay down his life to protect the one he loved?

Callin stepped forward. Not an attack, but an attempt to make Ethan flinch. He was trying to flush his prey from the bush. Ethan waved his hand. "Enough," he said and tried to push off the wall.

He could see disappointment on Callin's face as he realized the battle had not come to a climactic ending. Regrettable as it was to disappoint him, Ethan knew that the climactic ending would only be him bathed in blood, or lame from a broken bone. This fight was something his ego needed, but he certainly didn't need to take it to the bitter end. He was indeed capable of fighting a werewolf to the death.

His death.

"That's it?" Callin said, keeping his defenses high in case this was a tactical trick. "You were doing so well. I've never fought a human so long."

Ethan smiled. "I'm glad I could give you a respectable fight, but we both know that you could outlast me, so let's just call this what it was: a good effort." Ethan put out his hand to shake.

Callin examined his hand, as if questioning his honesty with the gesture. He slapped his palm into it for a strong handshake. "It was a great effort. Seriously, I've put men down with one punch before. You're right that I would eventually have beaten you. If I were wounded, though, you might have had a real chance."

"Thank you." Ethan glanced over at Leona and withdrew his hand. "You know I can only offer you my deepest sympathy in regard to your son." Callin looked back at Leona and his baby boy in her arms. "I can't justify taking him from you, but I also can't condone you taking him from her."

"It's a slippery slope, I know, but I understand what your obligations are. I don't begrudge you your duty. That's why you are still breathing. There won't be any need for that whistle. You don't need your backup. I won't stop you from accomplishing your goal. I don't want to upset Lynnius, but you should know that as soon as you're gone, I will simply track him down again and take him again."

"Yes, I imagined as much." Ethan frowned wishing he could just take the baby and go. Ethan pulled the whistle from his shirt and examined it. Callin tipped his brow like he figured Ethan was being overly cautious. "Unfortunately, it isn't going to be that simple." Callin narrowed his eyes. "I'm not a hunter, Callin. I'm the warden." Ethan pinched the whistle between his lips and blew.

47

THE WHISTLE, OF COURSE, made no sound. The triumphant attack of armed guards bursting through the doors would have been an exciting and dramatic culmination to the conversation, but that wasn't what happened either.

However, the lack of zenith to the situation didn't stop Callin's eyes from widening and backing away from Ethan like he had just been given the status of Judas in his mind. Ethan shrugged apologetically. Much as Callin had been chagrined to admit his superiority in a physical challenge, Ethan was remorseful that he was going to win this battle after all.

Had Callin suspected Ethan was from the prison, there would not have been a fight. With four werewolves, he was nothing more than a chew toy. Lynnius would have been stripped from his mother's arms again, and perhaps this time for good, if the men had known who was coming for them.

"Leona, keep still and keep him safe!" Callin yelled to her just before the lights went out.

Ethan had never witnessed the collectors at work. He wasn't actually witnessing it now, but the wafted breezes that whipped past him hinted at the speed of their work. He could hear growling and snarling, but he wasn't entirely sure who it was, werewolf or collector.

The smell of foul breath and sweat entered his nostrils. He could feel one of them right beside him. It sniffed him carefully, trying to decide if he was friend or foe. He most likely smelled like Callin from the fight.

Concerned that the creature would take him as well, he took a lesson from Nevia and plucked at his sweaty black shirt. The smell of his impromptu workout puffed up against his neck. The creature—and as it happened, creatures, because he only noticed the other one when it growled in his ear at his subtle movement—took in a big whiff of him.

The stink of breath was gone as fast as it had arrived. Ethan stopped hearing the sound of struggling bodies. He heard a screen door open and shut, but that was it. A few blocks away, the collectors would load the werewolves into the truck they'd come in on with ninja stealth. Ethan didn't imagine they could drive, but he was sure some well-paid driver had been designated to the duty of driving the creatures and their catches to the train. From truck to train, and back to truck, they would arrive tomorrow evening to be delivered to Danato, sans gift wrap.

Ethan felt bad about incarcerating a man who simply wanted to be with his son, but it wasn't his place to make decisions for the Council of the Moon. He only had one side of the story, and Callin was far from the norm in the werewolf population. If Randal had been the one fighting for his child, Ethan didn't think he would have quite so much sympathy.

"Leona?" Ethan called into the dark. He hadn't anticipated the collectors would take a fem-wolf, but when he didn't hear any movement, he got concerned.

"I'm here," she said from across the room. She hadn't moved from her position, and smartly so. Running while collectors were present was essentially volunteering to have your body slammed into the floor. Ethan hadn't been smart enough to avoid that with Callin, but he was smart enough with the collectors.

"Is the baby okay?" he asked.

"Yes, Lynnius is just fine." He could hear the contentment in her voice. Her baby was safe, she was safe. "How are you?" Her voice chimed with concern that surprised him.

"Ah..." He wasn't sure how to answer. A report of his injuries or just the standard 'I'm alive and breathing ergo, fine.'

"I can smell your blood."

"Oh, right." He drew in a breath and mentally tracked his pain. "My neck probably needs a turtleneck bandage, and my left eye is the size of a baseball, but just bruising after that. The only thing that really hurts is my head, but that's what you get when you try to head butt your opponent into submission." He chuckled, but she didn't join in.

"I noticed a candle on the kitchen table. The stove is gas. Why don't you get us some light, and I'll get you fixed up. I'd hate to send you back to Cori in such bad shape. She may never let you leave again."

"Right." He didn't mention that she barely let him leave this time, because it would have made Cori sound weak. Despite what Leona pretended to feel for Cori, or how she flaunted her sexuality before her, Ethan could tell that she respected Cori. Just as Callin had to respect him for putting up a good fight, Leona respected Cori for not taking "no" for an answer. Granted, it still pissed her off, but the one emotion didn't prevent the other.

48

E THAN RETURNED TO THE living room with his wide column candle in hand. He wondered why werewolves who spent their evenings eating pizza and beer might have a scented candle, but he couldn't deride a man for not wanting his house to smell like old pepperoni.

He found the couch and coffee table that had been shoved against the wall opposite Leona's chair. He pulled the table out and set the candle on it before falling onto the couch. Despite the half-assed, thrown-together decor, the couch was very comfortable, and didn't appear to be cheaply made.

"Do you need...?" Ethan paused, catching sight of Leona breast-feeding Lynnius. The image, albeit perfectly natural, threw off his train of thought. The candlelight shimmering against her bare breast was alluring to the eyes, but the baby suckling her made it so damned wrong to look at. The product of sexuality was a surprisingly strong turn off. "Guess not," he said in answer to his own intended question about feeding the baby. "Can you breast-feed while pregnant?" he asked, suddenly confused by the image.

"No, I'm not producing milk yet, but he falls asleep so well this way." She smiled, looking at her baby. "I confess I love the connection as well. You don't mind, do you?" she said, looking at him with concern.

"Of course not," he answered quickly, so he didn't sound like a jerk. "Bond all you like."

"You had me worried for a bit there," she said with a sweet voice that was only intended for Lynnius. "I thought you might have agreed with Callin."

Ethan huffed out an exhale and scratched his head. "I think Callin is a good man. I think he has some grandiose ideals, but I think he genuinely loves Lynnius... and you." She glared at him for that statement. "Hey, I don't know the guy, but any man that offers to make you queen and be at your beck and call must be in love."

She thought about that for a moment and smiled again. "Would you mind taking Lynnius upstairs to his crib? I'll gather some supplies for the first aid. I see well enough in the dark for that."

They both stood and met in the middle of the room. She handed Lynnius off to him without any attempt to conceal her breast when the baby slipped unhappily away. "Do you want the candle, or can you find your way?"

"I'll find my way." Ethan focused on the baby, so his eyes didn't wander beyond his marital vows of honor.

He took the baby upstairs, but he paused before placing him in the crib. He took a moment to feel the weight of the child in his arms. He had never really held a baby before. His life of small-time crime had never involved women, let alone babies. He hadn't really thought about babies, and he hadn't ever discussed it with Cori. He wondered if she would want one... or two.

The image of a miniature little Cori with wavy blond hair and a face burning red from a childish fit didn't scare him. It amused him. A little Cori that looked at him with the adoration that Cori reserved for Danato. Yes, that appealed to him a great deal.

Ethan shook himself from his revelry and made a mental note to ask Cori what she thought of children. He hoped she wasn't against it. Granted, they lived in the most dangerous place on earth, but what was life without complications?

Ethan tromped down the stairs and found Leona, thankfully fully covered, slipping the plastic seal off of a bottle of peroxide. He cringed at the sting it was going to cause. He sat down on the couch beside her and frowned at the toothbrush she was dipping into the peroxide. "He's asleep. What the hell are you going to do with that?"

"Clean those gouges on your neck," she said with a "no duh" attitude. "Do you know what germs are carried on hands and under fingernails?" He didn't, but he could guess it was some pretty nasty ones. "If you can brave a fight with an alpha male, you can handle a wound scrubbing."

"I wouldn't be so sure about that," he muttered before bracing for the pain.

He had hoped that she might show a modicum of sensitivity to his pain, but she brusquely scrubbed each of the scratches without remorse for the grunts of pain he pinched behind his lips. He was certain this was some kind of punishment for something, but he wasn't sure he had done anything to deserve this treatment.

When she'd finished, she patted the renewed hemorrhages with gauze and wrapped a bandage around his neck, making him look like a whiplash victim. She taped off the bandage and looked him over for more injuries. "Anything else?"

"I don't suppose you have an aspirin."

She pulled a small pack of pain pills from the pile. It was the single dose they stocked in hotel vending machines, but it was better than nothing. She went back into the kitchen and brought back a bottle of water for him to down the tiny pills.

She watched him gulp down the remainder of the water with gusto. He finished with a pleased exhalation usually reserved for soda commercials and laid his head back to imagine the pills taking effect on his throbbing head.

He was certain that he should refrain from sleeping for a while, but closing his eyes was a necessity. Even the dim light of the candle seemed unbearable. If he had any memory function left when this was all said and done, he would have to remember not to head butt anyone ever again.

"I was impressed by you," Leona said. He had hoped she wouldn't talk, but he wasn't rude enough to tell her to shut up. He grunted in response. "Cori always did have good taste in men."

He didn't respond to that. If she was hoping to bait him into being envious of a dead man, she was barking up the wrong tree. Ethan may have had an issue with Cori taking up with Vince over him at the time, but from everything she had told him about their relationship, it was vital for her to have been with him.

The benefit of dating a werewolf was their understanding of your emotions. Vince had accommodated for Cori's fears, irrational or otherwise. He always knew when to push her, and when to back the hell off. It took Ethan far more trial and error to get to that point, and even still, he had to make demands on Cori's honesty. Her insistence on keeping secrets needed to be resolved before he could be sure that his efforts to pacify her anxieties were building new trust and not just maintaining it.

"Did Cori tell you about her and Vince?"

"I know all about Vince," Ethan said.

"I bet there is one thing that she didn't tell you." Her voice hinted at a smile. She was getting a little too much amusement from this conversation.

"Cori has told me everything there is to tell about her and Vince without getting into details that would be too uncomfortable."

"Oh, I know, Ethan. I'm sure she is very honest with you, as she should be. A good wife should always tell the truth, and a good husband should always lie."

Ethan wanted to look at Leona. He wanted to see if he was right about the smug smile that he assumed went with that statement. He knew better than to ask what it meant, but that didn't stop her from expanding.

"That's how I know Vince loved her. It was the least he could do to not tell her the truth."

"He didn't tell her he was going to die because she would have been too guarded with him. She has long since forgiven him for that. She appreciates everything that the relationship offered her, despite the regrettable ending." Leona's chuckle took hold in her throat and turned into a villainous chortle. He at last opened his eyes and lifted his head to glare at her childish revelry. "What is so amusing to you, Leona?"

"That was only one of his secrets." Leona leaned back on the couch with him and put her arm behind him. She fiddled with his hair, all the while smiling at her secret. "Oh, Ethan, won't you please ask me what it is? I can't stand monologues. I like everything I do to have a partner."

Her smile was more than just villainous. It was venomous. Whatever the words were, she wanted to spill so badly; they were going to sting. He didn't want any part of it, but it was too late for that. He had taken the job. Part of that job was interacting with this psychopath.

Even with the image of her breast freshly in his mind, even with the caring mothering she showed to Lynnius, even with the glimpses of her character under Callin's gaze—he hated her. He was certain there was more to her than she showed the world, but that didn't matter to him.

In life, all that mattered was the side you showed. People want to believe that at heart, everyone is a good person, but even if that were true, why would it matter? What purpose does a good heart serve if the person you're interacting with is a complete ass-hat?

"I can't believe you're going to make me say it without a lead-up. How unsatisfying." She put her hand on his chest. He looked down at the offending hand, debating whether to move it. Since she left it on his chest, he decided not to react to her attempt to make him uncomfortable.

"Just say it, you overdramatic hack," he seethed.

"Well, that's not exactly the verbal foreplay I had in mind, but it will get me there nonetheless." She winked. "Cori, as you know, poisoned me so I couldn't procreate with her man."

"Yes, a gutsy move that I'm sure she's proud of."

"As am I," Leona added, losing her smile. "I was so impressed with her audacity that I kept my promise to never see her again. Well, until now, but I think even the sternest of promises have an expiration date, especially when my baby is the issue at hand."

"I think Cori was impressed with you, too. She respects strong women. I think in a strange, self-defeating way, she actually likes you."

"I like her too," Leona said it as if she needed it clarified before she continued. "She would have made a wonderful fem-wolf. If only the story books were right about werewolf bites." She chomped her teeth and smiled at Ethan.

Ethan gave a small smirk, even though he knew there was more to come. Leona stretched her body not unlike an animal, with all four limbs stick straight. When she relaxed again, her belly rolled over to touch his side. Her arm reached around behind him, resting on the couch. She had just pulled the yawn move that men did to women at the movies.

She looked down at her belly, overlapping his hand. She patted her belly. "Big tummies are a small price to pay for such a big payout."

Ethan shook his head. He didn't want to say it, but he couldn't resist. Some part of that chivalrous charm that Danato had practically force-fed him was irrepressible. "It's a beautiful transformation, nothing to be ashamed of."

She smiled warmly at him. "Well, don't you just make a girl feel good? Would you like to touch it?"

Ethan shook his head, and she laughed. "You said it's beautiful, but you won't touch it?"

"Leona..."

"I'm not asking you if you want to touch me, Ethan. I'm asking if you want to feel what a pregnant woman's belly feels like. You seem a little new to the baby thing. It can't hurt to familiarize yourself with it." She rolled up her shirt and patted her belly.

Ethan nodded his head and reached his hand out. He paused just before touching her, wondering what this scene would look like if Cori walked in. He rationalized that it would look like her very uncomfortable husband was touching the belly of her arch-frenemy. He touched her stomach.

He chuckled. "It's warm."

"Of course it's warm. It's not an alien." She laughed. "Press your fingers in, he might kick back."

"Won't that hurt?" he asked.

"No." She shook her head.

He pressed his finger into the belly. The tension was different than he'd expected: firm surface resistance, yet a pliable liquid center. A pregnant belly was one big water balloon, or a very small waterbed.

His fingers felt something hard when he dug into a different part of her belly. "Wait. What was that?" He looked at her, but she only smiled. He pushed in again and the hard knob pushed back on his fingers. He gasped. "Is that a foot?" Leona nodded.

All underlying thoughts about what Leona was going to tell him were gone. All that mattered was that the little knob inside of her was someone's foot. A baby, a real live baby, was inside there waiting to be introduced to the world. He wanted that. He wanted Cori to want that. If she had been there at that moment, he would have taken her upstairs and made love to her just to jump-start the endeavor.

He laughed and sat back away from Leona's stomach so he didn't take his liberties of poking too far. "Thank you, that was... enlightening."

Leona nodded. "I thought you might appreciate that." She leaned into him and kissed him gently. He didn't back away, partially out of shock and partially because it just seemed rude, since she had just presented her belly for exploration.

She pulled away and smiled at him. It was a genuinely warm smile. It reminded him of the way she looked at Lynnius. It was the way he knew she wanted to look at Callin, but refused to allow herself to.

She kissed him again, but only a short, simple kiss that didn't give him time to push her away and didn't give him room to object. By the time she came back for the third kiss, he was stuck in mid-thought. He wondered if this was what Cori felt like in the face of her enemy. Frozen and unable to make a decision.

He was kissing her.

Ethan didn't understand how he had gone from hating her, to touching her belly, to making out with her. His mind was stuck in a repetitive cycle of thoughts. He hadn't kissed anyone except Cori in forever, so the newness of her lips was appealing. He didn't like the way her lipstick tasted, but the mint on her breath was just that extra touch that made a stranger's kiss more acceptable.

When his mind came around to the guilt that he was feeling, his little shoulder angel was screaming at him to just stop kissing her. The little devil was stunned into submission. He couldn't believe what was happening, either.

Was Cori right? Was this woman a seductress? She had to be; he wouldn't let her freely kiss him for this long otherwise. How long had it been?

Why the fuck was he still kissing her?

He was enjoying it, that's why.

With that thought, Ethan shoved Leona away hard enough to make his point, but not hard enough to be concerned with how he was treating a pregnant woman. He looked her over and felt a flood of shame. She had no concealed skills of seduction beyond that of simply being a woman. He was just a man, allowing his brain to prattle on unintelligibly while his lips continued to cheat on his wife.

He took in a deep breath to calm his mind and refocus his thoughts on how much he loved Cori. How much he wanted to be with her now, instead of this tyrannous fem-wolf. Leona stayed quiet while he did. She probably expected him to find a way to bury his moralities temporarily so he could fuck guiltlessly like most cheating men did.

He could see now how pompous he had been in assuming that his love alone would keep him true to Cori. That wasn't enough. Danato was right, a man's body often worked against him. He had to not want her at all, if his defenses were going to work.

"Are you sure, Ethan? I would hate to leave you aching this far along." She reached out to grope him, but he grabbed her wrist.

"Don't." He tried to sound mad, but it came off as a plea. He shoved her hand away. He was only beginning to understand the trouble he was in. He was alone in a house with a fem-wolf that wanted him. He couldn't simply leave—she would stop him. He couldn't resist her—she was too strong. A flash of heat hit him as he realized he was about to be a rape victim.

49

"WHAT WERE YOU GOING to tell me?" Ethan asked, hoping to change the subject long enough to think of some way to either escape from her or completely knock out the function to his lower body.

She eyed him carefully, apparently considering her options before speaking. "Colloidal silver is a very painful poison. It won't kill a werewolf, but it's the equivalent of food poisoning; it continues through the body as an irritant for several hours. A strong enough dose could put a werewolf down for a couple of days. I'll spare you the details of my gastrointestinal distress, but suffice it to say that I spent the remainder of the day in and out of the facilities."

Ethan tried not to smile at that, but it sounded like a practical joke. He imagined that the pain of it was still not amusing to Leona. When her eyes narrowed, he bit back his lips to hide his amusement and cleared his throat. "I imagine there are few people who couldn't empathize with that experience."

"Cori worked so hard to get me to back off that I promised to stay away from her, but for all her forethought and consideration she never thought to ask me to stay away from Vince," Leona chimed in the amusement of that statement.

Ethan narrowed his eyes at her. She was once again overjoyed with her nearly spilled secret, nearly dished gossip, and nearly dropped bomb. "What did you do, Leona?" He hadn't wanted to help spin her yarn, especially when he knew it was only going to hurt Cori in the long run, but he needed to know what it was Vince had kept from Cori.

She chuckled. "I was better in a day and a half. I was past my prime conception time, but that didn't matter to me by that point. Vince knew immediately what he had to do. They were hiding out in a hotel just to be safe." She winked at him.

"I admit that I was mad," she continued. "I considered hurting Cori. I considered hurting both of them, but I stifled that rage into a more appropriate ladylike revenge. I simply checked into the hotel with them." She smiled broadly and arched her back, taking in the memory.

"The first night I arrived, I stood outside their door for a while so he could catch my scent. He made up some excuse about getting ice, or whatever. He tracked me to my room. I was pleased to see that he had not bothered to bluster or beg. He simply came in and sat on my bed. He made it very clear that he would cooperate with me as long as I did not hurt Cori, which included telling her the truth, or breaking my promise of seeing her again. I had no intention of breaking my promise, nor had I intended to hurt her by that point, but he didn't know that."

Leona rolled onto Ethan, straddling him. She eased herself high on his legs so he could feel her against him. He cursed himself and wondered once again if he could fight off a pregnant fem-wolf after already fighting Callin. That was probably a mistake.

"I should have thanked Cori for what she did for me. Vince was a very willing participant for me after that. He made sure all my desires were satisfied. I'm sure if he were alive to defend himself he would say he did it to protect Cori, but of course we both know he didn't leave unsatisfied either."

Ethan could see the pleasure she was deriving from this moment. Not just the sinister joy of telling her wicked back-story, but physically as well. Reliving the memory of forcing Vince to betray Cori was turning her on. That was the moment that he truly hated her. It was also the moment that he was conversely turned off by her.

"For a week and a few times after they left the hotel, I was not more than a hundred yards from her when I was fucking her boyfriend. He made simple excuses of getting ice and soda. He would even run out to buy her flowers." Leona laughed. "And all the while he was slipping away from her, he was slipping into me."

She ground her body against Ethan, and he was relieved that he felt nothing for her. His body, albeit still a man's body with a man's hormones, was, for the moment, impotent. "Do you know what the best part is? I get to relive that same torture with you." She leaned in and bit his earlobe before whispering to him. "I'm going to fuck you whether you want to or not, and then you can decide if you are a good enough husband to lie to Cori about it or not." She giggled and leaned back.

She took him in and noticed that his hands were neither pushing her away nor pulling her forward. He was sitting blank-faced, with his hands at his sides. "Are you playing the conscientious objector?" She smiled as she unbuttoned his pants.

"Something like that," he said with a cold stare of indifference and disgust.

"Good, I like..." He almost laughed when her hand slipped into his pants and found the last thing she expected. She glared at him and took a more aggressive hold on the focal point of her revenge plot.

He didn't stop her. He hoped Cori wouldn't begrudge him the amusement of watching a woman desperately trying to manhandle him into formation. In frustration, she even offered oral stimulation, which only made him laugh. His laughter finally broke her, and she backhanded him.

The searing pain was phenomenal, and he knew he would need to tread lightly around her temper to keep from losing his teeth. He tucked himself back into his pants and shook his head at her. "It won't work."

"It was working," she said. "What did you do? No man could withstand that much attention. I don't care how much he loves his wife!" Her teeth were bared and he could tell she wanted nothing more than to rip him limb from limb for insulting her sexual prowess with his flaccid response.

"Yes, it was working. You had me on the hook and I was in danger of being the man I had so vehemently promised my wife I wouldn't be. However, after speaking to Danato, I realized that it was not my morals that were at risk with you, but my body. So before I left, I took a trip up to Mezula. You don't know her, I'm sure, but she's my in-house love doctor. She's an eight out of ten on the scary scale, but she definitely fights for love when it's honest.

"I told her my predicament, and she told me she had just the right spell. She gave me the ingredients and instructions in the form of strawberry picnic sex and I was bestowed mental control of my lower half."

"What?"

"Yeah, she's that good."

"You can't tell me that you don't want me."

"For a minute there, when we were kissing, yes, I thought I wanted you, but if you think that I could ever want a woman that is turned on by the misery she causes others, especially my wife, you are wrong. Leona, you disgust me, and now..." he waved his hands over his pants, "I can show you just how much."

She stared at him, shocked by the banishment. She touched her belly, either to console herself or remind herself that she was still attractive to some men.

"Leona," he said, still a prisoner to his gallantry when it came to women. "I think you should seriously consider Callin's proposal of shared custody. He may be in prison for a few months, but I can't see any reason why you should turn down an offer that devoted just because you're afraid of being consumed by your love."

Her eyes widened, hinting at how dead-on his impression of her was. "You don't know what I feel."

"Actually, I do. Anyone who has ever tried to fight their own love knows what that feels like. I don't pretend to understand the social implications of a queened pack, but it sounds to me like you love your children with indifference to their fathers. Isn't it ideal to raise those children with their fathers?"

"You make it sound so simple."

"You're a powerful, beautiful, charismatic woman. Imagine if that energy was honed to guide the growth of your family instead of plotting revenge."

"You say such nice things for being disgusted by me."

"You *are* a powerful, beautiful, charismatic woman, but you're *acting* like a bitch." She raised her chin to that offense, but didn't vocalize her objection. "You need to stop flaunting your own self-importance and actually make yourself important."

She didn't respond to any of it, but she didn't outright attack him either. She sniffed the air. "There's pizza left in the kitchen. It's probably cold, but I can imagine fighting with Callin made you hungry."

He nodded. It *had* made him hungry.

"You should eat. You can stay here tonight. I'm sure Callin won't mind. I will go home though. I don't imagine I will see you after this, but if you see Callin... please tell him I'm sorry for... acting like a bitch," she said pointedly.

Ethan smiled a dismal smile. "I'll tell him. You know you can visit him. I'm not sure Danato would sanction an overnight stay, but I think I could talk him into a few visits a month, especially if you are bringing Lynnius."

"I'll think about it," she said. "Goodbye Ethan." She stomped upstairs to collect her baby. He made his way to the kitchen and collected his pizza until he heard the door slam.

He scarfed down a few slices in the living room, but without electricity and with the overhanging feeling of being an intruder, he blew out the candle, locked up, and headed out to his car. Fueled on pepperoni and about three hours of sleep, he drove to the train station to wait for the first one out. He was free of his gilded cage, but all he wanted was to be back in it as soon as possible.

50

E THAN ARRIVED BACK AT the prison in a truck full of live chickens. He'd been given the option of waiting for the next truck, but that would have put him out another twelve hours, and as it was, even with driving overnight to the train station, he had only shaved off a few hours from his trip.

By the time he arrived in the late afternoon, he smelled like chicken shit and looked like an imploded pillow. He would have been annoyed by it if he wasn't insanely tired. He stopped for a quick round of jibes with the dockworkers. When the levity dragged on longer than he had a tolerance for, he mentioned Danato might tar and feather him for real if he didn't report. They waved him off immediately.

The amount of fear Danato conjured in his employees still surprised him. He supposed they didn't know him as well as he did, but then again, there were people with tenures of twenty years here that still took on the same cowardly attitude to his presence. Perhaps they knew him better than Ethan realized.

With that in mind, he should have headed up the short stairway to Danato's office, but he didn't. He took one look in that direction and turned right to the exit. Danato didn't want chicken crap on his office chair even if it was a 1980s reject vinyl number. He decided to wash up and change before checking in.

Outside, he breathed in the cool arctic summer. The downside to living so far north was that summer was only a hiccup in the otherwise shivering climate. It lasted only a few months, and the really comfortable temperatures were only weeks. Nevertheless, there was beauty in the landscape with or without piles of snow. The variety of birds flourishing here always impressed Ethan. The grasses, though incomparable to the beauty of a forest, were prolific. They reminded him of lying on a picnic blanket, making love to his wife. That was definitely a beautiful scene.

His smile from that memory didn't fade as he entered the house. He let the door slam as he jaunted toward the stairs for a long overdue bath. He added up the hours on his stakeout, plus his time in the chicken truck, and the result was sounding unhygienic.

"Ethan?"

Ethan swung back around on the first landing and peeked down to the living room. Cori was lying on the couch in her usual jeans and t-shirt. The bold print on the front read: *I'm not a slut, but you are a dick!* It was one of the many t-shirts Danato had banned from entering the prison facility upon pain of death.

She looked a little disheveled, like she had been spending the day tossing on the couch. He couldn't tell at this distance, but he suspected she might have been crying at one point. "Hey, sweetness, why aren't you at work? I thought Belus was going to be keeping you busy while I was gone, so you didn't worry about me."

She gulped and looked down at something in her hands he couldn't see. He came down the stairs. She tossed the book in her hands on the coffee table. He squinted to read the cover. "Is that the hobgoblin lineage? Bloody hell, what did you do to endure that torture?"

"Self-inflicted," she said, standing up, "Ethan, I... what are you covered in, and what is that smell?"

"Sorry, I took the chicken truck home. I couldn't wait any longer to see you."

She smiled, but it quickly faded. He had hoped to have a loving embrace at their reunion, but she stayed on her side of the couch while they spoke. He didn't press it since he smelled like fodder and chicken shit. "What's up with you? Why aren't you happy I'm back? You were so sad to see me go."

She forced a smile, but he knew whatever she was feeling was beyond even his ability to cheer up. "I'm extremely happy you're back." He saw tears well in her eyes.

"Cori, tell me what's wrong." He leaned on the couch. If he had to strip down so she would let him hold her, he would.

"I had a little incident with Efrat while you were gone."

"Oh my God." He came around the couch, ignoring his own stench, to check her over. He kept himself at arm's distance, but he examined her for bandages or bruising. "Did he hurt you?"

She sighed. "Only my sympathy for humanity in general." She chuckled. "So, yeah, nothing that I can't get over in time." She backed away from him. He wondered if she was only doing it so she wouldn't cry. She had long since lost her ability to hide her feelings from him. It had left him with many wet shoulders, but he preferred it to be his shoulder than someone else's.

"Is everyone else okay? Did... you kill him?"

She laughed heartily at that. "Um... actually, I kind of saved the bastard." Her laughter left her with a smile, but it was wrought with worry. "I take it you haven't checked in with Danato yet."

"No, I didn't think he would appreciate my stench."

"He will want to talk to you and me regarding the details of my incident." She said it mechanically, like this was a statement Danato himself had told her. "I would rather just tell it all with him, if you don't mind," she added when Ethan started to form a question on his lips.

"Sure," he said, unable to hide some disappointment at her avoidance. "He's mad at you, isn't he?"

She shrugged. "He wants to be. He should be, but... it's just very complex, and I spent all last night telling Danato."

"Telling him?"

"My side of the story is a little different from his perspective. We'll get to that, but I have a favor to ask you."

"Anything."

"I need you to take me to see Efrat."

Ethan took a step away from her. His mouth opened as wide as his eyes, but he didn't find the words to speak for several seconds. "Cori, that makes no sense. You hate him. Why would you want to see him?"

"Ethan, I can't even begin to explain, but I will tell you that Danato would not want you to take me up there, so if we are going to go, it should be now before he knows you're back."

Ethan threw his head back, propped his arms on his hips and paced back around the couch, putting the distance back between them. "You are asking me to go against Danato's wishes."

"No, I'm asking you to take me up to see Efrat. Danato will tell you after we speak that you are not to let him near me. I'm asking you to take me up there before he officially tells you himself. I'm only telling you his feelings on the subject, so you don't feel like I've tricked you into something. I'm asking for your help. If you decide to abide by Danato rather than do so, I understand." She said it so straight that it came off as icy.

"Cori..." He clenched his fists in front of him; he wanted to grab her and shake her. "This isn't fair. I can't just knowingly go against what he would want just to help you... do what? What are you going to do up there?"

"I found some gloves in stock that are supposed to prevent electrical transference. I'd like to give them to him."

Ethan's face couldn't have scrunched any harder in confusion. "What the fuck for?" He hadn't intended to sound mad, but the statement by itself didn't translate his disgust at the prospect of seeing the man who almost killed her.

"He..." She shook her head. "Look Ethan, none of this will make sense now and maybe not even after Danato and I explain it, but my request stands on the merit of my character alone, not his. I'm asking for your help. The answer is either yes or no." She stood blank-faced, waiting for his answer.

"Son of a..." He started toward the stairs. "Let me change and I'll take you," he said without turning back. "I'll give you five minutes with him, but not alone and only if they are not feuding up there." He didn't look back to see if she was happy about his agreement or not. At this point, her being joyful might have made him change his mind.

51

THERE WAS VERY LITTLE conversation on the way up in the elevator. Ethan was boiling at the prospect of going against Danato's wishes, but he was madder that he was going to be the one to take the punishment for it because Cori's honesty put all the blame on him. He wondered if she'd known that when she did it. He hoped she wasn't capable of that level of contriving.

They even stood apart in the elevator like they weren't even intimate. He hated that he had rushed home to see her and he hadn't even held her hand yet, let alone hugged and kissed her. Considering what he went through to be chaste with Leona, he was feeling acrimony settle into his face and posture. Even if she wanted to be near him now, his body language would have repelled her.

The door *ponked, and* he started to stomp out of the elevator. She put her arm in his way. He looked at her, confused. She wasn't angry or happy, but the worry that had been etched into her face at the house was coming through stronger. "Ethan, don't do this if you're only going to hate me for it. It's not worth all that."

"Tell me why you're really doing this. I know it's not about gloves."

Her eyes flickered over his. "I can't explain it, but I need to see him again. If that's not enough of an explanation, then we should just go." She stepped back into the elevator. "I can't stand seeing that hatred in your eyes directed at me."

Ethan winced, and he leaned on the door to the elevator to keep it open. "No, not hate, Cori. Never ever hate. Frustration, confusion, and maybe a little disappointment, but never hate."

"I missed you so much."

He waited for her to come to him, but she still didn't. He wondered what had happened in the last two days that could cause her to restrict her connection to him. "How important is it for you to see him?"

"Important enough to risk Danato's wrath. Not important enough to risk yours."

"Are you asking me to keep this from Danato?"

"No, it won't matter. I've already screwed up enough. This will just be an irritation to an otherwise screwed up week."

"Okay, let's go." Ethan ushered her through, and he followed, punching the code into the upper level entrance. He wished he had brought his pistol, but for some reason Cori had requested he didn't. She didn't bring hers either.

They slipped into the ruined room. Two military men with elemental weapons immediately tromped up to them to investigate their arrival. "Can we help you, sir?" one said, standing in Ethan's path.

Ethan smiled at the broad shoulders that were tensely holding his weapon across his chest. He was about an inch taller than Ethan, but he was pretty sure his boots and erect stature were the majority of that inch. The man's face was plastered with severity, like the world might end if he wasn't there to stop it.

"My wife needs to give one of your inmates a present."

"Excuse me?" He broke character a moment to lower his brow at Cori.

"Gloves only," she said, showing him the pair of black gloves. "It's experimental. We're testing out fabric barriers for Efrat's powers. We suspect a number of power surges in the electrical systems are caused by your battles up here. We are hoping to find a way to dampen his energy. If this works, we may be able to put him in a type of gloved straightjacket. I imagine it might help you guys out as well." Ethan knew that was a lie, but only because she hadn't told him that. Had she wanted to, she could have given him that line and he never would have questioned her motives for coming here. In that sense, he was glad that she hadn't lied. At least she was honest about not wanting to tell him the truth.

"I haven't received any requests of this nature," the guard waffled.

"I know. The paperwork for crossover shit is horrendous. Plus, I don't even know if it's going to work, so I was hoping to skip all that and just try it out. If he'll cooperate, the braggart will probably try to fry me for the suggestion, but whatever, that's why you guys are here."

Ethan was a little impressed by how easily she slipped in that little compliment. He often forgot what a manipulator Cori could be. He supposed he should also be thankful she hadn't used that talent on him for this.

Or had she?

"I'll need to see the gloves," the guard said.

"Of course." She handed him the gloves. "They're a poly-vinyl..." she started to explain, but he ran off to show the General. The General eyed the gloves as the officer gave him the explanation. At the end, he looked at them and crossed over from the lookout booth to speak with them.

"I am in charge here. You want me to put these gloves on Efrat?"

"No, sir. Actually, I would like to give them to him. I'm concerned that he might see anything from you as a threat. This is purely a test. Pass or fail is all I need and then I will go."

The General chuckled. "You want to speak with Efrat? Aren't you the one that he tried to kill a year back?"

"Succeeded, sir. I'm not a threat to him, so I think he will cooperate. Just need to slip them on, test his electrical conductivity, and be on my way."

The General looked her over, trying to decide if this was a joke or not. "Nothing stops his power, but I'll humor you," he said and tossed the gloves back at her. "I take no responsibility for your welfare in doing this, but rest assured, my guards will escort you."

"I will too," Ethan stated rather than asked.

The General gave him a once-over before nodding. "As you wish, but make this snappy. I haven't had any complications from these guys in nearly twenty-four hours, and I don't want to change that because you want to perform a science experiment."

"Yes, sir," Cori said, playing the part of the good soldier.

Ethan glanced back at her as they followed the officers over. She barely glanced at him. She was too intent on her purpose to give him any indication of her thoughts. They approached an encasement—glass rather than metal—with scorch marks on the concrete walls within. There was no door, but Efrat was happily tucked inside on his bed. His feet were holding down a book that he was reading awkwardly from a distance.

Cori took the gloves from the first officer and stepped to the doorway. She was hiding it well, but Ethan could tell she was nervous. She tapped on the glass near the opening. Efrat looked up at her, first baffled, then curious, then amused. The smirk that settled on his face was enough to put Ethan on edge. "Hello kitten," he said, turning to face her on his cot. That was enough to make Ethan want to punch him. "To what do I owe this pleasure?"

Cori glanced back at the three of them looming in the door behind her. She couldn't exactly ask for privacy, but

Ethan got the impression she wanted it. He wasn't about to offer it, though. "I found a pair of antistatic gloves in the stockroom. I thought they might contain some of the unintentional static charge from your hands. Will you try them?"

He looked over the gloves in her hand. He seemed as baffled by the prospect as everyone else was. He stood abruptly, and Ethan took a step forward. Efrat caught the movement and smiled at him. He motioned to him with a tilt of his head as he spoke to Cori. "Your man, I take it?"

Cori nodded. "Yes, my husband."

Efrat nodded and put his hands out to her. "Does he know about us yet?" Efrat glanced at Ethan, but he held his ground. He didn't know anything about anyone, but Efrat didn't need to know that.

"Soon enough," was all Cori gave for an answer. She slipped the gloves on his hands. "I'm not sure if these will work. The fabric is the key." She tugged on the fabric. "I would have preferred something sturdier, but had no idea what to look for. Even if I knew, I probably wouldn't know where to find it." She shrugged. "How do they feel?"

Ethan watched Efrat play with the gloves. He touched Cori's hands, but she didn't seem to jump from any static. He touched his own arm gingerly and pursed his lips. "Not bad. Better than starting electrical fires with my reading material." He smiled at her. It seemed a genuine enough smile, but Ethan still didn't like it. He wanted to know what had happened between them to make this casual exchange possible. "You're alright, kitten. It's hard to know who to trust around here. Your motives seem pretty translucent, though. I think I might be able to file you with the good guys." He reached forward to touch her cheek, but she stepped back.

"Don't." She looked down to the floor. "Try those out. I'll see if I can find what I really wanted, but I can't promise anything."

"I understand. I appreciate the effort, Corinthia." Ethan didn't wait to hear her response to that. The fact that Efrat knew her intimately enough to know her birth name was too much for him to stand.

"Let's go, Cori." He patted the glass and extended his hand to her. Efrat didn't smirk as he expected. A glare was apparently all he could muster for the interruption. Cori took his hand, and he drew her out of the room.

"What, no kiss goodbye?" Efrat said, finding his smirk again. Cori tucked in beside Ethan and pulled him away from the cell as much as he was pulling her. Efrat gave him a smug wave even as the gloves Cori had brought him disintegrated from his hand.

Ethan waited until they were in the elevator before he spoke. Cori pushed the button for the main floor while he leaned against the back wall. "What the fuck is all this about? No more avoidance, Cori. How the hell does he know your name?"

"Belus was shot yesterday morning." She didn't turn to face him. "Efrat shocked his heart into rhythm for me. He nearly died, but Efrat saved him."

"What? He saved him? Who the hell shot him in the first place?"

She finally turned around and he could see the tears she was hiding from him. "I shot Belus."

52

C ORI WAITED FOR ETHAN to bark out a laundry list of questions. How? Why? When? Why? What? Why? Instead, he stared at her with his mouth open like a fish. She turned away from him, not wanting to see his face. She shoved her head into the corner of the elevator. "We need to go see Danato now," she mumbled. "We can talk about it all with him."

The elevator *ponked* and Ethan still hadn't said anything. His fish-mouth had luckily clamped shut, and he was looking at her with concern instead of shock, but he didn't say a word.

She led the way to the office and knocked on the door. She peeked in rather than barging in like she normally did. She couldn't afford to do anything that might offend anyone. Danato had already taken her gun and given her the day off.

Neither of them wanted to admit it, but they were stuck. She was miserable about what she had done, but she still felt justified that it had been the only option. Danato was pissed off that she hadn't told him, but he also understood why she hadn't bothered to the fourth time around. He wanted to punish her, and she wanted to be punished, but neither of them knew how to go about doing that without an understanding of what exactly they were punishing for.

"Ethan's here," she said. Danato looked up from his paperwork. "Are you busy?" He looked down at the forms on his desk like he had no idea where they came from.

"No," he said. "Bring him in."

Cori opened the door all the way and Ethan followed her in. He shut the door behind them while she took a seat, curling her knees into her chest on the chair. She felt butterflies in her stomach at the thought of retelling her yesterday mornings to Ethan.

He stood by his chair a moment before sitting down. He looked her over before turning to Danato. "She says she shot Belus."

"Yes." Danato nodded, looking at her with the same mixed emotions that kept him from deciding her fate. "She didn't mean to, of course. We had an incident with her, the time bubble, and everybody's favorite bug zapper, Efrat."

"The time bubble?" Ethan asked.

"Cori was jumping around in her own timeline yesterday. She also had a few skewed timelines. Suffice it to say she's a little shaken up by everything. Efrat bolted her next to the time bubble. Her reaction was to shoot him, and rightly so, but the reaction actually took place outside of that time and space. She ended up shooting Belus three hours later in a different area."

Ethan leaned back in his chair and cussed. "He's okay though, right?"

"Yes, he is awake and recovering. I've explained the bulk of the story to him. By the way, Cori, he's requested to see you."

Cori shook her head. "I can't."

"Cori, I'm not entirely sure you can say no to that request," Danato said firmly.

She nodded. "Right."

"Do you want to tell your side first, or mine?"

"Yours. I want to be the closing argument for my own trial." She smiled, but it fell away when Danato started right into the first 8:05 morning. The only morning he knew.

From his perspective, she seemed distant, surreptitious, and out of control. Ethan listened to the summarized story, not taking his eyes off Danato until he got to the end, where Efrat used her for mouth-to-mouth practice. The sidelong gaze he gave her was not just in objection to that kiss, but the fact that he had just taken her to see him.

When Danato finished, Cori began to explain her side. She explained her efforts to include Belus and Danato in this mystery. The details of her incarceration in the infirmary made Danato shift his gaze away from her. He wasn't any happier with that part of her story than Ethan was with the kissing part. She revealed her debate about letting Efrat die, or risking Belus.

She skipped over the subtle details of the conversation. She didn't mention the hard smack that Efrat had given her. It wasn't likely to appease anyone's doubts about her saving him. She didn't even go over the kiss again since that had already been established, and she certainly didn't mention the key he slipped into her mouth during that kiss.

In the end, Ethan took her hand and squeezed it firmly. He didn't seem to know what to say. His best consoling was usually done in private, so she wasn't surprised he didn't say much.

"Cori is on a temporary leave of absence," Danato explained. "I don't exactly know what to do in a situation like this."

Ethan cleared his throat and took his hand away. "Danato, Cori told me you wanted to see me when I came in, but I think it only fair to mention that we didn't come straight here." Ethan glanced at her, and she nodded. She never intended to keep her rendezvous with Efrat a secret. "If I had known all this before, we wouldn't have gone, but Cori asked to speak with Efrat."

"Excuse me?" Danato stared slack-jawed at her.

"I was with her. She just gave him some antistatic gloves."

"You were never to go near him again." Danato rose from his chair.

"I took her. I will take the responsibility." Ethan rose as well.

"The hell you will. She has no business up there. That's why she doesn't have a code. I didn't want her up there before this. I sure as hell don't want her up there now. You had no right to take her up there." Danato turned back to Ethan.

"I..." Ethan rubbed his face before turning to her. "Cori, why don't you go see Belus? Now. Danato and I need to have a little discussion about boundaries."

Cori looked between her husband and the man who had taken the place of her father. The similarity in their aggressive stares would have been amusing if she wasn't certain they might be at each other's necks as soon as she left the room.

She froze between them, unsure if she should interject to stop the argument. "It's alright, sweetheart," Danato finally said. "I think Ethan's right. We should talk."

She headed out, but stopped at the door and looked back at them both. She hated that she was causing them to argue. She also hated that even though they were both fighting to protect her, the outcome on each side meant very different things to two very different relationships.

53

CORI DIDN'T WANT TO be anywhere near the infirmary right now. She had hoped to wait out Belus's recovery and endure an awkward meeting over coffee in Danato's office while they talked about anything other than her shooting him.

She had hoped against hope that he would be asleep when she arrived so she could just go home and say she would try another time, but no such luck. The nurse ushered her into his room and announced her presence. His eyes fluttered open, and he took her in.

She stood in the doorway by the nurse, who hadn't left yet. The nurse was grinning at Belus like a smitten teenager. Cori frowned at her and she snapped out of her trance. She concluded her business with an offer to help Belus with anything he needed whenever he needed it. Cori didn't question the behavior, but made a mental note to ask him about it when he wasn't lying in bed with a bullet wound from her gun.

"Hi," he said when nothing had been said in nearly a minute.

"Hi," she whispered nearly inaudibly to him.

"Pull up a chair, kid. You look a little flushed. Don't need you passing out on me." She looked around dumbfounded until she saw the plastic school chair in the corner. She pulled it over and sat down. "Little closer," he said. She gave him a questioning look, but brought the chair close to his bed. She waited for his approval, and he nodded.

She sat down beside him and waited for the conversation to start, but it didn't. He laid his head back on the bed and closed his eyes. "Danato said you wanted to see me," she said.

"Danato misunderstood," he said.

"You don't want me here?"

"Don't jump to conclusions you don't have enough evidence for. I told Danato that *you* would want to see me."

"Actually, I was hoping to bury my head in the sand outside until the permafrost came back."

"Oh, chickening out, then."

"No, ostriching out, but the same principle, I guess."

"Mmm-hmm. Danato gave me the gist of the story. So, you finally start listening to me, and I get shot for it. Huh, that seems like pretty cruel irony."

Cori shrugged. She still didn't know what to say. She didn't want to apologize; not because she wasn't sorry, but because she wanted Belus to understand that it hadn't been an accident. She chose that path for the bullet. "Why did you tell Danato that I would want to see you?"

"Because I figured he was keeping you away. I half expected you to be beating down my door this morning, begging for my forgiveness. That didn't happen, though." He eyed her, and she tried her best not to evade him.

"I was at home..."

"Ostriching, I remember. So, no groveling, no confessions, no crying, no declarations of love."

Cori's eyes flickered between his. He sounded almost disappointed by her lack of drama, but he usually hated her drama. He could barely stand to look at her when she was in a state of breakdown. "No, sir," she whispered.

He raised an eyebrow. "Sir, even? I haven't heard that from you in a while. Good to know I can get some benefit from this incident."

"Are you okay?" she said, breaking her cold demeanor in frustration.

"Of course. You're a terrible shot." He chuckled.

"It's not funny. I could have killed you."

"Oh, stop, I don't want to listen to you pout about it. I'm jacked up on pain meds and I don't want you spoiling my mood."

"Why did you want me here?"

"I didn't. *You* wanted to be here," Belus specified again.

"I told you I didn't. Do you want me to leave?"

"Do you want to leave?"

"Belus!" Cori screeched in frustration.

"What do you want to do?"

"I want to grovel and cry!" she shouted.

"Go ahead."

"You hate that!"

"Then hold my hand and shut the hell up so I can go back to sleep."

Cori scooted her chair over, clamped onto his hand, and huffed into her silence. He gripped her hand and laid his head back on his pillow. She waited a few moments, allowing the connection in their hands to sink in. Belus was far from a touchy-feely guy. The fact that he was giving this affection to her was more than generous. It was probably his way of forgiving her, even though she hadn't technically apologized.

"Belus," she whispered.

"Don't ruin it," he mumbled.

"I hate you," she whined at the deprivation of marking the moment. He squeezed her hand, and she saw a smile on his face. After that, she didn't say a word. She waited for him to fall asleep and tucked his hand under his blankets before leaving.

She wasn't sure a session of handholding was enough to cure her guilt, or earn back Belus's trust, but at least that next coffee meeting wouldn't be quite as awkward.

54

As soon as Cori left, the gloves were off. Danato hadn't anticipated Cori going to see Efrat again, and that had been his mistake, but the fact that Ethan took her there without his permission was sending him through the roof.

"Let me get this straight." Ethan started in where they left off. "You don't think I have the right to take Cori to the upper level?"

"No, of course not. Not without my permission. You know that level is restricted."

"Yes, to personnel, but I'm not personnel. I'm the fucking warden."

"Successor!" Danato clarified.

"You left for two months, Danato! I was in charge. You're back, so suddenly that authority goes out the window. I'm your damn successor, but you still expect me to check in like an underling. I've been running the guard schedules and rotations for the last six months."

"You have full reign over the men."

"The men, but not Cori?"

"No, not Cori. Cori is my responsibility."

"She is my wife, Danato."

"Don't bring that into this!" Danato yelled.

"Why? Because your interests in this are strictly professional?"

"Watch it!"

"Watch what, Danato? You are still coddling her! You chastise me for taking her up there outside of your express permission, but I doubt she will have any consequences for talking me into it."

"I thought you two were over the jealous competition crap."

"That jealous competition crap was never dealt with. Cori and I have come to terms with our butting egos. You and I still have one area of conflict, and that's her. You can't expect me to take on the bulk of your duties, but stand back when it comes to dealing with her."

"Do you really want to be the one responsible for slapping her hand when she's done something wrong?"

"When will this hand-slapping begin, Danato? You left me to confront her about Cleos on our honeymoon! I had to tell my wife on the cusp of our life as husband and wife that she couldn't see her friend anymore because you told me to!"

"You agreed to that."

"Of course I agreed to it! I'm your fucking successor! You told me to jump, I jumped. I ripped her heart in two for you!" Ethan threw out his finger at him as he leaned over the desk. "She left me that night in a rage, and the consequences were her getting trapped in a transmorph!"

"Don't you blame me for that. You should have gone after her!"

"THERE!" Ethan turned around and kicked his chair over before returning with another teeth-bared accusation. "Right there! That's what I'm talking about!" Ethan pointed both fingers this time. "You make demands on me that hurt her, but then you turn around and blame me for not protecting her." Ethan's voice was shaking with the anger. Danato was glad the desk was between them. He had never once raised his hands to harm Ethan, but he wasn't entirely sure that it would stay that way if this topic continued. "You just said she is your responsibility, but that isn't true. You aren't making the same demands on her that you are me, and that isn't petty jealousy. I am more than willing to follow your instructions, but if you expect me to be the asshole just so you can maintain your father figure image, you've got another thing coming."

The desk became a nonissue after it flew across the room and slammed into the far wall. Danato didn't actually remember doing it, but he was face to face with Ethan, staring at him with the same shaky adrenaline high in his bloodstream that had caused the dent in the desk.

It took a moment for him to realize that Ethan didn't normally stand eye to eye with him. The red strain entering his face was another warning sign that he should take a moment to look over this situation.

Danato stepped out of himself to look at where he was at. How far had this gone? His right hand was clamped firmly around Ethan's neck. He had lifted him from the floor the extra few inches he needed for him to be eye to eye.

Ethan was struggling to breathe, but otherwise was not fighting the attack. Despite the same adrenaline in his blood, and enough strength to knock out an elephant, Ethan had not raised a hand to him. His loyalty was still strong enough to allow Danato to use him as a punching bag rather than disrespect him.

Danato dropped him to the ground and took hold of his shoulders to keep him from trying to bolt out the door in an angry huff before he could apologize. "Ethan." The adrenaline in his system was making his voice shake now, but for different reasons. "I'm sorry." He took in a deep breath to steady his voice. "Please forgive me."

Ethan coughed a little, but he was doing well to suppress his response to the assault. Danato stepped away for a moment. "When you're ready to be civilized, call me." Ethan headed to the door.

"Ethan, wait." Danato turned around, and Ethan stopped with the door ajar. "I'm ready. Please forgive me. I let my anger get the best of me. I hate myself for treating you so barbarically."

Ethan slammed the door shut. "I know you don't want to talk about this, but you can't just lose control when an issue arises with Cori." His voice was a little strained.

Danato winced, thinking of how much pressure he had actually applied, which made Ethan's holstered defenses that much more impressive.

"You're right. I am blindly devoted to her, and I can't entirely explain why, but it is interfering with my work. More importantly, it's coming between us, and I won't have it. I refuse to be on the list of men who have caused you pain.

"When I first brought the two of you here, I had no idea you would both become so integral in my life." Danato paused, unsure of how honest he should be. "I didn't imagine that I would love you both like my own children." Ethan didn't waiver at the admission, he was still listening. "I suppose when you married Cori... I think I stopped thinking of you as my son and started thinking of you as an employee. I suppose it sounds a little Freudian, but I think I was jealous that you were taking her away from me."

"I would never take her away from you, Danato. That's why we won't let you move out. Cori and I have both missed the benefit of a father. You are the only one who will ever have that job."

Danato nodded and looked at his desk, partially embedded into the drywall on the far side of the room. "And you guys wonder why my office looks like this? You know, I was just having this same argument with Belus yesterday, before he was shot." Ethan moved over to the desk and took a side while Danato took the other. They slid it back to its original position. "He was criticizing my approving Cori for a firearm so quickly."

Ethan gave him a questioning look. He must have seen the eeriness in the premonitory conversation. He picked up his vinyl chair and sat down to hear the outcome of the tale.

"He also thought that my disciplinary actions with Cori were lacking... existence. I blustered at him just the same and dented my desk." Danato moved his papers to show off another facet of his impromptu interior decorating. "He had much the same complaints as you."

"What did he suggest we do to resolve it?" Ethan asked.

Danato looked down. He didn't want to say it. He didn't want Belus to be right. He also didn't want to give up his control, but clearly, his obsession with Cori's welfare was becoming problematic. He needed to step back. Unfortunately, the solution meant Ethan would be stepping back as well. "He suggested that your interaction with her on duty be minimized as much as possible." Ethan shifted in his chair, clenching his jaw at that. "He also suggested that I step down as her primary superior and let him direct her duties. He wants to have full control of her, including enforcing any punishments he sees fit for her indiscretions."

Danato could see Ethan shift again. He knew as well as Danato that Cori would not like that. She did not bend to authority well. She was more likely to rebel more with Belus in charge than if she had one of them.

However, they were at an impasse. Neither of them wanted to give up the right to have a say in her life, but nor did they want to offend or irritate her. The only way they could stay on good standing with her, and protect her, was to let someone else be the bad guy. Belus was more than happy to fill that position.

"She's not going to like that," Ethan said. He wasn't exactly objecting to the idea, just pointing out an obvious flaw.

"I know."

"Belus will have to find a way to balance his need for militant structure and her need to fly by the seat of her pants."

"He'll have to figure it out, or... get shot again." Danato knew it was a callous joke when his best friend was lying in a bed upstairs, but he wanted to lighten the mood. They both laughed, letting the humor sink in a little as they did.

They had a moment of silence to think after the laughter. Danato let it pass so that Ethan could have an opportunity to voice any further complaints, but he didn't. "Are you okay with that?" he asked.

"We don't really have a choice," Ethan answered, sounding defeated.

"Are *you* okay with it?" Danto asked again. "She trusts you. Probably more than me right now. If you are on board, she will do better with this."

"Yeah, I think it's for the best."

"Do you want me to tell her? She might still be in the infirmary. I could tell them both together," Danato offered, so Ethan didn't have to be the bad guy again.

"No, if you don't mind, I need to talk to her about a few other things. This will just be the cherry pit in a bowl full of stems."

"Okay." Danato stood up and came around the desk. He raised his hand to shake Ethan's, but his protégé bypassed the peace offering and hugged him instead. Danato embraced him and squeezed a little harder than he should have. When they separated, they each shuffled around to make the discomfort of the sensitive moment vanish as quickly as possible. "Glad you're back, Ethan."

"Glad to be back, Danato," Ethan said as he slipped out the door.

55

THE EMPTY HOUSE WAS no surprise to Ethan. Belus wasn't much of a conversationalist, but if he wanted to see Cori, he probably had a few things on his mind. He ran upstairs, not willing to let his shower play second fiddle to anything.

Once he had shed the remainder of his two-day-old grime and thoroughly scrubbed the smell of farm animals out of his hair, he slipped into his oldest jeans and a button-down shirt. He didn't often get out of his usual black, but he knew it would give him the upper hand with Cori. She was a sucker for his Saturday-worst wardrobe.

He slathered on some cologne that once again was not his usual attire, but he had no intention of telling Cori that she had to answer to Belus from now on without a little sex appeal to soften the blow.

He tromped downstairs and headed straight for the kitchen. He had given up all hope of a welcome home dinner and decided to make his own. Two days of gas station coffee and cold pizza was enough to make him crave even his own cooking.

He rummaged through the cupboards and decided that the safest bet was a doctored hamburger skillet meal. He had never been a fan of the stuff, but Danato seemed eternally devoted to it. His epicurean nature had long since been lacking discrimination.

Before he finished, Cori arrived, seeming a little less stressed. At least until she looked at him. "Oh, God, what now?" she said, looking over his attire.

He looked down at his casual clothes and decided that it might indeed have been a dead giveaway to his bad news. He turned the skillet burner to low and came around the corner. "Cori, we need to talk." He probably should have phrased it differently. No one ever wants to hear those words.

She backed away from him, shaking her head. "No, just say it. I can't take anymore. Just tell me." She looked terrified, but he didn't understand what she was so concerned about. Even if she had an inkling about his news, she shouldn't have been afraid; she should have been mad. "Just tell me she made you, even if she didn't."

Ohhhhh.

"Cori." Ethan tried not to smile. He had nothing to smile about. He had come very close to unwillingly screwing her arch-enemy. If it hadn't been for her insistence, he may not have thought to go see Mezula before he left. He shouldn't have been amused by her reaction to a very valid fear. "I didn't want to sleep with her." He knew it was just downright mean, but he paused, letting her face cringe to near tears. "So, I didn't." Her face relaxed into a blank stare.

"You didn't. She didn't make you?"

"She tried. You were right. She's a conniving trollop."

"You swear? Because you don't have to lie. I would..."

"I swear." She looked him over as if she couldn't believe him. "Would you like me to go to Cleos?" Her eyes widened, and she smiled. His willingness to prove it beyond a doubt was all the lie detector she needed. He was glad that it was, since he didn't want to reveal everything about his time with Leona. There was no reason to hurt Cori with the truth about Vince postmortem.

Cori threw herself into his arms and hugged him. That was the welcome home he had wanted. He hugged her back. He opened his mouth to say as much, but she kissed him. She was frenzied to offer him a proper thank you for his devotion, but he knew he couldn't let her feminine wiles take him out of focus. He also wanted to talk to her alone. Danato would stay at work late to give them time together, but eventually, his stomach would call him home.

Ethan lifted her up and carried her to the stools at the end of the island. He would have preferred the couch, but that wasn't going to keep him away from her. He sat down and slid her off onto her own stool. She pulled away from him and stared at the surroundings like she was trying to figure out how they would make love on stools.

Ethan laughed. "I still need to talk to you."

She sighed and slumped back. "Does it have to be now?"

"You know we have some things to discuss."

She crossed her arms and gave him an angry pout. He smiled and squeezed her legs. "Listen, I just had a knock-down drag-out argument with Danato. This was the closest we've ever come to blows."

Her pout faded and guilt returned. "Because I asked you to take me up to Efrat?"

"Yes, but that was just a penny in a pig. There are much bigger issues at stake here than you and Efrat. Which, by the way, is never ever happening again?" She nodded. "I know it's going to be a moot issue soon, but you can't ever ask me to go against Danato's wishes. I know you warned me that he wouldn't approve, but you can't ask me. It's not fair to make me choose between you two. I know you think that I will always choose you, but Cori, I've committed to this job. At some point, I have to start thinking and acting like the warden. Do you get that?" He wrapped his feet around her stool and pulled her a little closer so he could reach more of her.

She nodded. "I'm sorry. I know it was a shit thing to do, but I knew he would say no."

"That's his right, Cori. He's the warden of this prison. *No* isn't a word he often exercises with you, but you should at least pretend you hear it when he does say it."

She nodded again. He knew she hated being lectured to. She especially hated it when he did it. "The argument we had was about who was in charge of you."

"In charge of me?" she castigated to the tune of all feminists.

"Yes, Cori. I'm not proud to tell you that we both seem to think we have a claim on you. Danato is just too overprotective and I'm just..." He let his hand slide up her thigh. "...too close to you to be objective." He could sense her losing focus on the conversation, and he knew it was better to drop the news on her like a bomb rather than let it drag out any further. Not to mention, he decided there was one more thing they should get accomplished before Danato got back. "That's why we decided that Belus should be your superior from here on out."

After a beat, she realized what he had said. "Belus?"

"Yes, the man you just shot is going to dictate, delegate, and discipline you from here on out."

Her brow dipped deep as she thought about that. "Danato agreed to that?"

"Reluctantly. Also, you and I won't be able to work together." He reached around her butt and slid her back onto his lap. "We'll have separate duties from here on out."

"They're separating us?" she asked, wrapping her hands around his neck. He could tell she didn't like that, but she was far too distracted by his hands slipping up the back of her shirt to voice her outrage.

She wasn't the only seducer in this relationship.

"Yes, they've forbidden us from being together." He unsnapped her bra, and she tensed like the change in pressure scared her. He hadn't really thought of the edict against them as being romantic, but in light of his own diversion, he was finding the idea of someone trying to keep them apart hot. Not hot like Romeo and Juliet, because that was just overdramatic, but hot like slipping into a broom closet for a quickie on coffee breaks.

Cori smiled at seeing the pleasure he was deriving from the decree. He reached around to her front and caressed her breasts softly. She leaned back slightly to let him have full rein. "I can't believe you used sex to break this to me."

He grinned. She had caught on to his tactics. He lifted her shirt and teased her with his mouth. "Would you rather I lecture you?" he said, switching breasts.

"No, this is much better." She wrapped her legs around him and clawed at his shoulders. He took that as a signal that it was time to move things upstairs. He gave the skillet a cursory glance and decided it would be fine until he could get back to it.

He carried her upstairs, continuing his dalliances under her shirt one handedly. By the time he got her upstairs, there was no debate about what he would do to her next. She pushed him down on the mattress, ripped at his clothes, continuing the interrupted "thank you" from earlier.

Like a good husband, he let her have her way, and she did. She demanded a few more affirmations of his love than she usually did, but they were otherwise right where they left off, before Leona and before Efrat.

56

CORI COULDN'T HELP BUT appreciate Ethan's way of breaking the bad news about Belus to her. To be honest, she wasn't sure it was bad news. They weren't the only ones to feel torn apart by their inconsistent trio.

Even though it didn't technically happen, Cori was disappointed by the way Danato had handled himself in her skewed timelines. She didn't like that he was willing to commit her rather than listen to her honest explanation. She also didn't like that he didn't believe her that General Clark would flat-out execute Efrat if he knew the truth. He'd obliged to her request, but he still hadn't thought it was necessary.

Belus, on the other hand, had been consistent throughout the time skews. He was indifferent to her suffering, but because he was, he was able to analyze the situation. Each time she was faced with questions, he was there, willing to answer them as best he could. He was also willing to sacrifice his own life to put things right again.

She knew what being under Belus would mean. It would be a lot of hard work, a lot of rules and regulations, and a lot less sympathy. Even though she hated the sound of all of that, at least she could depend on that each and every day from Belus.

Ethan slipped back into his jeans. She watched the tight denim slip over his muscular legs and butt. She bit her lip, checking the clock. If there was time after dinner, she was definitely going to have to get those pants off again.

He caught her eying him and buried her smile in the blankets. She hadn't bothered to get dressed again. She liked the feel of being naked under the sheets. Ethan moved to her and sat on the edge of the bed. He pulled the sheet away from her mouth and still farther until her chest and tummy were exposed. He openly ogled her, as she had only moments before done to him.

He touched her stomach. He stared at her as his hand caressed the flesh around her belly button. She wasn't sure what he was thinking, but when he finally snapped out of his trance, he pulled the sheet up to cover her body again. "You cover that up before you make me ruin dinner."

She laughed, but she could see another thought crowd into the romantic moment. He stared down at nothing until the thought was too overpowering to keep in. "Cori, about Efrat."

"It meant nothing." She'd already been prepared to defend this part of her morning. "He just did it to mess with Danato."

"I figured as much," he said, sounding distant in thought. "But that isn't my question." He looked at her, with all hints of romance gone from his eyes. "The gloves, the conversation. It all seemed very... conspired."

She suddenly wished she had gotten dressed. She felt more naked than ever. "What do you mean?"

"I need you to be very honest with me. Is there something more going on between you two than just gloves and provocative kisses?"

Cori hated lying to him. She didn't exactly want to tell him the truth, but she needed to be as near honest as she could before this situation got away from her, like so many others before it. "Umm..." She played with her sheet. A sure sign of guilt. "I'm not sure. I mean no, but there were some conversations that made me question some things."

"What's the question?" He tipped his head, innocently querying about her dilemma. She loved him for that. He wasn't prying or coercing, just asking.

"Ethan, do you know anything about the elementals? I mean, do you know why they are here? What did they do to get incarcerated here?"

"Well," he took a deep breath before answering. "I know they were part of an elite military operation in the U.S. They were recruited to be a new special ops division, like Navy SEALs. I think the U.S. thought they had superheroes. As it turns out they just had a bunch of wild, supernatural beings with the ability to create chaos. I don't know the specifics of their crimes, but given the laundry list of lives they've cost in the prison, I can only imagine what they did in the real world."

"Oh." She was disappointed, but she wasn't sure why. It all seemed very simple. Militant soldiers incarcerated for war crimes. Very simple. "I guess maybe Efrat was just bitter about being locked up. He must have been trying to get my sympathy. Like that would do any good. I don't even have a code to go upstairs."

"You thought maybe he was really a good man because he helped save Belus?"

"I guess. I know he's such an ass, but... I really am gullible."

"No, you're just a natural born hero. But trust me, he's not worth saving."

"Have you read his file?"

"No, Danato keeps those under lock and key in the office." He looked her over, trying to see if she had any more to say or ask. "Is that all? Nothing else is bothering you?"

Cori knew she should tell him about the key. She knew it was a violation against him and Danato not to reveal it, but she just couldn't. Until she knew more, she didn't want anyone to know about the key. She wanted to know what Efrat thought would change her opinion of Danato.

Efrat probably was still just a bad guy, incarcerated for doing bad stuff, but the image of his brain being blown out by a point-blank gunshot made her question the motivations of the military. Until she had answers, she would keep her secret firmly stifled.

"That's it." She shrugged with a contented smile to ease his concerns.

FELICIA JEDLICKA
TENANTS & TYRANTS
Book 5
THE WARDEN

TENANTS & TYRANTS

Sneak Peek

DANIEL MCGRATH SPRINTED UP the second to last flight of stairs. His throat burned from the effort of sucking in excess air while ascending the five flights of hospital stairs. He was pretty sure if he made it to the top without puking, it would not be viewed as a triumph by his stomach.

On the last landing before the roof, Heaton popped out of the sixth-floor door, looking alert and un-winded. Daniel conversely thought his heart might explode if it thumped any faster. He pointed a finger at Heaton, threatening to say something as soon as his breathing was not overpowering his vocal cords.

Heaton looked up at the next flight, and back at him. He had finally given up his efforts at long dreads and floppy mops, and settled on corn rows to manage his thick black hair. Daniel had objected fervently to this new hairstyle. Not because he wasn't pulling it off, but because it, along with his new black leather sport coat style jacket, made him look like a mobster thug. However, since this look had increased the attention he got from women at the pubs, he had no intention of making any changes. He had even threatened to grow a goatee like Daniel's.

"Where the feck have you been? I thought you were right behind me," Daniel spat out between breaths.

"I was. I took the elevator," Heaton answered, motioning to the door he just arrived from.

"What? I thought you said we had to chase it up the stairwell."

"Yeah," Heaton said, implying the "no duh," "not both of us."

"Are you off your nut? I just ran up five flights of stairs."

"Yeah, you did good. Jordan said he popped out on to the roof. Let's go get him."

"You wanker! You made me climb these stairs?" When Heaton didn't respond, he clarified his outrage. "You run marathons, you plonker!"

"Yeah," he offered the "no duh" implication again, "on roads, not stairs. Who wants to run up stairs?"

Heaton opened his mouth to let loose a deluge of Irish curses, but his cell phone ring interrupted him. The ring was a high twittering noise. It was annoying as hell, and he chose it with the very specific intention of pissing himself off every time he heard it. So far, it was working.

He tugged it from his pocket and clicked to answer it. "What?" He croaked into the phone.

"Are you two coming?" Nevia asked on the other end. They had only been working together for three months, but she was already ruling the roost. She made the plans while they did all the dirty work.

"Yes, we're fecking coming, you narky woman!" He clicked the phone off and shoved it back in his pocket. "Whose damn idea was it to keep her on?"

"Yours," Heaton answered, jogging ahead of him on the stairs. Daniel felt hot in his long jacket, but as soon as he got onto the roof, the night's early autumn breeze cooled him down. Most people hated to see summer go, but he was much happier in a cold climate. If he hadn't hated the idea of being nearly celibate, he might have considered opting for Ethan's job. He was basically an indentured servant, anyway.

"Where is the blood sucking bastard?" he asked, scanning the roof. There was a helicopter on the landing pad on the other side of the roof. They had a special entrance to take the emergency victims into the hospital, but those doors required I.D. badges.

"He has to be up here. He's not a flier." Heaton surveyed the roof, taking in the scene with the precision of a soldier. Daniel only knew a little about Heaton's military background, but it was enough to know not to ask about it. Heaton wasn't exactly proud of the roles he had played. Heroism always looked different depending on what it required you to do.

"Then he's hiding. Search or lure?" Daniel asked, not sure which answer he would have preferred. He was tired enough to hope for lure, but no one really wants to be vampire bait.

"I'm up for search, if you take the cut."

"Damn it, I always take the cut," Daniel grumbled.

"You heal faster."

"Barely!" Daniel didn't really heal faster, but something about his system allowed for quick clotting. It was a pretty useless talent, but it had saved his life on one occasion. The occasion was New Year's Eve. The life-threatening offender was a broken bottle that he impaled himself with when he passed out. Even with the quick clotting, it wasn't a happy new year.

"Fine, I'll do it," Heaton said, pulling out his knife. "Can't feel anything on this arm, anyway." Heaton rolled up his sleeve to reveal his melted flesh. Ever since he had confronted Daniel about it at the prison, he had been passive aggressively taking shots at him about it. However, Daniel no longer held any sympathy for his affliction. Rule one: stay the fuck out of a dispeller's way!

Daniel had never known what to call himself. He had rejected the phrase exorcist, for obvious reasons of blasphemy and inaccuracy. He hadn't really thought of himself as worthy of an official title, but Nevia had started referring to him as a dispeller and it just sort of stuck.

Heaton cut through his scarred flesh before Daniel could voice an objection. It was just another in a long list of things he would complain about later. It was getting tiresome, but Daniel wasn't in a position to take the high or low road, so instead, he would just sit in the middle and ignore it all.

"Walk it around. I want to get to the pub before closing."

Instead of walking around, Heaton milked the wound, letting the gash pour blood on to the graveled roof. Daniel looked away as he did. He wasn't particularly sickened by the sight of blood, but he was sickened by Heaton's severity. He was generally a calm mediator, but recently his sudden outbursts of bravery, violence, and on occasion sexism were starting to push the envelope. He had even had Nevia sniff check him for parasites. No luck. Heaton was just becoming an ass.

"Maybe if I gash my throat, I could get you there before the good tarts are taken."

Daniel turned back to him. His face was smiling like he was joking, but his voice had said otherwise. "Really," Daniel nodded, lowering his voice to a level that allowed him to keep his temper in check. Outside of being mad drunk, he didn't have a problem keeping his anger management issues in check. He always wondered why it was so important for him to keep himself under control when no one else did. "Was that supposed to be funny?"

"I don't know. Are you laughing?"

"No, as a matter of fact, I'm quite the opposite of laughter."

"I don't see any tears." Heaton weaved his head to see.

"Crying is not the opposite of laughing," Daniel objected.

"What? Yes, it is. Have you ever seen drama masks: happy, sad."

"Laughing is not happy."

"Of course it is." Heaton raised his voice to help make his point. "You're happy when you laugh."

"Not always. I've laughed when I'm sad. You laugh when something is funny. You laugh through tears. Laughing is just an extension of an emotion. Just like you can cry when you're sad, or you cry when you're happy."

"Only women cry when they're happy."

"Only woman cry when they're sad," Daniel pitched. "Men drink when they're sad and laugh when they're drunk. They might be sad and laughing, and still not crying. So, no, crying is not the opposite of laughing."

"So, what is the opposite of laughing?"

"Yelling!" Daniel technically raised his volume for that statement, but only for effect.

"In what world is yelling the opposite of laughing?" Heaton asked, going so far as to get in his face.

"Laughing," Daniel heard his cell phone tweeter from his rear pocket, but he ignored it so he could finish explaining. "Happy and sad are the polar opposites of one spectrum. That's why you can laugh when you are happy or sad. Angry and jealous are opposite ends of a completely separate spectrum of emotions. Those emotions cause yelling. Therefore, yelling is the opposite of laughing."

"Son of a bitch!" Heaton yelled.

"Hey don't—"

"Behind you!" Heaton pointed with his wide eyes.

Daniel whipped around, hoping that Heaton would have a good laugh at his well-played joke, but the stark white elongated face behind him was no joke. The open mouth mere inches from him held sticky yellow fangs. The creature hissed and dove for his neck, even as he stumbled back into Heaton.

Daniel heard a pop and the creature's head bobbed to the right, followed by its body. Daniel fell back as the creature fell to the side. Heaton caught him and steadied him. A small pool of blood gathered around the head of the vampire. There was no need to check for a pulse, not because the vampire was undead like the story books said, but because he had a bullet through his brain, and that just wasn't survivable.

Daniel cleared his throat and straightened his coat as he righted himself. He turned back to Heaton and looked him over. "You okay?"

Heaton looked at him with the same concern. "Yeah, you?"

"Good, good, never better." He pushed his fingers through his hair reflexively to check for flyaway strands. "That was a good shot."

"Yeah." Heaton nodded.

"Nice to have her around," Daniel said, surveying the damaged body.

"Yeah," Heaton did the same, "I'm glad I decided to keep her on."

Thank you so much for reading. I hope you enjoyed the ride and if you aren't getting off here, I encourage you to sign up for my newsletter so I can return your generosity with new release updates and special offers.

Sign-Up

You can also find me on Facebook or visit my website. Keep reading!

Website

Facebook

AUTHOR

As a Nebraska native, and a small-town girl at that, I have very little to occupy my time beyond imagining a world outside of my own reality. By the grace of God and the seat of my pants, I have kept my waning attention span on the task of becoming an author.

So here I am, an indie author, peddling my words in cyberspace and enduring my comeuppances with an unwavering determination. I may not be a professional, and I certainly am not perfect, but if you've made it this far, you have to admit, this smartass yokel does spin quite a yarn.

From the self-inflicted sweatshop conditions of my unairconditioned childhood home, to the arthritis reaping positions of a sedentary lifestyle, I bring to you: my sarcasm, my oddity, and my heart. Take it with a grain of salt or a teaspoon of sugar, but take it for what it is: a story born of the mind, translated to paper, and gifted to you.

I thank you for your readership and even more for your support. Please recommend this book to your friends and family via any social media that you use. Word of mouth is still the best advertising and is greatly appreciated.

Most importantly, keep reading. I'll keep writing.